Cast of Characters

Matthew Weir. A former professor and the owner of Spanwater, who was acquitted two years earlier of poisoning his sister-in-law.

Catherine "Kate" Weir. His frail, wealthy wife, fond of brewing tea from wild herbs she gathers. She lives largely in the past and is ten years older than Matthew.

Augustus Weir. Matthew's brother, a poet and literary editor.

Dinah and **Nick Terris.** Weir's orphaned niece and nephew, who are his wards.

Aurelia Brett. Mrs. Weir's newly hired young companion.

Dr. Sandy Smollett. Mrs. Weir's doctor and Matthew's close friend.

Miss Leith. Dinah's tutor, from Oxford, rumored to be Weir's lover.

Alice Gretton. A shadowy older woman friend of Mrs. Weir, who recently abandoned her rented cottage, Titt's Cote, with no explanantion whatsoever.

Esther O'Malley. A disreputable old gypsy woman befriended by Mrs. Weir.

Bessie Kingdom. Weir's housekeeper, an angry, self-righteous woman who was a close ally of the late, equally despicable **Leah Bunting**, Weir's supposed victim.

William Mond. A manservant at Spanwater, who may not be who he says he is.

Joyce Murray, aka **Fenella Pagan.** The chief legatee to Mrs. Weir's estate, who fled to Australia. If she is still alive, Matthew inherits almost nothing.

Andrew Pitt. A student at Savile College, Oxford, and best chum to Nick Terris.

Freddy Borth. Son of the local squire who's injured in a suspicious auto accident.

Lou Blessitt. The cheerful, good-tempered new cook, who keeps her own counsel.

Flora Hickley. An observant schoolteacher from Indiana, U.S.A.

Chief Inspector Dan Pardoe. A tall, spare, keenly observant detective who, notwithstanding his white hair, is the youngest Scotland Yarder ever to achieve his rank.

Detective Sergeant Salt. His shrewd assistant, old-fashioned despite his atheism.

Superintendent Creed. Head of the Cottle

Plus assorted servants, doctors, farmers, vil

Books by Dorothy Bowers

Postscript to Poison (1938)
Shadows Before (1939)
Deed Without a Name (1940)
Fear and Miss Betony (1941)
The Bells of Old Bailey (1947)

Shadows Before

by Dorothy Bowers

Rue Morgue Press
Boulder / Lyons

To my
Mother and Father
with love

For information on our titles see
www.ruemorguepress.com
or call
800-699-6214
or write
The Rue Morgue Press
P.O. Box 4119
Boulder, CO 80306

ISBN: 0-915230-81-X

Printed by
Johnson Printing

PRINTED IN THE UNITED STATES OF AMERICA

About the author

Dorothy Bowers (1902-1948) was well on her way to establishing herself as one of Britain's leading mystery writers when she succumbed to tuberculosis at the age of 46. Her first Inspector Dan Pardoe novel, *Postscript to Poison*, was published in England in 1938 to enthusiastic reviews ("She ranks with the best."—*The London Times*). Three more Pardoe books followed, one a year until 1941, when Bowers left her longtime home in Monmouth for London, to do war work for the European News Service of the BBC. Her fifth and final novel was published in 1947, and she was elected to the prestigious Detection Club in 1948, shortly before her untimely death.

She was born on June 11, 1902, in Leonminster, Herefordshire, the second daughter of Albert Edwards Bowers, a confectioner who moved his family to Monmouth in 1903. He operated his own bakery on Agincourt Square in that city until he retired in 1936. Dorothy's early education was at the Monmouth School for Girls. She went up to Oxford on October 13, 1923, when she was twenty-one, a somewhat advanced age for a first-year student, though one should also remember that Oxford only started awarding degrees to women in 1920. She took a third honors in Modern History in 1926 from The Society of Oxford Home Students (now St. Anne's College) and returned to Monmouth to pursue a reluctant career as a history mistress, although her first love was writing. Her happiest memories during that time were of her days at Oxford.

In addition to her writing and substitute teaching duties, Dorothy compiled crossword puzzles for *John O'London Weekly* from 1936 to 1943 and for *Country Life* from 1940 to 1946. Like her sister and many of her Oxford friends, she never married. She died at Tupsley, Hereford, on Sunday, Aug. 29, 1948, at the age of 46, with her sister May at her bedside, and was buried near her mother.

For more information on Bowers see the introduction by Tom & Enid Schantz to The Rue Morgue Press edition of *Postscript to Poison*.

CONTENTS

PROLOGUE

SHADOWS

We delight to anticipate death by such shadows as night affords.
CHARLES LAMB: *Popular Fallacies*

SHADOWS

Being the greater part of a letter written by Andrew Pitt, Commoner of Savile College, Oxford, to his aunt, Miss Muriel Hart, of Stalley House, Bath, in the County of Somerset, July 5th, 1939.

SO IT'S ALL OVER, Mew, or nearly. The shouting and the tumult dies, the captains and the kings depart. Only this time it's the murderer who departs. Old Coffin—gosh, what a name for *defending* counsel—did his usual stuff unusually well, but he couldn't pull the wool over their eyes this time. I mean the jury's. After all the mystery and darkness we've groped in the light's been too beastly clear. Do you remember how it was always me who had the urge for murders and blood and general nastiness? Poor wretched little mutt that I was, I actually *wanted* to find A Body! Well, I found it. And now I'd like to roll time up neatly like a map and start fresh at the beginning. Say sometime early in the spring. This is sheer, cussed, hoggish selfishness, of course. I say so first because if I don't you will. But I feel flattened out, floored, devitalized. I've lived in a funk as though it was a tunnel, and I'm not properly out yet. Do they still run up a black flag for everybody to stare at?

Besides, look how it's messed up the summer term. Hang it all—what a vile ring the phrase has—but, Mew darling, this is the end of my second year and I'm still a free man. Next Trinity's going to mean work (*work*, WORK, woman!) and schools, and old Froggy going all broody, and a little white tie. I *knew* I had to be all het up then. But this was going to be different. And now I shall have to het up for two summer terms. That has squashed the last fragment of altruism I may ever have had. I'm not sorry for anybody but me. I'm a brimming urn of self-pity, and make no apologies for it. All I want is my yesterday given back.

Not that I think it would really do any good. The other night when I was lying winkless going over for the umpteen millionth time what I'd have to say in the witness box the next day, an idea came to me. (Derisive laughter off.) You know how one says the future lies in the lap of the past? Well, suppose it wasn't that at all? Suppose it was the other way round, and the future was everything, holding and controlling the past. Then the past would never have been a free agent molding what was to come, but only a shadow of it. Zoe warns me this is too highbrow to be safe for me. But I think perhaps it's more Donne-ish than donnish. Anyway that's how I see it, the light of a larger and always unguessable future shining behind *our* future and laying the darkness of it over the past.

Couldn't it be? Think of it—these murders huddled in Time, planned though still inactive, and their hateful approach misshaping the past. All the evidence goes to prove it. Think of the Rev. Micah Paskin, poor old sucker, stirred to a little bit of greed and a lot of childish pleasure at the thought of storing *some* treasure on earth, being plucked clean by that eyrie of share-pushers, with his kids flung out to be anybody's responsibility and nobody's. That was years ago, before the gold mine peddling gents engaged the serious attention of our abstracted House. Ten years ago, in fact. A long shadow that. But you see it fell full upon him.

And you can have shorter shadows than that one. Look at that wet afternoon in June only two years back, and Matthew Weir leaving the Old Bailey, a supposedly free man. They'd shifted the trial there, hadn't they, because of bad feeling against him in Penmarket? Penmarket, where Leah Bunting nursed the poor without loving them, and died from a dose of weedkiller. Old Coffin got home by a neck that time anyway—gosh, what's wrong with me, or is the scaffold the home of all our metaphors and idioms and suchlike? Twelve men believed him when he said Matthew hadn't done it, and Matthew drove away into the rainy streets that weren't half as dark as the shadow that lay on him.

Think I'm crazy, Mew? It's how I see it now. A group of events, people, conditions strung untidily across the years, their only common factor what touched them all, the shadow of a place and its deeds yet to be. Little Fenella Pagan (glorious name!) dying of T.B. in a Sydney lodging house. Buried out there in New South Wales, all those years and miles away from the Paskins, but sharing their darkness. Then Alice Gretton coming to Titt's Cote. And Bill Fennick leaving his job as hall porter in old Benedict's cramming establishment in the Mendips because he was caught up in it too. Doesn't it thrill you, even if it is beastly, to think of all those independent lives in common bondage to a hideous future?

My own share too. Why did I holiday in Malvern three years ago and try to be a callow Galahad? Because I'd walked into the shadow too.

Do you believe that the peace and freedom Zoe says we shall all feel now will ever have the reality of what's gone? I can't. I've a horrible feeling I'm bound to wake up soon, in that police-ridden house, and all to do again. I did wake up the night before last, in my own room here. But it was too dark and smothering to know it was my room, and where I'd been was back to the wood. For what seemed hours, but perhaps wasn't, I tried to know I was Andrew Pitt, safe and sound and in my right mind, in my uncle Edward's house. I'd be too ashamed to write this blue funk to anybody else but you. But I could *feel* the earth in my fingernails.

Freeman and Tim are going to Italy about the middle of the long vac. Raikes may be there too. All of them my year. They've asked me to go. I think perhaps I will. It's sure to be hot as Hades, but grand fun.

Winny and Edward send their love, and of course Zoe. Zoe is going all maternal lately. By the fuss she makes you'd think it was me that had been in the dock. The girl's only nineteen, too young to be so soppy yet.

You didn't like it, Mew, because you couldn't get a line from me. Well, I've written plenty now. Can I come and see you please before I see Italy?

Your funky, faithful

ANDY

PART I

COMING EVENTS

I met Murder on the way—
He had a mask like . . .
P.B. SHELLEY.

CHAPTER 1

SITUATION VACANT

We are yet but young in deed.
WILLIAM SHAKESPEARE: *Macbeth.*

FIVE MONTHS AFTER the death of her employer Aurelia Brett walked up from Cottlebury station in search of Dr. Smollett's house. It was an afternoon late in March, cold and windless, with a special purity in the air that must, she thought, betoken another fall of snow. Crusts of an earlier one still lingered on the hills, as she had seen from the train, waiting for more, as the country folk said. She crossed the wide handsome promenade, glancing up and down its almost deserted length where the chestnuts and limes were uncurling their first leaves, and went briskly past the succession of glittering shop fronts that extended their lures with impeccable taste. They were not for her, and she had schooled herself to disregard what was out of reach, a discipline that simplified life and fortified singleness of aim. But what she could not avoid glimpsing was the repetition of her own image in the polished glass, pale, anxious, resolute, keeping pace with her up the street with a shadowy relentlessness that made her uneasy, she could not have said why.

Directions in the letter she had received were so clear that there was no difficulty in finding the house. Across a main thoroughfare that was the business center of the town, and down a narrow entry that widened all at once into an old churchyard planted with pollard ash where three railed paths ran in the form of an arrowhead, the Norman church between two of them, Aurelia hurried, taking the middle walk and coming out into a small close framed in houses that seemed to have shrunk a little into their own respectability. The doctor's was on the corner, facing two ways, brighter than the rest, green shuttered and with well-scrubbed steps.

When she had rung the bell she found that her hands were trembling. She got the impression that a curtain at a bay window close at hand was flicked aside for a moment, but when she looked there was nobody there. The door opened noiselessly, and a maid who looked at her with impersonal interest brought her into a light square hall and thence to a room on the left that was plainly a study.

"The doctor will be with you in a few minutes, miss," she said, and withdrew.

The room was at the back of the house, lined with books that were both used and cared for. Aurelia did not sit down but walked past the closely stacked shelves to the window that looked on a tiny walled garden, so carefully ordered it appeared far larger than it was. Her eyes traveled unseeingly from clumps of daffodils shining in dim corners to the first radiant flowers of an almond tree against the end wall. The only sounds behind her were the ticking of a clock and the sly whisper of the coal fire.

She sighed, tapping her foot restlessly, deliberately checking the forward movement of her thoughts that were ready, she knew, to sap her resolution at the first wavering. She had always hated an interim, none the less because experience had again and again forced upon her these periods of suspended action. Opening her bag she took from it the mirror and surveyed herself dispassionately. If her new, carefully chosen clothes did their best to camouflage poverty and gave her an appearance that went far to hide the importance she attached to this interview, the face that looked back at her was not reassuring. She wondered if she had judged wisely in employing neither powder nor rouge today, then decided that their use would only have emphasized the high bones and hollows of her cheeks. But the faintly bruised flesh beneath her eyes startled her in the wan light. It was, she thought, like the dark cavities in a skull, and gave to her look a sort of desperation she would rather be rid of. Her thick shingled hair drawn smoothly back behind her ears was oddly placid by contrast. Funny how yellow and halo-ish it always looked when her face was colorless. She smiled grimly at the angelic allusion that went so ill with her hungry features, and putting the mirror away shut the bag with a snap as the door opened to admit Dr. Smollett.

He came forward quickly with a cordial greeting and pushed a low chair closer to the fire. "Forgive me for keeping you waiting, Miss Brett. Please sit down."

He was a small man with pale, dry features and deft movements that achieved their purpose without fuss. Beneath thick sandy brows his eyes moved restlessly. He seated himself opposite Aurelia but got up immediately, and going over to his desk took from it a letter and some papers attached. He stood on the hearth rug between the two chairs and tapped the papers lightly with his finger.

"The letter you wrote Mr. Weir was admirably to the point," he said abruptly.

A short silence closed on his remark and Aurelia wondered if she was expected to reply. Glancing up she intercepted a curious look. Without turning his head the doctor, who held himself perfectly still, was watching her shrewdly. The bright, keen regard from the corners of his eyes gave him a crafty mien. When it met hers the look, with the taut bearing, vanished, and turning he sat down again facing her.

"You understand," he resumed in a normally brisk voice, "that I am acting for Mr. Weir in this matter. He has asked me, as Mrs. Weir's doctor, to see any suitable applicant for the post. So your letters and testimonials were passed on to me. They seem very satisfactory, but I had better hear a little more about your late post—you've not been too informative."

He smiled as he spoke. Aurelia flushed.

"I wrote shortly, I know. Nowadays I've cut down my application to the mere essentials. The fact is," she went on more bluntly, "I've found that after mentioning my lack of qualification as a nurse an interview is seldom required."

"You were not expecting an interview in this case?"

"Not really. Though I hoped that being in Gloucester so close at hand might help to get me one."

"It did," the doctor admitted. "But more than that, Miss Brett, I liked what you call the 'mere essentials,' being a busy man with only the average memory." He drew out a piece of typewritten paper from beneath the letter and looked down at it. "The writer of your most recent testimonial states that you were with her aunt at the time of her death?"

"Yes," Aurelia said. "Mrs. Kempson died at the end of last October. Her niece, Mrs. Friend, was with her for the last month or two and wrote me that testimonial when I left."

"Did Mrs. Friend nurse her aunt?" the doctor asked.

"No. A trained nurse came in. But Mrs. Friend was very anxious about her. Mrs. Kempson caught the chill which in the end caused her death while she was staying with Mrs. Friend. That was in the early part of September when I was away on holiday. The nurse was brought in nearly six weeks before she died, as neither I nor Mrs. Friend was competent to deal with a grave illness. There was really very little for me to do in the last month, but I was naturally of some use and Mrs. Kempson had grown accustomed to me, so I was kept on till after the funeral."

"I see. Why were you engaged in the first place? Was your employer in poor health when you went to her?"

"Yes. Mrs. Kempson had a weak heart. She wasn't ill enough to need a nurse, and besides she strenuously opposed the idea, but her doctor decided she must have a companion. She was never well, nor really ill until the last two months. My duties were light." She stopped suddenly.

"But what?" Dr. Smollett took her up quickly on the word she had not uttered.

Aurelia looked at him unmoved. "I might have added that they were not in practice so light as they sound, perhaps. The usual companionship, some shopping, little household jobs. But Mrs. Kempson was highly nervous, and irritable as people with heart trouble often are, I believe." She hesitated, and feeling she had been too frank explained. "I don't think the sort of little social round that is all the thing in Fycliff and places like that was any good to her health. It can be exhausting, you know."

"Oh, yes, I know Fycliff," the doctor said contemptuously, with the mental reservation that Mrs. Kempson had probably been a tuft-hunting old tartar, "snobby little dugout, close enough to Bournemouth to bask in reflected glory but failing signally to make any mark of its own. Well, Miss Brett, you acquired patience there at any rate, eh?"

He looked at her narrowly, observing the signs of strain on the clear-cut face and admiring her steady poise that was still not sufficiently at ease to be reposeful. She met his gaze squarely.

"Yes, I am patient," she agreed with such clear emphasis that the doctor gave a short laugh.

"The indispensable handmaid of the major virtues," he said lightly. His tone changed. "I think you will probably handle this case well, Miss Brett. Mrs. Weir is an elderly lady, getting on for seventy, with heart trouble of a not very serious nature. Indeed, we are not looking for a companion for her mainly on that account. She leads a quiet, healthy life, no social frills and furbelows there, and is very placid and amenable. But a year or two ago she suffered a great shock which has enfeebled her intellect a little, a death in her family and a complete change of residence soon afterwards."

He paused, his head slightly bent, his glance roving uncritically over the rug. Aurelia detected a subtle change of tone in the last remark, and in the silence that followed it she got the idea that though his eyes were not on her he was all attention for any reply she might make. She said nothing, however, and after a minute he went on.

"Her mind is hazy and adrift, though at times she can be as rational as you and I."

"I've no qualifications at all for looking after a—a mental patient," Aurelia said, boggling a little at the term.

The doctor shook his head impatiently. "None such as you mean are needed in this case. You misunderstand me, Miss Brett. Mrs. Weir's trouble is childishness. Most of her time she is living in the past, a fairly remote past when she herself was a child living in the country. It appears that all her adult life until the last couple of years was spent in towns and cities, associated for her with tragedies. Now that she is back in the country, after a shock which has unsettled her, she identifies her present surroundings with those in which her childhood was passed. That's all. Mental trouble in any disturbing sense you won't find."

Aurelia contrived to look relieved. "Is Mrs. Weir confined to her bed?" she asked.

The doctor smiled wryly. "Quite the contrary, I assure you. That brings me to the real reason why it has become necessary to get a companion for her."

He got up suddenly and pushed the letter and testimonials he was still holding behind a tobacco jar on the mantelpiece. Then he put his hands behind him and looked down into the dull glow of the fire. Aurelia was disconcerted by the feeling that his thoughts were running in a channel other than his words.

"Mrs. Weir is devoted to the country where her home is now," he explained carefully. "She goes for a great many walks, and her belief that she is living again her early years has revived in her a knowledge of some of the things her mother used to do in those days. For instance, last spring and summer, the first in which she was living at Spanwater, she was very keen on picking various plants, making an infusion of them with boiling water and drinking it. Mr. Weir and the others, I too, tried to dissuade her in case she should be careless about what she gathered. But it is the one point on which she is completely stubborn, and I don't think it is wise to bother her about it. It was, as she practiced it last year, a very innocent fad, though it naturally caused the family some anxiety. With spring at hand now it's probable that she will devote herself to it again."

"What sort of plants does she pick?" Aurelia asked.

Dr. Smollett put his toe to a crumbling log and sent up a shower of sparks. "Dandelions and young nettles," he said indifferently, "and things like that. Perfectly harmless. Even beneficial, I've no doubt, in a mild way. Better than edible fungi that turn out inedible anyway," he added grimly.

"But if Mrs. Weir is not to be checked——" Aurelia began tentatively.

The doctor waved his hand brusquely. "I know. But we shall naturally feel less anxious if Mrs. Weir has somebody with her when she is out walking. Besides," he hurried on with a sideways look at her, "I am sure you would know anything definitely poisonous, as the plants she gathers for this brew are among the most easily recognizable. But she seems remarkably sensible on that score, and knows a good deal more about the properties and so on of wild flowers than do most people. I consider that the upset which might be caused by depriving her of a simple pleasure would be greater than any risk she incurs because of it."

"I see," Aurelia said, in her tone little relish for the kind of supervision expected of her.

The doctor gave her a quick look. "That's not all. It hasn't been easy for the family always to accompany Mrs. Weir when she goes out or even to know when and where she is going. She slips away quietly, with no intention of hiding her movements from the household but forgetting that they don't know where she has gone. This has meant a lot of worry for them. Not only does she go too far, or at least covers too much ground by vague wandering, with bad effect on her heart, but she apparently picks up acquaintances her family knows nothing about." He hesitated, then added, "You can well understand that in her present state of health she is likely to be imposed upon by unscrupulous people to whom she is kind."

Aurelia agreed, recalling that facile friendship with strangers was characteristic of those troubled with Mrs. Weir's mild affliction.

"Are there any particular people you would wish her to avoid?" she asked involuntarily, realizing in the same moment that she had not been engaged for the post and that the doctor would hardly supply names.

He shook his head. "Mr. Weir will give particulars, of course," he said cautiously. "I believe there are some gypsies in the neighborhood that she seems to have taken to, but," he added with an acid little smile, "by what I hear the poultry houses have more to fear from that quarter than Mrs. Weir."

In spite of a frank manner he had been speaking with the kind of abstraction Aurelia had noted before; as though, she thought, there were something more he did not say but which occupied his mind. All at once he glanced at the clock, looked at Aurelia as if seeing her for the first time, and shot at her in a brisk, incurious tone questions relating to her capacity for taking a temperature, being observant, and knowing how to combine sympathy with firmness in the case of a patient who lacked concentration and memory.

"I call Mrs. Weir a patient," he said, "because she definitely needs looking after and is herself unable to give orders. But a qualified nurse is not required. It might sometimes be necessary to give a little attention in the night."

"I am used to that," Aurelia said. "And I am a light sleeper."

He nodded with careless assent as if he had already assured himself on that point. Aurelia, who doubted whether he had listened to her replies, had the notion that the questions he had put to her were to him mere formality.

"Very well," he said. "I think you are the right person for the post, Miss Brett. The salary is three guineas weekly, and you would live with the family. Do you find the terms satisfactory?"

She did not answer immediately. Her bag slipped from her knees to the rug, and as she stooped to pick it up he peered at her closely.

"I think you are tired," he said quietly, watching the play of firelight on her white cheeks as she lifted her head. "You should take a short rest before beginning fresh work."

She shook her head. "No, it's all right," she replied a little unsteadily. "I felt overwhelmed for a moment, that's all. You see, I have been out of a job since last October, and hardly an interview all those months. Work at the present time means everything to me. I couldn't have gone on. Living on one's capital is no joke when you can't see any prospect again of living on an income. And London isn't the happiest choice of place to do it in."

"London?" Dr. Smollett echoed. "But you're in Gloucester now?"

"Only for this interview," Aurelia explained. She had recovered composure. "I thought it would be most improbable I should hear anything more about the post if I stayed in London. So I came to friends in Gloucester for a day or two and applied from there. I'm very glad I did so now, for you admitted that being so near Cottlebury was a point in my favor."

The doctor was silent for a few seconds. "I admire your pluck, Miss Brett," he said at length, "and your perseverance. And I am glad luck has changed for you. No," he added quickly as she half rose from her chair, "please stay where you are for a few more minutes. I must explain that Mr. Weir himself is in Cottlebury this afternoon, and is here at the moment. I should like you to meet him and settle final details before you go."

She could not altogether hide the surprise she felt, though she acquiesced in a matter-of-fact manner. Dr. Smollett with murmured apology for leaving her was already at the door and hastily gone. The moment she was alone Aurelia noticed an electric bell beside the fireplace. She wondered why he had not rung for the maid instead of himself fetching his visitor.

She felt disturbed, suspicious of a cordiality on the doctor's part that she thought was not native to him, yet annoyed at her own suspicion; not because she wanted to think well of Dr. Smollett, but because this prompt wariness of hers told her only too plainly how close it was to fear. And fear at the outset without tangible roots could, unless sternly dealt with, be somehow more disquieting than a well-founded fear later on. She had always held premonition in contempt, but that did not make its power any the less real.

She glanced at the door, her mind in these uneasy regions. They were a long time. She got up and, crossing the carpet without making any sound, cautiously opened the door an inch. It would not close, the pile of the carpet kept it ajar. A murmur of voices came from across the hall. She returned to her place and sat down again composedly.

In a minute there were steps outside and the voices louder this time and close at hand. The doctor came in quickly, followed by a man dressed in badly fitting tweeds, to whom Aurelia, as she rose from her chair, gave all her attention. When the doctor had introduced them Matthew Weir stood looking at her for some moments in a difficult silence. He was a man of middle height, about as tall as Aurelia herself, without pretension to good looks but with an indefinable attraction. His lean build, intelligent brow from which wiry reddish hair receded, and a certain withdrawn, unobservant look in the prominent eyes gave him the appearance of a scholar. They were the eyes of a sick man, Aurelia thought, uncomfortable, strained, filled with unspoken questions.

"I am glad you are coming to us," he said in a quick soft voice that made his pleasure sound apologetic. "Dr. Smollett tells me you are not a nurse."

For an instant Aurelia fancied that in spite of his first remark a nurse was what he wanted her to be. Then she saw that it was satisfaction he was expressing.

"No," she said, "not in any professional sense. But Dr. Smollett has made clear to me what is required in Mrs. Weir's case, and I think I can cope with it as you would wish."

"I am sure you will," he said, with a mixture of diffidence and eagerness. "When can you come?"

The doctor who had moved over to his desk and was going through its contents in a swift, methodical manner spoke without looking up.

"Miss Brett will probably want a day or two before she is ready," he said firmly. "We ought not to hustle her."

"Of course not," Matthew Weir replied, as though reminded of something. "I understand you have come a long way, Miss Brett?"

"Well, not today exactly. Only from Gloucester. But I am living in London, and it is there I must go to pack my things before coming to Spanwater. But it won't take me long—I can be ready whichever day you like."

He looked pleased. "What day of the week is it, Sandy?" he asked the doctor.

"Saturday."

Matthew Weir turned to Aurelia. "Will Tuesday be too soon?" The note of eagerness was more apparent.

"No," she said. "I can manage that easily. Tuesday, the 28th of March? Very well, Mr. Weir, I will come that day. I get the Cottlebury train again, don't I?"

He was fumbling in an inner pocket. "Yes. We live more than twelve miles from here. In the heart of the country. Off the main line. Otherwise I—that is, I would have suggested Spanwater for this interview. But it's a long way, and an awkward journey."

He had taken out his checkbook while speaking, and now walked across to Dr. Smollett's desk and seated himself at it. The doctor had moved aside and was standing, hands in pockets, looking thoughtfully out of the windows and paying no attention to either of them.

Matthew Weir rose and approached Aurelia with a folded check in his hand. "I shall write and confirm the engagement, Miss Brett," he said. "Meantime, please accept your first week's salary—and a small additional sum for the expense it has been to you in coming here today."

Aurelia, who had expected nothing more than her fare, and perhaps not that, thanked him and placed it still folded in her bag. He held out his hand abruptly, his long, sensitive fingers holding hers in a tight grasp. In the moment before he turned away, his hard nervous stare again looked its mute inquiry. The tension communicated itself to Aurelia, who felt constrained to say something.

"If you are writing to me," she said, "will you please send to Gloucester? You have the address, I think. As you have been good enough to give me till Tuesday I shan't be returning to London before Monday."

He agreed, wishing her a hurried and, as she thought, relieved good-bye. It was the doctor who accompanied her into the hall and to the front door. He said nothing until she was standing on the threshold. Then, eyeing her askance, he spoke with some urgency.

"You will find, Miss Brett," he said, "that Mr. Weir is reluctant to discuss his wife's health. That is natural, of course, because, though not particularly serious nor at times even apparent to a stranger, the turn it has taken in the last year or so has been very grave in his eyes and caused him much distress. For this reason I think it advisable if you should want enlightenment on any point to refer the matter to me rather than to Mr. Weir. I call at Spanwater every week and shall certainly be down there in your first weekend."

Aurelia assented without comment. When she had left him and was crossing the deserted churchyard the conviction that there was during the interview something which he had expected her to say and which she had not said nagged at her mind. Before reaching the station she knew what it was.

CHAPTER II

ARRIVALS

I and my fellows
Are ministers of fate.
WILLIAM SHAKESPEARE: *The Tempest.*

MISS FLORA HICKEY, of New Albany, Indiana, U.S.A., got up from the thankless task of trying to make a neglected fire burn in the third-class waiting-room on Cottlebury platform. She was a large woman, and the effort entailed in kneeling to poke and jostle the discouraged embers had been greatly in excess of the result obtained. They went on sulking as if aware that April would be here in a few days and a frugal management unlikely to summon their help again for another six months. Miss Hickey relieved her feelings in thoroughly Middle Western terms that were a mixture of impatience and good humor, and applied her vigor to more congenial occupation.

She was in sole possession of the waiting-room, a fact which from her sociable standpoint was an added reason for resentment and the shivers. Her small suitcase stood upright on the dusty bench. On the table reposed a hat and a sticky bottle and brush, a group of alarmingly post-impressionist appearance at first glance. The hat had originally been gray straw. It now presented what seemed to be a map of the northern hemisphere painted savagely on its crown in lustrous navy blue. The rest of the dye was still in the bottle or congealing miserably on the brush. Miss Hickey decided to remove the instruments with which she was trying to improve an hour not particularly shining, out-of-doors, a region that could scarcely be colder than the one that housed her now. This was not a date to choose anyway for hanging about Cotswold platforms, nor if it came to that for respectable and aging schoolteachers from the States to go chasing their ancestors (in the form of registers and headstones, of course) halfway across the English shires. Outside, the keen Gloucestershire wind came hurrying to meet her through the wide arch she could see on the other side of the line, beyond it an inviting miniature of budding trees bounding a pavement; eddied soundlessly round the pillars and seats; trickled through every interstice in the roof where sparrows, permanent residents regardless of season, fussed and bickered. Well, if the British could stand for it, Flora Hickey would too, and judging by the phlegmatic unconcern with which a fair sprinkling of them stood about the station it did not seem as if they intended taking cover.

She sat down on an unoccupied bench beneath one of the pillars supporting the roof, a yard or two past the parcels office, and uncorking the bottle renewed her onslaught upon the hat. In between she amused herself with watching the few passengers who, in varying degrees of discomfort, waited for their trains. It was the kind of diversion she loved above all else, a sort of fleeting speculation about individual characters, intentions and destinations that never let her down because she had never been in a position to put her fancies to the proof. What she did do was to give them more or less permanent setting in the diary she had kept lovingly since she had been fifteen years old. Its present volume rested now in the suitcase beside her, a fat little book bound in a demure outer cover of chintz that served at once to preserve its inner gloss and to disguise its true character. She thought of it tenderly, in rare flashes wondering what the long procession of unknowns it chronicled would think if they knew of their involuntary contribution to her pleasure.

There were several here now who would unquestionably find their way between its modestly clothed boards. Only a few feet away a white-moustached man stood, irritably totting up figures in a notebook and grunting at intervals into his muffler. Some worn leather bags at his feet seemed to proclaim him a commercial traveler, none too pleased perhaps with the day's business. Farther off, scuffling their toes at the edge of the platform, two boys with schoolbags on their backs waited with a blasé air for the train that meant teatime to them. But in spite of her profession, perhaps because of it, children were flat images; it was impossible, she thought, to visualize them in the round. Instead, she turned her head and looked a little higher up the platform at a girl who was leaning on the rails which at that end separated the station from a group of allotment gardens. A handsome creature, she thought, in a tall, gaunt fashion. Fine bones in a proud, composed face. That hair was lovely too, bleached, of course, but probably a case of art improving on nature. She could see her profile only imperfectly, but the square shoulders and straight, taut body in the long green coat gave the impression of loneliness and even of fear sternly repressed. Miss Hickey's romantic instincts persuaded her that it was perhaps disappointment in love that had added the touch of implacability.

"Your property, I believe, madam." The voice above her head made the words a caress. She looked up with a start to receive from the hands of a gigantic stranger her hat which had bowled to his feet. He handled it fastidiously, aware of its delicate condition, surrendering it with a bow so graceful as to be almost comical if there had been anything in him to provoke mirth. There was nothing, she decided, as he moved noiselessly away. The immensity of physique and catlike step impressed her strongly in this sparsely peopled place. The delicacy with which he moved drew her eyes instinctively to his feet. They were small, narrow, beautifully shod, looking insubstantial supports for the mass they had to bear. He was a mountain of flesh, though not unfortified by muscle. In a tight corner possibly a tough customer. He had stopped in front of a bookstall and with bent head that set a roll of flesh beneath his chin was contemplating its load indifferently. In the great smooth face and loose jowl, the eyes that seemed all lid, the unshapely lips and heavy pallor, Miss Hickey detected nothing but grossness and felt only repelled. But some potency beneath the superficialities made her shudder a little too. He was hatless, his gleaming black hair curving rigidly back from a meticulously drawn center parting and cut *en brosse* behind. An enormous coat with an astrakhan collar hung open nearly to his ankles, exaggerating height and bulk. She tried, with something less than her usual zest, to place him. Probably an impresario, she concluded. Surely not British, hardly American, possibly Russian. She wondered where he had been hidden all this time, and thought by the look of him that it must have been in the first-class waiting room.

"I will say he has a fine voice," she muttered magnanimously, with enough audibility to draw a suspicious glance from the commercial traveller who moved away hastily. Miss Hickey smiled and picked up her damp hat, regarding it with doubtful appreciation. As she stretched out a hand to the brush her attention was again diverted.

A woman had come out of the refreshment room and was hesitating a moment, looking up and down the platform. She was tall and dark-haired and, in spite of the winter, showed in her face the warm coloring of the South. Her slender figure was so rightly treated by the clothes she wore that neither their cut nor their color, Miss Hickey reflected, would be remembered afterwards, but only the vibrant personality dominating them. Miss Hickey loved words like exotic, passionate, alluring, seductive, because she would never be any of them herself. Her diary abounded in them, and they were, she found, instantly applicable to the newcomer. But the frigid bow with which the lady had just acknowledged someone's greeting tempered Miss Hickey's epithets a little. It was as cold as March in Cottlebury. She looked to see who had been so repulsed and, discovering that it was the large stranger who had bought a magazine at the stall and was smiling at the dark woman, felt there was probably some justification. Neither of them after that seemed disposed to make further advances. The lady at least was not taking any risks, for she slipped back into the restaurant and disappeared from view.

Miss Hickey sighed and twiddled her unsatisfactory creation round on her fingers. A vague feeling of depression stole over her. It had been there, she knew, for some minutes, but exactly when or whence it had come she was unable to say. Its source was somewhere on the station, of that she was sure. She ran her eye over the passengers, the girl by the rails, the boys, the grumpy man with the bags stamping up and down now in a fret of cold and impatience, the cat-footed giant examining the timetables with an air of lofty wonder, and the door of the refreshment rooms which was the nearest she could get to the woman who had shown herself an instant before vanishing. It was no good. She was getting old, certainly cold, and much too ready to let slip her cheerful spirits. But Miss Hickey prided herself on a little Scottish blood that had brought in a still smaller portion of second sight. And this doubtful gift told her there was something not quite wholesome here.

Aurelia Brett leaned against the rails and beat her gloved hands together gently on the wood. Not that she was acutely alive to the cold; her mind was too busy for other intrusions. She had noticed the big man who minced in his walk, and recalled having seen him at Paddington three hours earlier. She would have liked to dismiss him as a mere outsize in gigolos, but could not. When he had passed her a few minutes ago she had been conscious of a careless scrutiny that seemed to hold a degree of recognition, and had had the uncomfortable feeling that the recognition should have been mutual. It was absurd, even despicable, to see the hand of fate in every trivial incident, but she found herself nevertheless linking things up with her own project. Because it was of such importance in her eyes she could not help feeling that it was the center too of everyone else's hopes and fears, that she herself was the cynosure of them all.

What she ought to be experiencing was a sense of achievement in having secured the post at all. It was a matter for fervent self-congratulation now—it might have been for self-reproach if she had failed—that she had insisted upon her lack of qualification as a nurse. It looked like plain sailing, but there were one or two things she did not understand: why the doctor had first referred her to Matthew Weir for details of Mrs. Weir's idiosyncrasies, but on taking leave of her had suggested that she apply to him rather than to Weir on questions of health. Reasonable, of course, to expect a medical man to be the better informed on the latter point, but her hypercritical faculties were disturbed by what looked like inconsistency. She had been glad of the check. The new clothes she had bought and the journey to Gloucester had taken the last of her money.

Thought of the money brought bitter reflections of her late employer and the catty, untruthful circle of which she had been the center. They had told her, one and another, in the last weeks of Mrs. Kempson's illness, that she might expect a legacy of five hundred pounds. Fool that she had been to pay any attention to the gossip. Expectation had left realization far behind. The five hundred had turned out to be fifty, soon swallowed up in months of living and scheming how to live. But she had the work now and she would see that she did not readily let go.

A sound at her elbow made her turn her head.

"There," an unself-conscious voice exclaimed happily, "a new hat for ten cents! If I hang it out here your nice English spring breezes will soon dry it, won't they?"

Aurelia decided that one would know she was an American before she spoke. The cut of her plain, expensive suit, and the assurance of voice and glance gave her away. She posed her hat on top of one of the posts, heedless of Aurelia's stare, and laughed with a show of strong teeth.

"I expect so," Aurelia replied shortly. She did not enjoy being addressed by strangers. In any case she did not like Americans. They were the world's true extroverts, and their frankness offended her. Her own inclination was for secrecy and reserve, and she mistrusted their candor, often wondering how a race so eager to give itself away had ever produced a formidable crime record. This woman here was clearly quite undeterred by her reception. She was only thinking up a new method of attack. If she should be traveling on her train she would have the devil's own job to shake her off. She must be firm at the start. Salvation in the tall spare form of the stationmaster was approaching. Aurelia went a step or two to meet him.

"Is there a station for Steeple Cloudy?" she asked.

He looked at her thoughtfully through gold pince-nez that had slipped a little. "No," he said, his pose suggestive of that blend of knowledgeable condescension and proprietary pride common to his office, "there isn't. You've got to get out at Steeple, and that's two miles this side. Where would you be going?"

"To Steeple Cloudy," Aurelia said curtly, knowing quite well what he meant.

The American woman laughed. She had not withdrawn. The stationmaster tried to cover up his inquisitiveness with a faintly indulgent smile.

"I was thinking," he said, "it's a very small place, and unless you know beforehand you're being met you'll not find it easy to get a conveyance."

"I'm going to a house called Spanwater," Aurelia conceded, "and I am being met, but—"

She was caught up by the expression of disapproving interest on his face. Before the coldness in her eyes, however, his stare wavered.

"Well, if somebody's meeting you," he said rather testily, "I suppose they told you the station to be at."

"Of course," said Aurelia, quite unruffled. "But the letter said Steeple, and I wasn't sure whether that was short for Steeple Cloudy or if it was a different halt altogether."

The American cut in with the inoffensive brusqueness of her race. "Spanwater? Isn't that a little Jacobean manor house in these parts? A gem of a place where Henry VIII stayed?"

The stationmaster took pleasure in trotting out a more accurate chronology.

"Henry VIII couldn't have put up at a *Jacobean* house, ma'am," he said reproachfully. "They say it was Charles I, trying to raise some money for his war. And it's not open to the public. Oh, *no*. Oh, dear me, no."

The disagreeable note in his final remarks escaped neither of the women, but it passed unquestioned.

"You know your history," the American observed admiringly, but her tone was a little absent. Aurelia, looking to see where her attention had strayed, noticed that she was gazing with insistence at the triangle of green woolen jumper appearing between the lapels of the coat she was wearing. Here Aurelia had pinned at the base of the throat a heavy brooch of unusual design. Carved in ebony it represented the head of a Mænad, the short wild hair rippling up and back. It was a fine, impassioned bit of work, and she supposed that the other, with the childish acquisitiveness of her countrymen and their flair for spotting an uncommon thing, had had her curiosity aroused. She prepared for the customary barrage of intimate questioning, but none came. The American turned and seized her hat just as a particularly wild gust wobbled it into jeopardy.

"I suppose your station never saw a funnier sight than this," she cried, gaily brandishing her creation in the air.

"I wouldn't go so far as to say that, ma'am," the stationmaster said guardedly. "But, if you will excuse me for saying so, we can always rely on the charming citizens of your country to give us something fresh and interesting—"

Aurelia moved away, sure that his gallantry to the other woman was a kind of inverted displeasure with herself. She had gone only a few steps when there was a rumble, a rush, a tearing whistle, people from nowhere in apparently aimless pursuit of one another, and a train clattered in.

Aurelia pushed her suitcase in front of her into a carriage in the middle coach, sat down in the corner by the door and kept an eye on the handling of her trunk. There were only two others in the carriage, a woman seated diagonally to herself and next to her a little boy who swung his legs and watched Aurelia with the budding resentment of the traveling English in his eyes. Everyone seemed to be leaving on this train except the American who had returned to her bench and, with her suitcase open beside her, was preparing to write in a little book with flowery covers. The guard's flag had already been flapped and the first tremor run through the train when a slim dark woman whom Aurelia had seen for a moment outside the restaurant stepped without haste into the carriage and sat down facing her as they ran smoothly out of the station.

For a minute or two Aurelia let her eyes rest on the usual unplanned collection of railway environs gliding past. A tall church of uncertain denomination, a succession of low-roofed buildings of definite board-school architecture, and on the crest of the next embankment a row of red and yellow brick villas by turn darkened windows and carriage. Then all at once they were running with gathered speed past Cottlebury playing fields and a rush of chill March light flooded the glass. She turned her head and looked at her companion.

Her face was bent over a mass of handwritten foolscap paper which she had taken from a portfolio beside her on the seat and was supporting on her knee. She was scribbling red ink corrections inexorably with a fountain pen and in a savage haste her poise did not suggest. Aurelia saw that she was probably not more than thirty, with an elegant figure admirably set off by severe tailoring. As the train bumped over the points two or three of the papers slid off her lap and floated to the floor. She handed them back, receiving a smile that tilted the corners of the inscrutable mouth without touching the eyes. It was a small face, the skin like warm ivory, the eyes almond-shaped and dark, but too cool and watchful for their color. Long unplucked brows that slanted at the outer tips gave a faint, rather attractive cynicism to her expression. Her hair was drawn off her temples and coiled neatly on the nape of the neck.

Aurelia, admiring her self-possession and something else she could not so easily define, put her down to be a schoolteacher correcting end-of-term examination papers. But did schools break up quite so early? Easter was still twelve days off and nothing but the papers was evidence of academic interests. Feeling suddenly irritated at her instinct to probe into other people's business, surely in itself a sign of apprehension, she gave her attention to the country outside.

They were leaving behind the great uplands that had brought her to Cottlebury, and the low stone walls that dipped and climbed mile upon mile over the turf. There the track had seemed at times to soar, slung midway between the austere curves of sky and pasture; here it ran for the most part between humpy banks that sank at intervals to disclose a less uncompromising landscape. The unadorned sheep ranges were giving way to acres that in a few months' time would bear cabbages and peas for the consumption of Cottlebury, Coventry and Birmingham. The meadows began to have a lush, more amenable aspect, the clumps of trees were not so wind ravaged. The journey was quicker than she had thought, and something, perhaps the unfaltering beat of the train, perhaps the functioning of habitual self-control, had restored her calm. An unemotional detachment that had been her standby before enabled her again to view with equanimity past and future alike. She was not so much Aurelia Brett traveling to new employment as an independent observer watching Aurelia Brett doing it. She began to feel sleepy, and was soon drifting into an uncharted region where enormous strangers incongruously endowed with transatlantic accents gyrated round her, beckoning her on through one dark archway to another. She awoke with a jump as the train jerked to a standstill. They had just run through a tunnel, and the little boy, scrambling out in the wake of his mother, was complaining with repetitive vigor of the absence of light in the carriage.

Aurelia saw that the station was Placton. Her own would be next. The woman opposite had put her papers away and with hands folded in her lap had turned her face to the window. Her shining gaze that reflected the clear afternoon light was focused unseeingly on a distant point of the horizon.

Five minutes later they had pulled up at Steeple Halt. The other woman got out first. As Aurelia stepped down on the wooden boards a girl who had been standing uncertainly in the background came forward quickly.

"Are you Miss Brett?" she asked. "But I think you must be. Hardly anybody gets down here. I'm Dinah Terris, Mr. Weir's niece—and my other uncle is somewhere on this train."

So that was it. An obscure resemblance to Matthew Weir. The girl's eyes were roving up and down the train as she spoke. She was a small, coltish creature, little more than a child, wearing what looked like a masculine overcoat buttoned round her throat and with dark wispy hair blown all ways by the wind.

"Please excuse me a minute," she cried, and was off down to the end of the train from which the large stranger was just emerging. Aurelia saw her fling her arms round him as far as they would go, while he stooped and gave her a solemn kiss. Then she clutched him by the wrist, leading him up the platform much in the manner of an indomitable little trainer conducting a dancing bear.

She effected a quick introduction. "Miss Brett is coming to look after Auntie. You can bring her case down to the car while they get your luggage out. Miss Brett, this is my uncle Augustus—we call him Uncle Weir for short. It's a pity you didn't know about one another earlier, then you could have travelled down together."

Weir looked at Aurelia unsmilingly, and bowed. "I fancy some sort of mutual instinct warned us we were to meet," he said. "I even think Miss Brett may have been looking for the cloven hoof."

His voice was astonishingly musical. But Aurelia was not in the mood to appreciate it. She met his gaze without enthusiasm, and turning to Dinah remarked that her own trunk was still in the train. The porter, returning from taking down Weir's luggage, received instructions, and the three of them moved down the steps leading from the halt.

Near the bottom stood a Hillman saloon, Weir's trunk on the back. Dinah looked at her uncle.

"You saw Miss Leith, didn't you? Walter met her. I don't think she recognized me. She went by without speaking."

She opened the door and motioned Aurelia to the seat next to the driver's.

"Will you please sit by me, Miss Brett? My uncle and your trunk will go in the back, and that won't leave any more room."

They seemed the only people astir in this patch of chilly countryside. Behind and above them the platform and rails crowning the embankment had sunk back into somnolence from which it was hard to imagine they had ever been roused. In front the road they were to travel disappeared behind a group of whitewashed houses above which a great barn towered, the lichen spread like gold-leaf over its tiles. A few yards away a gray goose cropped the grass at the side of the road with commendable concentration while a rush of homebound starlings threw a shadow for an instant across the windscreen.

Once they had negotiated the bend and left the homesteads behind it was a straight road that lay before them. On their left a steep bank ran, dusty at the base and covered thickly with the sharp green of dog's mercury; overhead hung the new buds of beech and hazel, and beyond them lofty and invisible meadows from which came the thin cry of lambs. On the other side the village of Steeple reclined in a sort of hollow that was almost a miniature valley between railway and main road. Very soon the habitations dwindled to a straggling cottage or two, and then a farmhouse in acres of arable land.

Dinah drove with cautious skill. "We're almost there," she said. "It's amazing how different the car makes these two miles and a bit seem. When you're in Cloudy, you know, you feel in a world of your own, leagues away from everybody."

"That must be uncomfortable sometimes," Aurelia said slowly. She felt cold, and the rhythm of the car was renewing her drowsiness. She fought against it, but though she wanted to keep her senses alert she did not want to talk to the child beside her.

An aged and efficient Ford rattled past them in the direction of Steeple, a cloud of dust trailing in its wake. Dinah lifted a hand in greeting to the driver.

"That's Walter Cox," she said, "coming back from taking Miss Leith home. His father keeps the pub in Steeple, and the way he drives that old bus sometimes makes your hair stand on end!"

"I thought he looked rather wild," said Aurelia.

A sleepy chuckle came from behind them. "He's probably as frightened of Miss Leith as I am," Weir drawled.

They had reached the corner of a narrow, stony lane. Dinah drew up to let half a dozen milking cows and their drover emerge. One or two of the creatures rolled their great innocent eyes at the windscreen and puffed sweet breaths on the radiator.

"Don't be silly," she said to Weir, and turned to Aurelia. "Miss Leith is a tutor from Osney Hall, one of the women's colleges in Oxford, and she has a cottage close to us where she comes in the vacs. I cannot make my uncle understand that being frightened of women with brains went out with crinolines, didn't it? And in his case it's specially idiotic because he edits a very abstruse quarterly and ought to welcome intellect wherever he can find it."

"But who said my fears were on intellectual grounds, little one?" Weir's voice had a still silkier quality when he himself was invisible. "And crinolines are back again."

Dinah made no reply. The first rough gradients of the lane overcome, it developed into a road where two vehicles might pass one another. A larch plantation bordered it on the left-hand side, terminating abruptly at a grassy track, obviously unused by wheeled traffic, debouching at right angles from the one they were following.

Dinah was crawling along, her thoughts plainly elsewhere. She turned her face to the little lane, and Aurelia's glance followed hers. The larch wood, a fragile vision in its mist of new green, curved towards them at the top, about fifty yards up, but it was difficult to see in the wan, diffused light shaded by trees and the hedges of the fields on the other side whether or not the road continued past the curve. There was certainly a dwelling of sorts just visible on the corner.

"Miss Leith's house?" Aurelia asked lightly, for want of something to say.

"Oh, no," said Dinah, accelerating a little. Her expression conveyed a mixture of pleasure and anxiety. "That's a mystery. An elderly person has been living in that cottage for months. A Miss Gretton. She was rather a mystery in herself, but you'll hear all about her soon, I expect. My aunt, Mrs. Weir, knew her well. And now she's gone away—not a word to anybody, and nobody knows where on earth she can be."

"How very odd," Aurelia murmured politely.

Augustus Weir leaned forward and whispered mockingly in his niece's ear. "Another case of fright in flight, my pet?"

Dinah rubbed her cheek crossly and ignored him. The hedges on their right had given way to an old brick wall, small dark ivy clustered thick on its summit. It turned on a sharp corner. Round it, ridden fast, came a bicycle. The youth on it, who bore a striking resemblance to Dinah, swerved neatly round them, called out something incoherent, and pedaled furiously along the way they had come.

"My brother Nick," Dinah said briefly.

They had turned the corner and in front of them lay the small and beautiful front of Spanwater Manor. A pair of wrought-iron gates stood open between stone piers, and Dinah drove quietly through, along the straight, short drive to the front porch. Two women were in the drive, walking slowly side by side at the edge of the lawn. One was stout and slow of movement, with a queerly mottled complexion and gray hair round which a chiffon veil had been loosely tied. Her companion was a little spare thing, tight-lipped and quick of eye, dwarfish in stature. Dinah smiled at them but did not stop the car.

"My aunt and Mrs. Kingdom, the housekeeper," she said.

At the top of the drive where it branched in front of the windows, two men were examining the topiary of a yew close to the verge of grass. The shorter of the two was evidently a gardener; in the other as he turned his head to look at the car, Aurelia recognized Matthew Weir.

The door of the house opened the moment the car stopped. A manservant came down the steps to deal with the luggage. He was middling in height, fairly young, with a pale skin and a mouth that was a blend of weakness and impertinence. He kept his eyes down and moved round to the back of the car as Aurelia got out.

"There's another trunk inside, Mond," said Dinah. "You had better get Comfort to help you."

"Very well, miss," the man said almost inaudibly.

Augustus Weir had already extricated himself softly and delicately as a cat and was making leisurely progress towards his brother.

"Come in, Miss Brett," said Dinah, and walked with her up the round, shallow steps to the open door. She glanced at Aurelia with a concerned expression. "You look desperately cold. You must have tea directly. I'll send it up to your room. You don't need to meet anybody yet—I mean, you seem to have met us all already."

CHAPTER III

ENCOUNTERS

What country, friends, is this?
William Shakespeare: *Twelfth Night.*

"Well, now, if that isn't a funny thing," said Mrs. Kingdom, with satisfaction and some asperity. "A *very* funny thing. Dr. Smollett attended her himself each time she was sick, and yet you're telling me he never said a word to you about it!"

She looked at Aurelia Brett as though she held her to blame for the omission. Indeed, if the satisfaction in her tone was for confirmation of the belief, expressed with frequency and emphasis, that all doctors were either noodles or knaves, the asperity was purely for Aurelia. She had looked upon the arrival of a companion for Mrs. Weir as an insult aimed at herself, and two days of the new order of things had served only to convince her more strongly than ever that people of the newcomer's ilk were uppish, opinionated misses remarkable only for inefficiency when it came to the push. Well, like as not they would have to fall back upon old Bessie Kingdom—as they'd done before. She watched Aurelia grimly with hard little eyes that had always invented what they missed.

"He certainly didn't mention the matter to me," Aurelia said with feigned indifference. "Perhaps the attacks were too slight for him to think it necessary, especially as I'm not a nurse."

They were talking in the housekeeper's sewing room on the first floor, a place that looked as if it were given over to ruthless polishing more often than to the activities of needle and thread. It was true that a sewing machine stood in a corner, but so protectively draped with a cover knitted in crimson wool that there was an appearance of taboo about it. For the rest of the room was as scrupulously clean and as bare of comfort as Mrs. Kingdom herself. Aurelia had come there after breakfast with a message from Mrs. Weir, and had got drawn into her first real conversation with the housekeeper.

The formidable little woman snorted at her last remark. "Not so slight, miss, as for them not to call in a doctor," she said with heat, summoning her negatives haphazardly. "She was never the one to be sick before. And seeing as how you've been brought in to look after her it's only right you should have been told."

"Of course," said Aurelia. "But I made it clear to Dr. Smollett that I couldn't undertake nursing, so perhaps as he was engaging me he didn't think there was any point in touching on it."

It sounded to herself a feeble explanation. Mrs. Kingdom demolished it at once.

"Stuff *and* nonsense," she said. "And what sort of folk have you had to look after if you can't put a body to bed with a sick turn? And what would you have thought if she'd had another as soon as you came?"

"But Mrs. Weir hasn't had another," Aurelia said coldly. Some of the hostility Mrs. Kingdom felt for the doctor seemed to be directed at herself.

"No, and *that's* funny too." The housekeeper twisted her locked fingers slowly in one another, as though she were wringing the life out of something.

"As you've said so much," Aurelia went on, ignoring her remark, "please tell me more. How long has this sickness been going on?"

Mrs. Kingdom thought for a moment. "The best part of six weeks."

Aurelia raised her eyebrows. "How often?"

"Not above seven or eight times. But twice in a week at the beginning of this month. And other times too when she's not been sick I've heard her complain of queer pains after eating and drinking—especially after drinking."

"You mean Mrs. Weir complained to you?"

"Certainly I do, miss. I couldn't say who else she may have talked to about it."

"But you reported it to the doctor, I suppose?" Aurelia asked. "I mean the occasions when she wasn't sick but had pain."

"And *that* I didn't!" Mrs. Kingdom exclaimed. "Peppermint water and a long face to hide up all the things he don't know would be the doctor's cure for stomach ache. And she'd still have it. She can cure herself better. Or I can. No, miss, I don't hold with doctors, and I'll not move my little finger to help get one inside the house."

"I see," said Aurelia, who certainly saw a fanaticism not to be shaken. "Can you remember the last time Mrs. Weir was sick?"

"I can. It was a week last Tuesday. March 21st, the day two or three things happened. She went up and had her tea with that artful hussy that's been living over at the cottage—the place they call Titt's Cote. She was sick by supper time, but of course no doctor came till morning. In the night there was a big fall of snow. It wasn't till Thursday she got out again—"

"Do you mean to say," Aurelia interrupted, "that after being ill and having the doctor Mrs. Weir was allowed out in snowy weather only two days later?"

" 'Allowed' is not the word," Mrs. Kingdom said defensively. "There wasn't any keeping her in. We didn't know when she went. It was only old Daniels from the farm telling our gardener she didn't ought to be up at the cottage with only her bedroom slippers on and no hat or coat that made us know where she was. Then Miss Dinah, she went and fetched her."

"What had she been doing?" Aurelia asked curiously.

"Trying to make that Miss Gretton hear, of course. But she wasn't there. She'd gone." Mrs. Kingdom compressed her lips in jealous triumph as though she had been instrumental in the departure. "And she's not been back since. *The Lord be praised.*"

There was none of its usual formal lightness in the last ejaculation. It rang with such Old Testament fervor that Aurelia started.

"Well, I must go," she said with some relief, for the housekeeper wore an air so militant as to look positively destructive. "I have to get ready to take Mrs. Weir out. And if I were you, Mrs. Kingdom, I should let the doctor know directly another time if she has any pain whatever."

Her admonition had a bad reception. "Well, you're not me, miss, nor ever likely to be. And when I want advice I'll ask for it—in the right quarter too. What's more, seeing as none here was thought fit to look after Mrs. Weir and you had to be got in to do it, it'll be *your* place to tell the doctor what you think he ought to be told!"

She flounced out in Aurelia's wake, and went down to the kitchen to vent what remained of her indignation on the new cook. She got small satisfaction for her pains. Lou Blessitt had not been there long enough to find Mrs. Kingdom anything but a rather tedious joke. A placid creature herself, jealousies arising out of human relationships were to her merely funny.

"Get along with you," she said with open disrespect, grinning at Mrs. Kingdom's derogatory remark about lady's maids that thought themselves too good to be called lady's maids. "It was all wrong when the old lady took up with that there Miss Gretton that's gone and done a flit—and now you haven't got her to pick on you must start pulling this other to pieces! I dunno what's the matter with you, I'm sure. You ought to be *glad* to have the poor old lady taken off your hands for a bit. Anybody 'ud think by the way you go on as you wanted her tied to your starchy old apron strings!"

She continued with renewed vigor beating up the eggs she had been engaged on when Mrs. Kingdom had come in.

The housekeeper gave her a bitter glare. "I'll thank you to keep a civil tongue in your head, Blessitt," she said, "and to remember your place."

"Aw, go *on*," the cook flashed back at her, whisking the yolks into a frothy whirlpool, "talking to you makes me real glad I'm in the kitchen. Folks don't fight about food. Leastways not when they can get it. They eats it. As for my place"—she burst out into frank laughter before which Mrs. Kingdom retreated with what dignity she could muster—"there's few as want it, as *you* ought to know for sure!"

Catherine Weir sat alone at the window of the morning room waiting for Miss Brett to come and tell her it was time to go for a walk. She liked this aspect better than the one from the front of the house which looked westward across the lane and over the well-disciplined park to Titt's Cote. There she had found her friend many times in the past few months, and now could find her no more. The view before her was homelier, less acutely reminiscent of recent pleasure. Midmorning sunlight, thin and veiled, but with the promise of spring, lay warm on stone and leaf, spreading like a gentle tide over the whole country, pointing all the shadows towards her. Past the sweep of the drive and the peacock yews her eyes wandered, to the bowling green and the old brick wall. Toadflax clung there, ivy-leaved and with blue-pink flowers that shone like shells in the more somber growth. On the other side the meadows fell away steeply to the main road that ran here from Cottlebury and Steeple and thence on its southeastern ramble to such faraway places as Chipping Norton, Oxford, London itself. From the house it was not visible until it had left Steeple Cloudy a mile or two behind, when it reappeared, a thin white filament threading unerringly the lovely formless pattern of meadowland where the shires of Oxford, Gloucester and Worcester stretched hands to one another.

All that distant landscape under the tender sky made an easy picture for Catherine Weir. Mileage presented no difficulty to her eyes. That was one of the compensations of age. It was easier to see into the distance than to discern the faces that often seemed to hem her in. She might be growing deaf, it might be harder nowadays to fix her mind on the present, more restful to drift like a spent swimmer into the security of the past, but she could still watch to the farthest horizon the march of seasons across the country she inhabited. South of the road the land rose again. Her gaze rested on the sheep-speckled pastures that climbed in a low, continuous swell to the dark plumy wood on the ridge. It clung there like a rook's nest in a spring elm, like a tuft of black feathers on the first green of the hedges; and below, the dazzling white of the lambs that moved beside their elders was easy to mistake for the snow that had so lately melted on the turf they cropped.

As she looked out on it all she experienced again the sensation that had possessed her more and more frequently in the last year or so, that the whole record of events of the past half century was only the idle phantasmagoria of a dream, and that life now was the simple continuance of a childhood spent in the country. She knew quite well that they all, even Matthew, thought that her memory was going, that she spoke vaguely, comprehended imperfectly, and at times confused them one with another. Of course it must seem like that. But how could she explain? How make clear to them, even to Matthew, the one plain, absorbing fact, that Spanwater Manor, where they had lived now for nearly two years, was the same as the cottage on the Welsh border of Herefordshire that had been home for the first ten years of her life? She could not tell them this, not in any way to make herself understood. To them the sign of a fading memory, a failing mentality, a second childhood—she knew what they said though she did not always remember it—was to her a truth so unalterable that it was not to be proclaimed where it was not apparent.

Where peace was, and the happiness that rested on impersonal things, it was the same peace and the same happiness. It did not matter if it was called cottage or castle. But they could not see this. They were blinded, even Matthew, with personal frets and anxieties, with the foolish belief in old age and illness, and the still more foolish surrender to their claims. So it was that they had all in some degree become strangers of late. Even Matthew. Dinah too bright and cheerful to conceal the impatience underneath, Nick too quiet and watchful, Bessie Kingdom more fiery and persistent in her chapel attendance, Mond increasingly evasive and eyeing her from a distance. Matthew's brother too, quiet and urbane, who came only at intervals and was in consequence hard to place. Her mind got a little tired nowadays when it came to sorting out people with migratory habits, and by the time she was quite sure of him Augustus was always gone again. But he had the art of being kind in a casual, oddly patient manner that touched him hardly at all but was soothing at the moments he exercised it.

Life was stirring in the distant pastures. She could see small black dots that had emerged from the wood and were moving swiftly down the field. Those would be the O'Malleys, whom she called her friends but who rarely approached the house these days. But old Esther O'Malley, with no words spoken, understood this fusion of past and present that in the eyes of the family had made her seem ill and in need of attention. Sometimes she had thought too that Miss Gretton understood, and then she would wonder if she really had, because she talked so much, and too much talking was only confusion to ears as deaf as hers had become. But wondering, too, was a fatigue; and it was easier to accept friendship gratefully than to question its sympathies.

She could see by moving her head a little the curve of the oriel window at the south end of the library, its mullions bathed in sunshine that drew the warm yellows to the gray surface of the stone. How often she and Leah had pretended the cottage was winking at them when the sun had struck a thousand tiny sparks from its rough face. Those were the mornings when they had gone to school across the fields, while in the paved kitchen at home their mother made from nettles and bedstraw and the little blue flower the country folk called jill cooling herb tea in a big brown jug against their return. It was strange that memory made it always summer.

At thought of Leah the mirror in which she was reviewing the days that were so clearly part of these grew dim. She groped in vain for the clean thread of her thought. It was gone, into that maze of darkness which seemed to have engulfed Leah. In wretched, familiar fashion the obscure figures, the voices that struggled to be articulate, were there again, in a large room that was a sea of faces. Somebody addressed her in a loud voice, then somebody else, then a third, who spoke little and was dressed in scarlet and white. Try as she would to make sense of it, there was nothing coherent in the scene. And Leah, whose name alone conjured up the confusion, was not there. Her absence gave the vision the absurd inconsequence of a dream, a nightmare in the oppression it left behind. For there remained every time the knowledge that from the first visitation of this picture to her bewildered mind dated the change that had taken place in Matthew. But Matthew, it was clear, believed that it was she who had changed.

She got to her feet in involuntary protest at the fear which always assailed her at this point. The placid train of her thoughts had ended in chaos. She muttered a little, her breathing was difficult, her hands went ineffectively to the bodice of her dress. Then she saw that the door stood half open. Nicholas Terris, her husband's nephew, was inside the room looking intently at her.

Her eyes were void of recognition. "What do you want, Mond?" she asked in a voice hardly above a whisper.

Nicholas moved over to her quickly.

"It's not Mond, Auntie. It's I, Nick. Don't look so worried. Aren't you feeling well?"

She had put her hands tightly on his arms as if the feel of his blazer would establish identity. Then all at once she sat down again in her chair and broke into quiet weeping.

"Here now," said Nick anxiously, casting a look at the door. He had taken a step towards it when it was pushed wide open and Aurelia Brett came in. She was dressed for walking, in the green skirt and jumper, long green coat and small hat to match that she had worn on arrival two days before. Her face was pale beneath the light blonde hair, but when she saw Mrs. Weir in tears and her nephew hesitant in the middle of the room a quick flush came to her cheeks.

"What happened?" she asked. There was a slight edge to her voice.

"I don't know," Nick replied coolly. "I came in here looking for my sister, and when my aunt saw me and I spoke to her she started to cry."

There was a touch of resentment in his tone. He had been conscious of the suspicious note in the girl's inquiry, and the faint implication that he was responsible for his aunt's distress. Just like a nurse, he thought, to assume this proprietary air before she had been five minutes in the place. The woman wasn't even ordinarily polite. No wonder his uncle Matthew had such a distaste for the species. Though he remembered them saying that this one wasn't a proper nurse. Certainly she wore no uniform, but there the distinction appeared to end. For he had to concede with grudging admiration that the results she achieved were every whit as effective as those one would expect from the most thorough training. With that impersonal attentiveness and economy of touch and voice characteristic of the best type of nurse, Aurelia Brett succeeded in soothing his aunt. Mrs. Weir stopped crying, and started cheerfully tidying her person and tucking in a wisp or two of hair preparatory to going for a walk. Nick, whom they both ignored, went quietly out of the room.

Ten minutes later Aurelia, convinced that fresh air and a change of scenery were the most reliable remedies, had got her charge dressed in her outdoor things and was walking with her down the drive to the lane. Mrs. Weir's rambling conversation had about it a brightness due to the revulsion of feeling succeeding her lonely mood.

"I'm going to take you across the park," she said in a pleased voice. "We shall look in on Alice too. I mean—I mean——" Her eyes wandered uneasily and she put a hand to her mouth, then smiled suddenly. "Yesterday I showed you where we always played," she added as they turned into the lane.

Below Spanwater gates it was narrow, greener, less of a road. Entrance to the park was about twenty yards down on their left, along which ran a ditch filled with delicate cuckoo-flowers, the color of spring skies. A stone lodge in which Comfort, the gardener, and his wife lived, stood at the park gates, built in the classical style of a hundred years later than the manor house, for the park had been an eighteenth-century addition to its demesne. Something of the correct symmetry of that age still prevailed in the colonnades of beeches that traversed its few acres. The smooth gray of their soaring trunks gave them the appearance of cathedral pillars, and the new-budded branches the lofty fan tracery of the nave. The grass beneath them was of the usual thin, discouraged variety, though out of range of their boughs it grew emerald green and velvety. Clusters of creamy primroses were springing up everywhere, in the shady places still glistening with beads of moisture. Between the boles bordering the main walk the earth was dry and flaky with the leaf-mold of centuries. Farther off oaks and chestnuts came into view. Round some of them rustic seats had been constructed, and as the two women walked on down the beech avenue they could see not far away between the trees Nicholas Terris sitting on one of these seats, some books beside him and a few more at his feet. To Aurelia at least it appeared that he was not making use of any of them. He caught sight of them immediately, waved a hand, then drew one of the books towards him. He opened it on his lap, stuck an elbow on either knee, and thrust his hands up into his hair so that his face was hidden. It was a gesture precluding the possibility of interruption.

"They have a lot of work to do at Oxford," Mrs. Weir said vaguely.

She waved her stick round a little to indicate the hushed aisle down which they were walking.

"I come here almost every day to see Alice," she went on. "I mean—I came this way every day. She isn't there now, you know. But I think she will be back any time."

She spoke equably enough, but in the flat tone of one to whom words have little meaning and are lost as soon as uttered. Aurelia, glancing at her profile, decided she looked calm enough to be questioned.

"Didn't Miss Gretton tell you she was likely to go away, Mrs. Weir?" she asked.

Catherine Weir looked up at her, startled. Her lips formed soundlessly the words of the question. Aurelia repeated it.

"Oh, no," she said with emphasis, looking ahead along the dappled reaches of the park. "I had tea with her. She told me how wise I was to believe in herbal remedies. She always told me that. And next day the cottage was locked and nobody came to the door. Nobody came," she repeated quietly.

"She was probably called away suddenly," Aurelia said indifferently. "What was she like?" she added curiously.

They were crossing the open park, the grass bright and tender underfoot and still lightly strewn with the copper of last year's leaves. In front of them was a little gate nearly opposite Titt's Cote.

Mrs. Weir gave her a slow puzzled look, but she spoke normally. "I am rather deaf, you know," she said anxiously. "It is very trying—to me and to the others. I cannot tell one voice from another. Sometimes I even think—"

She left her remark unfinished, and Aurelia put her question more loudly.

"Oh, yes," Mrs. Weir nodded. "She is tall, and getting old," she said with surprising clarity, "but not so old as I, I am sure. Her hair is still dark. She wears glasses, and always something warm round her neck because her throat is weak. She feels the cold very much, and wears a great many clothes too."

Her voice was trailing away a little, as it was apt to do, as if she were confiding in herself. Aurelia did not answer, but pushing open the gate followed her into the lane.

At this point it had dwindled to a mere path. A few yards to their right it narrowed still more, terminating in a stile that gave access to fields adjacent to the park. In the other direction it turned at almost a right angle to join Spanwater lane fifty yards farther down, and became wider in that part of its course along which Dinah had stared on the journey to the house.

Titt's Cote stood back a little from the elbow of this grassy track. It appeared at a distance to be crowded on all sides by the ranks of larches that had about them such an air of windless calm and delicacy as to seem artificial in contrast with the less orderly, more varied growth around them; but on approach the wood was seen to be set far enough back to allow for a small garden behind the cottage as well as a piece in front. There was no way to the plantation from the lane, but the thorn hedge was broken by a wooden gate that led straight to the front door of Titt's Cote.

Mrs. Weir put both hands on the top of the gate and looked at the cottage.

"There's nobody at home, you see," she said regretfully.

The only indications of this from where they stood were the closed windows and the absence of smoke from the chimney. The ground sloped downward from the gate, so that the cottage was on a slightly lower level than the lane. Flagstones formed the path and continued under the windows. The eaves jutted out from a tiled roof that was patchy with close yellow lichen. A certain amount of reconditioning had evidently been done not long before, for the walls were cleanly whitewashed, there was some new spouting, and a letterbox had been inserted in the door. An old brick dovecote, still charming in neglect, was visible from where they stood, on the right of the cottage. The place, renovated and tricked out a little now, must have been at least two hundred years old, which explained why the larch wood, of comparatively recent planting, had deferred to its presence.

"Let us go in," Mrs. Weir said, lifting the latch of the gate. Aurelia followed, and they walked slowly down the uneven flags. The small garden grew in uncontrolled and spasmodic fashion, large patches of uncultivated earth where groundsel and petty spurge flourished alternating with clumps of daffodil and jonquil, and here and there bluebells in bud growing between the stones that sprawled everywhere. The one beautiful feature was a mass of dark blue and white violets growing along the base of the wall under the windows and between the chinks of the paving stones.

Mrs. Weir paused near the door and drew a deep breath. Her face was relaxed and happy.

"This is the most peaceful place I know," she said simply, in a voice more conscious of her immediate surroundings than any Aurelia had heard her use. "Yet Alice isn't much pleased with it. Now I come to think of it," she added, looking at Aurelia brightly as recollection, so often evasive, came to her, "she said she wouldn't be sorry to leave."

"It's probably damp," Aurelia replied, eyeing it distastefully. "Perhaps Miss Gretton felt she couldn't bear it any longer."

Mrs. Weir moved to the window and bent forward a little to peer inside.

"Look," she whispered, "you can see there is nobody there."

Aurelia's height made it necessary for her to stoop more than Mrs. Weir in order to confirm a fact that was obvious since they had come in. She rested her hands on her thighs and gazed inside. What she saw was an extraordinarily tidy room, low-ceilinged, very barely furnished, clean, and of superlatively uninhabited appearance. A single discordant note was struck by an object visible on the sill of a smaller window overlooking the back garden; this was a jam-jar half filled with brown water and containing some very defunct flowers, probably snowdrops. It seemed the sole relic of the late occupant.

Aurelia did not notice that Mrs. Weir had moved away until she heard her exclaim suddenly:

"Oh, Miss Brett, she must be coming back! She hasn't told the post office to send on her letters. Here's one pushed in, but it didn't fall down. Now do you think I ought to take care of—"

"No, I don't," Aurelia said sharply. She was at her side as Mrs. Weir put up a timorous hand to the letter-slit, from which the thick white end of an envelope protruded about a quarter of an inch.

"It wouldn't be right to meddle with her correspondence, Mrs. Weir, as long as you don't know where Miss Gretton is nor how long she will be away. Better push it right in and make sure it's safe."

Her hand went firmly to the slit, and there was a little thud on the floor inside as the letter dropped.

Mrs. Weir felt unhappily that she had put herself in the wrong. She wandered round the house for a few minutes, disturbed a couple of rabbits nibbling the depleted winter greens, and remained silent. Presently, by mutual and unspoken consent, they left Titt's Cote.

"Would you like to go home by the fields?" Aurelia asked to break the constraint. She, too, felt ill at ease, ridden by a nameless oppression. She recognized it for the return of that foreboding first sensed at Dr. Smollett's house. The silence and void of the deserted place they had just seen enveloped her like a cloud.

Mrs. Weir, on the other hand, was happy once more as soon as they were in the sunlight again with the prospect of the meadows before them. There was no room for obscure anxieties in the open sweetness of the pastures which, running narrow for a short distance between park and woodland, seemed suddenly to bound away east and west in successive waves of daisied turf. The slope was eastward, where not far away Spanwater was visible and the lane winding past. On the other side beyond the edge of the plantation the ground was higher, ending about half a mile away in the bank that ran down to the road from Steeple.

Mrs. Weir looked fondly down upon the chimneys of Spanwater. Then she drew Aurelia's attention to the roof of a trim little stone house at the bottom of the fields, fronting the lane and about a quarter of a mile from the park lodge.

"A friend lives there," she said dreamily. "I—I cannot remember her name. She is often away, but Dinah says she came home a few days ago."

"Oh, yes?" Aurelia returned. "That would be Miss Leith, perhaps, from Oxford?" But she spoke a little absently, for her eyes were on a figure that was approaching from the middle of the next field.

It was a tall, thin woman, etched darkly against the northern sky. She was still some distance off, moving with a slow, lithe stride, an oblong basket on her hip. She was hatless, and the clothes she wore, a full skirt and three-quarter waisted coat of some dark material had an antique, unmatched air. On her feet were a man's boots. As she climbed the intervening stile and drew closer, it was plain that she was a gypsy. Her features became discernible, a high-boned face that had once been handsome and was now ravaged and predatory, black, enigmatic eyes, and coarse hair knotted loosely on her neck. A near view disclosed that her age was greater than might have been at first supposed. She was an old woman, the brown skin wrinkled and tired, her hair more silver than black, though she still retained a grace of build and carriage inconsistent with her years.

From the moment she had entered their field her gaze had been intent on the two women walking towards her. While still some yards away she stepped off the path and made a detour across the grass on Aurelia's side. She kept her head turned in their direction, her eyes on Mrs. Weir. The sun glinted on two thin copper rings hanging from her ears and played on the gaunt face with a strange light and shadow effect. It gave to her brooding expression a look of profundity oddly disturbing, for it was patient only with the unsubmissive patience of her race.

"Good morning, Esther," Mrs. Weir said, rather uncertainly, conscious of something disquieting in the encounter.

The woman muttered an inaudible response. Then she hastily crossed herself and, as if to invoke all available aid, thrust her hand out a little towards them, forefinger overlaid by middle finger.

Aurelia felt a cold pricking of her skin as she passed them, a momentary darkening of the bright landscape. Mrs. Weir, though she had not interpreted the gesture, glanced at her nervously.

"Old Esther is not so friendly lately," she said in a tremulous voice.

They walked in silence down the next meadow and out by the gate into the lane that led home. On the way back, past Miss Leith's house, through a door into the shrubbery of Spanwater, and over the small stone footbridge that gave the manor its name, Aurelia was silent, burdened with a kind of cumulative anxiety she was unable to analyze. So preoccupied was she that she paid scant attention to the variety of plants Mrs. Weir plucked and carried home from the banks in the lane.

CHAPTER IV

STEEPLE CLOUDY TO THE WORLD

Consisting of some letters posted in Steeple Cloudy on various days between Palm Sunday, April 2nd, and Easter Sunday, April 9th, 1939.

No Body knows how to write Letters; and yet one has 'em, one does not know why——

CONGREVE: *The Way of the World.*

1. *Dinah Terris to Avice Morgan.*

SPANWATER, ——SHIRE
April 2

DARLING VICKY,

Why don't you write me a real London letter, exuding art school and

Bloomsbury and all the old crowd? Not that I know any of them, of course, but you used to turn them into such lively letters they were enormous fun. Have you become such an important person with brush and palette nowadays that you can't pick up a pen? Anyway, here's something for you! Old thing, I've really pulled it off! Not a schol, *that* I knew it wouldn't be, but they're at least admitting me. The letter doesn't give you the idea it's with open arms, and there's a frigid reminder that I'm still faced with Responsions in July, but that trifle being overcome I can, if I like, be an undergraduate of Osney Hall in October. Do I like? Shall I? Shan't I? I don't know. I daren't whisper these heretical doubts to Uncle Matthew, who is overjoyed. He never expected or even, I believe, wanted the schol., which would have been desperately useful. I imagine he looks upon a commoner's gown as being more becoming (not sartorially!) to the female young, and is already transported at the thought of carrying out improvements in my Latin by the end of the summer. Complete alterations would be an apter description.

But it's just because of him that I'm doubtful if I ought to go to Oxford. I don't honestly think he can afford it, and if he can, I don't see why he should. He has the expense of Nick, and that is going to be really worthwhile. And now, you see, they are pressing Nick to put in a fourth year, partly, I suppose, because of that silly business that made him waste the Michaelmas term. Uncle Matthew, bless his unworldly soul, is all for it, never stopping to count the pounds and pence, and I know Nick wants it in his heart. One doesn't know what to do. At eighteen and nearly twenty-one both of us feel it's a bit thick to go on being dependent on Matthew who has done such a frightful lot for us. You see, he isn't rich. The money is Aunt Kate's, and even if things were different with her from what they are at present, one couldn't really ask her to do things for two people that are not her own nephew and niece. I mean, I think she most likely would, but there's no question of bothering her with that now, and anyway, Matthew would never ask help for his own relatives. Quite right too, when you think we're both of an age to be earning for ourselves. Higher education's all very well, but the people who get it don't pay for it.

My uncle made a bad mistake in buying Spanwater. That sounds horrid, as if I grudged him the pleasure. I don't mean that, and I know Aunt Kate helped to pay for it. But Matthew sank nearly everything he had in it, everything that was left, I mean, after that ghastly business two years ago. He bought it for two reasons that were all mixed up with one another, partly because he had to find a retreat for us all from that unspeakable Penmarket, and chiefly because he wanted the perfect gift for Aunt Kate—you know she always longed for the country—so as to make up to her a little for what they'd both been through.

Well, it didn't work. I mean she's been happy in *her* way, but not in Matthew's. There's been a terrible change in her ever since we took it. It has sort of separated her from him. That is another reason why I don't think I ought to go away. I hate bleating about duty, the Victorians made such a monstrosity of it, but I do believe my place is with them here, especially with Uncle Matthew. Besides, I haven't the brains for Oxford. I'm not big enough, and it's awful to risk disappointing Matthew in three years' time. What shall I do? Oracle, pronounce.

Aunt Kate hasn't been well for a long time, but she seems a little better since the nurse came. I don't mean she's a proper nurse, only a companion. But she's marvelously efficient. Uncle Matthew thought Auntie ought to have one because she wanders about so much and insists on picking weeds that she makes into the most awful brews. Witches' potions. Dr. Smollett says it's quite O.K., but I hae ma doots, having been prevailed upon to taste them! And she'd go so far away and to such weird places, even to Pie Wood more than three miles off, where those awful gypsies live. She hasn't been there since Miss Brett came, but a day or two ago they met the old woman gypsy in the fields and Auntie came back with a tale of how she did something or other, not exactly pulled faces at her, but by what I could gather, sort of shooed her off. Miss Brett, too, said she looked quite unpleasant. It's funny, because old Esther, as they call her, seems to have been rather partial to Auntie in the past. But of course you can't trust gypsies, all that smarmy insincerity on top and very deep waters underneath. I hate them anyway. They roast hedgehogs alive.

I thought when Miss Brett came it would be rather fun to have somebody young of one's own sex in the house—youngish, at any rate, for I suppose she's about twenty-five. But she isn't the companionable sort (that isn't meant to be a pun). She's *very* good-looking, in an uncomfortable way. You would make a fine portrait of her, I expect. But she makes us feel we've got to know our places, because she knows hers so well. I don't think she can have had a very decent time somewhere.

Does it seem to you simply *years* since we were at school? I don't yearn to be back. I've more opportunity than you of popping in to Cottlebury and viewing those austere walls that repressed our youthful ardors. Augustus is with us again. Do I hear you snort? Funny how you and Nick loathe him. But you only met him once, and I do assure you he improves upon acquaintance. And he *is* a poet. I wish you'd paint *his* portrait. After that I'll stop!

This is a whacking letter. Write me one back with some real news. Love to Bunny and Tigs, and lots to yourself.

A happy Easter to all.

DINNY

2. *Nicholas Terris to Andrew Pitt.*

SPANWATER, ——SHIRE
3/4/39

DEAR ANDY,

Sorry I missed you at the end. Old Skippy kept me dangling round for the devil knows how long over my essay which seemed to have struck a chord in him somewhere. Gratifying, of course, but not quite the thing for the last morning of term. I can tell you I felt like King Charles, an unconscionable time a-departing, and when I did get away, Savile, like the little gents they pretend to be, had all cleared tidily off.

This is to ask you to come and stay with us over Easter. You know you've never been, one thing or another seemed always to crop up to prevent it, and I want you to meet my uncle and to see this place. We haven't been here two years yet, and we've no what-d'ye-call-ems, ancestral ties or traditions to bind us to it. But it means a good deal to me, and I want to know what you think of it. So be a good chap. Come Thursday if you can. Saturday at latest.

I saw you so seldom in the last week or so that I didn't get the chance to tell you that Skips wants me to do another year and take schools the summer after this. He was by turns emphatic, urgent, supplicatory, and plausible. And it isn't "all along o' doing things rather-more-or-less" that he would like me to put in more time, because I worked like a dog in my second year, and Skippy knows it. What he's really afraid of, though he doesn't say so in so many words, is that being sent down a term lost me just enough ground to miss a First. And the poor old blighter's more or less counted on me bringing that off. He thought I was very edgy this term ("Don't cherish resentment, Terris—you'll sour your work.") hence the desire to keep me till I've mellowed, I suppose. Well, I grant I did lose ground, not so much because I was out of Oxford all Michaelmas as because I felt, unreasonably perhaps, too bitter about it all to work decently on my own. I felt, and still feel, that exactly the same treatment was meted out to me as would have been for a silly rag like alpine stunting on the Martyrs' Memorial and breaking off Latimer's nose. My campaign for euthanasia wasn't like that. I admit I was a bit green to go at it as I did, something like Amanullah experimenting in westernization. But if I forgot the gentle tutelage I swear I never meant to hurt any tender consciences.

Well, it's over now, and I'll confess I don't need much persuasion to stay on at Oxford another year. We should be going down together then. But a grave objection is the added expense it will be for my uncle, especially as Dinah has got an entrance now and ought to be given her chance. Like a silly ass I blurted out Skippy's arguments in favor of a fourth year as soon as I got home, and it was thumbs up with Matthew directly. Yet I know,

Andy, that the old thing's near the end of his tether. His generosity to Dinah and me has been terrific. Sometimes I think it's incredible a man should be quite as unworldly as Uncle Matthew. In sheer self-defense he ought to develop a mean streak. Dinah and I both want to do something about it. I would do anything in my power for Matthew. That isn't sentiment, or if it is it's the sentiment of an average honest debtor. Money is said to be the root of all evil, but I know that lack of it is the very flower itself. A smothering curse.

And look how the stuff gets wedged in the wrong hands. You remember Freddy Borth? Failed his Mods three times, poor little oaf, and is now with a crammer (not for the first time in his young life) in Cottlebury trying to get back to the fold, God knows why. They live there, in Cottlebury, I mean, and Freddy asked me to lunch the other day. I wasn't keen, and if I'd known beforehand what Papa Borth was like, all Mazeppa's horses wouldn't have got me there. I hate being forced to suppress rudeness to my host. It's a harmful form of discipline. I tried to console myself most of the time by thinking out exquisite, subtle, painful and quite undetectable means of murdering him. I'm quite good at that sort of thing. The trouble is he has a down on Freddy. He talked *at* him the whole time. The boy doesn't want to go to Oxford, knows in his muddled way that he isn't cut out for it. Old Borth had set his heart on it, having the dibs to pay, and now that he sees Freddy's not the lad for his money he's turned nasty. There's another son, you see, older than Freddy, who grew up before the shekels rolled in and never went to a university but got a rattling plummy job before he was twenty and is now piling it up like the old man. There's nothing against that. But hence old Borth's sneers at education, which he thinks is a mug's game if it isn't a preparatory course to commercial success. You'll say I'm a fool to be angry with such folly. But, do you know, I *knew* he was hitting at Uncle Matthew. I could see the Weir Case revolving round inside his head in streamer headlines, and his tacit belief that by condemning culture he was justifying his contempt for people who got tried for their lives. I could have murdered him. Gladly and coldly, and oh, so neatly. Instead I hit back good and hard by quoting Matthew (he didn't know it was Matthew though) and said that a university education never had made for quick results and shallow apprehensions, nor was it *calculated* to produce the materially successful. It served an older god. But that didn't mean that having it didn't emphasize the value of worldly success.

I got a trifle incoherent, I imagine, enumerating the legacies of a liberal education, but as old Borth was completely at sea and Freddy horribly miserable, it didn't matter, and deadlock soon ensued. Then he thought to bait me by attacking euthanasia. Didn't I believe in killing off the physically unfit like so many sick dogs, was his gracious way of putting it.

"Certainly," I replied, "but the mentally unfit first." I gave him a pretty eloquent look, but, bless you, he didn't take the thrust. He thinks *his* brain, which put half the industries of the Midlands in his pocket, is the cat's whiskers.

That's all till you come. My uncle Augustus is down here, as usual to sponge on Matthew. We are given to understand that *The Archon* (also as usual) is going through a specially perilous passage. Dinah, who always liked him, of course, says he would be easier to hate if he weren't such a fine poet. I experience no difficulty.

Let me hear which day you can come and I will be at Steeple to bring you forth into the wilds.

Yours ever,
NICK

3. *Augustus Weir to his sub-editor, Sir Ronald Edwy.*

SPANWATER, ——SHIRE
April 5

MY DEAR RONNIE,

Blast Rice. My instinct is to tell him to go to hell, but as a super-civilized product who knows which side his bread is buttered, though he can't reach the butter, I don't. We want his stuff and he presumably wants our money. Mutual satisfaction, so rarely obtained, is now fulfilled. I enclose the coveted pelf. Don't swoon. It's quite all right (or at least it soon will be). Please note that I have postdated the check. But let him have it immediately. It will stifle his cries.

You will be curious about this sudden affluence, or rather the promise of it. I prefer to tell you when I see you, which should be this month. I may be on to something good. It would be risky to say more at the moment.

The country here is all lambs and larks. I like it.

Yours bucolically,
WEIR

4. *Aurelia Brett to a former landlady, Eliza Lessing.*

SPANWATER, STEEPLE CLOUDY, ——SHIRE
April 6, 1939

DEAR MRS. LESSING,

I promised to let you know if and when I got a new post. You must have thought that I had either forgotten the promise or else that I was still out of work. The second idea would have been nearer the truth. I have thought about you often and hoped that business was good and both your rooms let.

You will remember that Mrs. Kempson died in the autumn and that as soon as I came to you a few days after her funeral I started looking for another post. But nothing came along week after week until I was in complete despair. I cannot tell you how often I have wished that I had not left you after Christmas to go right into London, for if more opportunities offer themselves there it is also true that there is very much keener competition. The fact that I have such few qualifications as a nurse was a stumbling-block in several instances. I had very little to do with Mrs. Kempson in the last month of her life and a trained nurse had to be got in for her. So in cases where my prospective employer was an invalid, even the good testimonial I could show wasn't enough to secure me the job.

Things went on like this all through the New Year and after. Each day I was searching the papers for ads and answering everything likely and at last even unlikely. Usually I got no reply. Until a fortnight or more ago. Then, when things seemed at their lowest ebb, I came across an advertisement for a companion for an elderly lady. I wrote, feeling only apathy as I did so, in fact less hope on this occasion than several times before, for the notice was worded so briefly, specifying nothing in particular, that I was positive there would be a great many snags. To my surprise an interview was arranged. Still more to my surprise I got the post.

You would think I ought to be highly pleased now. I am in a way, but all the same I have never felt easy about this place. Directly my interview was over I remembered where I had seen the name Weir before, which is the name of the people who have engaged me. You will probably recall it too when I tell you. The Weir Case, two years ago. You remember? The professor from Penmarket who was tried for murdering his wife's sister with some poison or other. He got off, but a great many people still believed he had done it and thought that he owed his life entirely to that clever Sir Kenward Coffin, who defended him. It all came back to me, and I remembered it had been impossible for him to go on living in Penmarket, and how he had resigned his post at the university and bought a manor house north of the Cotswolds where he and his wife live nowadays. I wished I had not thought of it, because I was in desperate need of work and had gladly accepted the post.

And though I have been here over a week, I still cannot shake off the feeling that all is not quite as it should be. A nurse was in the house, you know, when Mrs. Weir's sister was poisoned, and had been engaged a short time before. The coincidence makes me uneasy. And Mrs. Weir was sick on and off for a few weeks *before* my arrival, though nothing was said to me about this, but since I have come she has not had one of these turns, though she is a bad color and the doctor says her heart is not in a healthy condition.

All the servants appear to be local people engaged since the family moved here, but the rest of the household, including the housekeeper, who is very jealous of her privileges and belongs to some fanatical religious sect, are the same as were at the house in Penmarket, an orphan nephew and niece, and a brother of Mr. Weir, who writes poetry and edits some London journal. The last three seem to me to be living on the bounty of the Weirs. Mrs. Weir is a harmless soul, much older than her husband, I think, rather deaf, and a little feebleminded. Her most dangerous habit seems to be gathering plants from hedges and fields and making what she calls "herb tea" with them, as her mother used to make it, she says. I don't understand why the doctor doesn't forbid it. But they seem resolved to humor her, and he says there is no harm in it. I don't feel at all sure myself, for she is hardly responsible for her actions and may easily pick something poisonous, cuckoo-pint, for instance, which I have seen growing in several places. But there is a stubborn streak in her.

She is also prone to wander about a lot outdoors, and in this way picks up a number of chance acquaintances, gypsies among them, that the rest of the family either don't know or won't acknowledge. One of these people who has been living in a cottage close by has gone away without telling anybody where or why, and Mrs. Weir is rather bothered about it.

The house and grounds are beautiful, but very isolated. There is a doctor in the next village, but the family doctor comes from Cottlebury, a distance of twelve miles and more. A curious arrangement. My duties are light, so I have plenty of time to observe things. I notice that the servants seem to prefer Mrs. Weir to her husband. That, of course, may be only the natural prejudice of their class against a man with a past. The housekeeper is odd in more ways than religious, and very mistrustful of everyone. For instance, yesterday afternoon a lady who lives part of the year in this hamlet and is a tutor at Oxford called to see Mrs. Weir. Mrs. Kingdom (that is the housekeeper's name), finding she was with Mrs. Weir, came hurrying upstairs to my room where I was changing my frock to urge me to go down and join them. She conveyed the impression, and I suppose meant to convey it, that they were not to be left alone together. I didn't take much notice of her, but she was so emphatic and mysterious that I felt uncomfortable all the same.

I must close now and see Mrs. Weir safe to bed, so will post this tomorrow. I sleep in a room communicating with hers, but she gives little trouble. A good thing perhaps, for I have been sleeping *very* heavily for me of late. It must be the country air.

I hope I have not bored you with so much about my new place, but you were always kind and interested in my doings. It has been a relief to write. Will you please keep my letter for a time? One never knows what the future may hold, and this contains a few of my early impressions.

Does Miss Aveney still live with you? And do Cappy and Sam sing with the same gusto? They must be the oldest canaries in the country!

Yours affectionately,
AURELIA BRETT

5. *Bessie Kingdom to Mary Purvis.*

SPANWATER, ——SHIRE
8th April

DEAR MARY,

Thank you for the recipe you sent the beginning of the week. But it was not the one I meant. I've had this before, and the one I asked you for was that you gave Bertha Dunn's girl when she went as cook to the Platts. A rare good one she was too, different from some I could name, and they not a hundred miles away, neither. The baggage we've got is not worth the salt she leaves out of things. And the airs they give themselves, well, I told her the other day, Lou Blessitt, I said, if I had presumed in my time above my elders and betters as you do I wouldn't be where I am today, a respectable widow looked up to by all and with a nest egg to retire on when occasion do arise. Sit on it then, she says, and see what you can hatch. And that Gracie titters at all her bad sayings.

It's a pity, that it is, you're not in the same case yourself. It don't seem decent you shouldn't have a penny to turn to. Let Tom be my brother but I will say he was a poor thing and a godless one too, always making a mock of them as worshipped the Almighty in fear and righteousness. And as I look at it the Lord took him off sudden like because it was a waste of time letting him be around any longer. There's a many that could be said of, only some are not gone yet. You should have been firm. Kingdom was one of Tom's kind when I married him, but in the end of his days he was as upright a worker for the good cause as any could wish.

Well, *she's* better than when I wrote last. They got the companion they were after for her, and *not* a nurse this time, and she's been pretty well since. But nothing to do with this new girl, mark you. Don't think to put the credit there. She was improving *before* my lady come. In fact ever since that Miss G. went off. I told you about that. We may think what we will, but there was more in it than meets the eye. Why else would she take to her so and have none of the rest of us by, but that she knew who had the money? Glad I am she's gone, the schemer. It's getting on for three weeks now, and no sign of her back. She was more of a worry even than they O'Malleys, sinful livers as they are. They don't come nigh the place since I told Esther she was trying to sell us one of Comfort's own galeenies. They ought to be cleared from Pie Wood like a nest of hornets. It's a puzzle why old Birchall has them living like pagans on his land and thieving off it. They say the old woman saved his children once in a barn fire out there, but that was before our time here and all their stealing and badness since should have wiped that out. If she did get burnt it was but a taste of punishment to be. Not but what they'll turn up at Steeple church tomorrow in all their ribbons and nasty dirtiness, I've not a doubt, and take part in the popish goings on. Our good lady will get out there too, or my name's not Bessie Kingdom. But some as have need to ask pardon won't be there. His fine cock of a brother has landed on us again, and the colleges have broken up and Master Nicholas come home, so with this new madam they've got there seems plenty here. That other one you've heard me name, the Miss Leith from Oxford, has come back, too, and opened up her house. I haven't actually seen her with him again yet, but it's early days, and she was brazen enough the other day to call on the old lady. But Mr. M. happened to be out then.

I'm surprised you should think I write harshly to you. What I say is only for your good. I never did like improvidence.

Your affectionate sister-in-law,
BESSIE

6. *William Mond to his sister.*

(No address)
April 9

DEAR DORA,

It won't be much longer now. Keep your head and hold your tongue. You know what you have to do. Don't leave anything behind. It's F.P. for you now, but keep the name quiet as yet. M. can corroborate some, but we have everything. *No more letters* whatever happens. You might have wrecked it all. *A. is here*. Get that into your head. I don't like it, but I'll see it through now. You will be told what to do as soon as possible. Till then not a word, and stick where you are.

BILL

PART II

HERB TEA

To bitter sauces did I frame my feeding.
WILLIAM SHAKESPEARE: *Sonnet 118.*

CHAPTER V

THE WEIR CASE

Uncharitable woman! thy rash tongue
Hath raised a fearful and prodigious storm:
Be thou the cause of all ensuing harm.
JOHN WEBSTER: *The White Devil.*

"AND SO," the assistant commissioner remarked in conclusion, "enough arsenic being found to kill a household, the police are taking no risks—*this* time. I don't blame 'em. Shift it on to our broad backs, eh? I know their chief—nice old johnny, but in rotten health nowadays. Won't be at it much longer, I shouldn't wonder. Anyway, the Penmarket mess is deterrent enough to any local force wanting to handle this job, if you ask me. Better get down there in the morning, Pardoe—take Salt with you if he's available."

Chief Inspector Dan Pardoe returned to his room with, it must be confessed, none of that exhilaration and excitement commonly supposed to arm the amateur detective on the brink of a new inquiry. To tell the truth, he felt a little reluctant and worried. The sensation was familiar when murder, or what appeared to be murder, presented itself, though it would soon pass away. Routine, with the way it had of habituating one's personality to whatever conditions or issues arose, would see to that. Like slipping into a brand new overcoat, reflected Pardoe, who liked the tried in clothes as in most other things; you felt uncomfortable and conspicuous at first, but a compromise was soon reached by which body and garment worked in harmony. But there was certainly for him a unique factor in the particular job to which he'd just been assigned. He was going to investigate a death by poisoning in the house of a man acquitted only two years earlier of a charge of murder by the same means. That staled the ground a little at the start.

What he would have constantly to guard against was an initial, perhaps almost inevitable prejudice that given its head might distort the whole affair and result in a monstrous perversion of justice.

Inspector Pardoe was tall and spare, with lean, intelligent features that were handsome in the least showy sense of the epithet. His face was weathered like that of a man whose waking and working life is spent in the country, its roughened tan in agreeable contrast to the white, curly hair above it. Even his eyes had the remote look of those who are not, as he himself was, bounded by close horizons. Actually, in London he was a fish out of water. Born on a Gloucestershire farm forty years ago, his adolescence had coincided with the birth of the new, unquiet era, and a succession of what were nothing more than accidents had landed him at New Scotland Yard with an occupation that in the eyes of the uninitiated spelled romance, of the initiate a job of work as frequently tedious as any other. It gave him a shock sometimes to recall with what little planning his life had been ordered. No single-minded ambition there, forging ahead on a clear track to a cherished goal. Achievement had come by hard work, it was true, but not by design. He was, he supposed, where the personal factor was involved, unambitious; the only thing he had ever desired ardently was that peace which was apparently the one thing the world intended to withhold. Yet he liked his work, rejected nothing he thought would promote its interests, and had the wisdom to respect intuition equally with reason. He was a clever man whose abilities never scintillated nor owed anything to histrionics. Facile emotion, like facile judgment, was not for him. But he himself was privately grateful for a dissatisfaction which few suspected that made him acutely sensitive to the responsibilities of his work; for if it sometimes came near crippling his action and gave him some bad moments, in learning to subdue it he had recognized that this very sensibility was a two-edged weapon that sustained while it threatened.

He pressed a bell, and when it was answered sent for all available material bearing on the Weir case of 1937. It was rather less than it might have been; the local police had judged their own fingers sufficient for that pie, and Scotland Yard had not been invited to a share. It was enough, however, to keep the light burning in the inspector's room for nearly two hours, while he absorbed press reports of the inquest and subsequent trial, reading, remembering, making notes, considering in the light of the past the deadly facts of the present which the A.C. had been able to supply this evening. At the end of that time he pushed the papers from him and sent for Detective Sergeant Salt.

"What do you know of the Weir case, Salt?" he opened without preamble.

The sergeant, used to his chief's direct introductions and appreciative of them, sat down in the proffered chair without betraying any surprise. He was a shrewd, old-fashioned officer who had reached his present position through unostentatious work on sound, conventional lines. Pardoe, who admired both type and individual, found him easy to work with and extraordinarily reliable, with a retentive mind that was often a storehouse of apposite information.

Salt, not given to wasting words, was silent for a minute. Then he slowly indulged in a rare smile. The touch of childish malice in it gave, Pardoe thought, a surprising look of old Silenus to his comfortable face.

"Not so much as I ought to, p'r'aps," was his reply. "But that's neither here nor there. The Weir case wasn't one of *our* mistakes. A schoolmaster, wasn't he, murdered his sister somewhere up in the north country?"

"Not one of your brighter days, old man," Pardoe said with a grin. "He wasn't a schoolmaster, and she wasn't his sister, and they didn't live in the north country. *And* he was found not guilty." He laughed outright at the sergeant's bewilderment. "But you're perfectly correct in saying it wasn't one of our mistakes.

"No, Matthew Weir was a professor and tutor in Classics at Penmarket University. Penmarket is a dull, straitlaced, rather sordid little city in the Midlands with one excellent feature it doesn't deserve and has never appreciated, a thoroughly progressive university. Matthew Weir and his wife lived in the suburbs, in a comfortable house that was like scores of other comfortable houses round it, smug, circumscribed, set on keeping up appearances, the happy hunting-ground of the dabbler in poisons—"

He pulled himself up. "Sorry. I've been soaking myself in a pretty grim story. Only the middle-class really knows how to produce its particular brand. Squalor and luxury alike know very little about it, but suburbia—yes. I'll give you the facts. The Weirs were childless. They lived in a semidetached house a mile from the city, with a garden that a jobbing man attended to and a little built-on garage. They kept two maids, and Mrs. Weir's sister came to live with them about five years before this thing happened."

"Ah. Sister-in-*law*," Salt grunted, as if it explained everything.

"She was a couple of years younger than Mrs. Weir," Pardoe went on. "And Mrs. Weir was nearly ten years older than her husband. Her name was Miss Leah Bunting. By all accounts, piecing this, that, and the other together, taking off a slice here and supplying a bit there, she was one of the most difficult, though not the most uncommon, types of maiden lady, given over at the same time to good works and to the exercise of an uncharitable tongue. In short, it seemed as if the good works had wrung all the goodness out of her."

"I've known women like that," said Salt darkly.

"Well, whatever charity she may have dispensed in Penmarket, none found its way into the house where she lived with the Weirs. Matthew Weir was an agnostic, and his sister-in-law, preferring precept to example every time, gave him no peace. She nagged and bothered and fretted unceasingly, more, it seems, because he wasn't worrying about the pit that opened before him than because she actually wanted to save him from it. Her chief occupation appears to have been making people miserable."

"Wait a minute," said Salt with more interest, warming to sudden recollection, "I remember now. There was somebody else in the house you forgot when you said two maids—who was it, a cook, or a housekeeper, or suchlike?"

"Quite right," Pardoe said. "There was. I forgot to mention her. She was the housekeeper, Bessie Kingdom by name. And I know why you thought of her then. She had the same kind of religion as Leah Bunting, and was the only person to speak a good word for the dead woman at the trial."

"That was funny, though," said Salt. "Wasn't the place pretty hostile to Weir? They tried him at the Bailey, didn't they?"

"Yes. But when I said the only one to speak a good word, I meant of those whose evidence was heard in court. Penmarket wasn't asked for its opinion, for all that it gave it freely enough. Penmarket esteemed Leah Bunting as a good woman who had busied herself among its poor and 'fallen'—into neither of which categories the speaker could be placed. Penmarket didn't live with Leah Bunting, you see. Besides, don't you remember the other reasons for the place hating Weir?"

Salt shook his head. It was old stuff, anyway, he thought. He wondered why it had suddenly assumed enough fresh importance for the chief to rake him out at this time of night. But he wouldn't hustle the pace. He would hear in good time.

"He'd married a very rich woman years older than himself," Pardoe reminded him, "and thereby committed a double offense. Poking nose into other people's business is one of the major occupations of the world, and there's nothing like disparity of age in marriage for becoming everybody's business instanter. Add to it disparity of worldly goods, and you bring down on your head the satisfied disapproval of the whole community. Human nature being what it is, it finds it impossible to conceive a comparatively poor man who will marry a rich wife for any motive other than that of getting a clutch on the moneybags."

"I see what you mean," Salt said slowly. He had a vague idea that the inspector was putting up a kind of defense of such marriages, and the fancy was not quite to his taste.

"And you must remember," Pardoe continued, unaware of the sergeant's disapproval, "that not only was Mrs. Weir herself rich, but she had expectations of greater wealth still on the death of her sister. The story of their inheritance is a curious one, with a nice touch of the fairy tale about it—except that ultimately they didn't live happily ever after. There were three sisters, Hannah, the eldest, then Mrs. Weir, whose name was Catherine, and Leah, the youngest. They were the daughters of a farm laborer in Herefordshire, earning in the days before the deluge his sixteen bob a week with a cottage thrown in. His lot would have delighted the heart of the bygone lady novelist, for he turned out to be the heir of a very comfortable fortune made by a great-uncle out in Australia at a time when it was still possible to make one there. Well, he came into all this money at an early age, when his daughters were still little girls, and as far as business acumen goes he seems to have deserved his surprising deal. He probably had more than a bit of great-uncle in him. Instead of losing his head and generally going to the dogs, he invested the bulk of his fortune sensibly, and with the remainder bought an ironmongery business up in Sheffield. Oddly enough—I mean from my own point of view it's odd—he seems to have jumped at the chance of leaving the country and hurling himself into the competitive hustle of city life. They say money makes money. It certainly did with Tim Bunting. When he died he'd added considerably to the original fortune, and left his daughters three of the richest heiresses in the north of England."

"It's a wonder, isn't it," said Salt, "that the sister—I mean the one who was poisoned—didn't leave her pile to the charities she thought so much of, instead of to Mrs. Weir for the husband most likely to get his hands on?"

"I expect she would have if she could," Pardoe rejoined. "But she hadn't a free hand. Old Bunting tied it up—at least nearly all of it—so that each childless daughter's share had to go on her death to the surviving daughter or daughters. See what I mean? Hannah, the eldest, married and had two children, so her portion didn't pass to her sisters. But Catherine—that's Weir's wife—was childless, and Leah was a spinster, so whichever predeceased the other her money would go to the survivor."

"So that Mrs. Weir was a good deal richer still when Leah was dead?" the sergeant put in bluntly.

"Yes. And there was more than that to Bunting's will. Its provisions extended to the grandchildren of each daughter, that is, to the testator's great-grandchildren. The old man intended his lucky windfall, and the additions he'd made to it, to stop in the family. He meant to establish its fortunes all right, and to make an acquisitive suitor think twice."

"What d'ye mean?" said Salt. "The husbands never had a chance of the money?"

"Only the incomes. Whatever they did with those the capital stayed intact. But of course the incomes were considerable, and Penmarket, which condemned Matthew for marrying a rich woman wouldn't have bothered to look further or work out the implications of the will, even supposing it knew about it."

"But it still left this professor chap with a motive for poisoning the Bunting woman?" Salt questioned hopefully.

"A money motive? Oh, yes. Their income practically doubled itself when Leah Bunting died. And there were things at work even more powerful than money—the hatred she had for her brother-in-law, and the release her death must have meant for him from a peculiarly vicious persecution. She was undoubtedly an unbalanced woman. He coached some undergraduates at his house, you know, and there was unpleasantness on different occasions. She was evidently of the opinion that the young, especially the masculine young, are all heathen and ripe for conversion, and she'd start advances along these lines. But it seems that in one case at least her friendly interest wasn't altogether prompted by missionary zeal. Weir had to come down heavily when she started waylaying the youth in the town and outside the college gates, and so on. After that any possibility of reconciliation with her brother-in-law seems to have been out of the question where she was concerned. For a time she lost control of herself completely and even circulated absurd stories about Weir and the women students, which unfortunately got credence in certain quarters."

"I remember," said Salt. "That made a row, didn't it?"

"Yes. When it got to angry parents removing daughters who had never so much as spoken with Matthew Weir—and this happened in two cases—the university authorities thought it time to step in. Mind you, they never appear to have lent a credulous ear to any of the spiteful nonsense. From a weight of quite disinterested evidence Weir emerges a gentle, guileless kind of man, absorbed in his work, devoted to his wife, and with no misadventures of any description to his discredit. To the end the university was as loyal to him as he seems to have been to it."

"But he left it, didn't he?" Salt remarked.

"There was nothing else he could do but resign after the stink and notoriety of it all. But we haven't got to that yet. The university took the matter up, and pointed out to Weir that as the scandalous rubbish going around was traceable to his own sister-in-law, he must find some means of stopping it. If it couldn't be checked privately without a fuss, then they would be compelled in the interests of the university and all its members to make Miss Bunting leave Penmarket altogether as alternative to meeting a charge of slander in open court."

"Well, he—somebody found a means of stopping her good and proper," Salt said.

Pardoe nodded grimly. "Somebody did. But not for a few months after that ultimatum. That is, she didn't die till three months later. And a curious feature of that intervening time was that the malicious gossip *did* come to an end. All at once, like turning off the gas. Questioned on the point, Matthew Weir said that he had spoken to her and told her that unless she kept quiet she would have to leave Penmarket or be faced with a slander action. He hadn't been much impressed with the way his warning was received, but something, anyway, must have found its mark, for that particular trouble came to an end. There was no more tittle-tattle."

"And directly that stopped the woman started being ill," Salt supplied.

"Well, not directly. About three weeks later. But as soon as Weir had told her of the university's decision a queer change, to which all the witnesses testified, came over Leah Bunting. Instead of being militant, domineering and garrulous, she became all at once self-contained and almost humble. At first she ignored her brother-in-law entirely, neither addressing him nor mentioning his name. It must have been a refreshing change. Then, in a variety of meek little ways she began to acknowledge his presence and, or so it seemed, to curry favor. Mrs. Kingdom, the housekeeper, said that in her opinion, Miss Leah was anxious for a reconciliation."

"Funny thing, you know," Salt broke in, "seeing how she hated him, that she hadn't cleared out and gone to live somewhere else long before."

Pardoe shook his head. "She was a spinster with few relatives. Notoriously hard to live with too, so when alone she'd found it difficult to keep a servant, and at last impossible to get one. She was comfortable in Penmarket, where she'd built up the sort of reputation she strove for. And you must remember she was the kind of person whose satisfaction is incomplete without a victim to nag. The ideal one was probably her brother-in-law."

"Well, she got what was coming to her by staying on."

"The illness began simultaneously with this change of front," Pardoe continued. "After Christmas she complained of pain, sickness and aching limbs, and according to the housekeeper—there was no corroborative evidence of this—confessed that she went in fear of someone unnamed, saying that 'they would not be happy till they had got rid of her.' The defense, which was frankly skeptical of Mrs. Kingdom as a witness, suggested that this ambiguous phrase, if it was ever made, meant that the university, and Matthew Weir if you like, would have been pleased if she'd elected to leave Penmarket. The prosecution put a deadlier interpretation on it."

"What was she *doing* there, anyway?" Salt sounded aggrieved. "If she thought somebody was poisoning her, she could still have got away before she was too ill to go."

"Exactly. The preliminary stages of the illness went on for some weeks before she was confined to her bed consecutive days on end. Kenward Coffin made a good deal of the point. Financially, he said, here was an independent woman, bound to the Weir household by no ties of affection, as was only too clear, so that if it were true that in the New Year she was living in dread of someone *in the house*, why didn't she leave it? And if the source of her fear was *not* in the house, then the case against his client fell down."

"Neat," Salt said. "But somebody gave her the stuff, didn't they?"

"Oh, yes. Weedkiller. A brand called Clerepath, which the Weirs used. The gardener's evidence was pretty important. He swore he missed a tin that still had some in it. Well, by the end of January Leah Bunting was so ill that she took to her bed and a nurse was got for her. Nurse Geary seems to have been a sharp-eyed, waspish woman, efficient up to a point, a pronounced feminist and fairly bristling with the more negative virtues—an ideal ally for a sick woman who believed a man was poisoning her. Anyway, it was an ill day for Matthew Weir when the doctor engaged her, for her testimony was the most damning of all.

"Leah Bunting died late in February, and the doctor who was attending her refused a certificate. Yes, I know what you're going to say," Pardoe added at a movement from Salt—"that he had plenty of warning beforehand, and should have taken some action that would have checked the game of a slow poisoner. To a certain extent I agree. The discovery of arsenic after exhumation is a different matter—it usually means that the doctor either had no doubt at all of the genuine nature of the illness, or that his suspicions were not strong enough to be voiced. But in the Weir case Dr. White's suspicions were grave enough for him to put the affair into the hands of the coroner there and then, though it was no sudden death but one from the cumulative action of poison. She had been ill for seven weeks, and in the care of a nurse during the last month. Both Dr. White and Nurse Geary came in for some rather severe grueling, for the autopsy showed that a pretty stiff dose of arsenic had been taken only thirty-six hours or thereabouts before death. The doctor's answer was that he had, more than once, given veiled hints to the household that there were peculiar features of the illness, and that he had done all that was humanly possible by insisting on a trained nurse, whose presence, he supposed, would deter anyone who might be 'trying to hinder the patient's recovery.' That was his euphuistic phrase for the deliberate poisoning of Leah Bunting. What isn't at all clear is why he never called in a second opinion."

"They found out, did they," Salt asked, "that it was arsenic she'd been having before the nurse came?"

"It was in the nails and hair. Of course, that isn't irrefutable evidence, you know. A good many people may have minute quantities of the stuff in their system without anybody's nefarious attempts to bump 'em off. But taken in conjunction with the symptoms of the long-standing sickness and the quantity found, there could be no practical margin of doubt that arsenic had been administered to her as far back at least as the first week of January."

"I forget," said Salt, "was it put to the professor johnny that the doc had tried to tell 'em 'hands off'?"

"He was asked in the witness box if he had not noticed that Dr. White was puzzled by the severity of the illness. He said, no, he thought the doctor was simply taking a justifiably grave view of the case, and that he himself was as anxious as Dr. White for his sister-in-law to have a nurse, but that he never realized there were features in the illness which bewildered the doctor.

"On such facts as were established, White seems to have been a vigorous, overworked, rather irascible G.P., with the average skill and perhaps really rather less, after all, of the average reluctance to delve beneath the surface. I think myself he was unjustly censured, except for his omission to get a second medical opinion. After all, it isn't easy to say what else he could have done in the circumstances. He must have hoped up to the end that he was going to pull her through. And when all's said and done he *did* do what a good many haven't done, saved them the expense and pother of an exhumation."

"And Nurse Geary? How'd she explain the arsenic being taken while she was in the house?"

"Well, she couldn't. But the ruthless cross-examination she was put through turned up an odd story. She said that in the last fortnight of her life Miss Bunting had on several occasions asked if her brother-in-law would come and sit with her. He had done so, twice in the nurse's presence, twice alone. The last time was on the afternoon of the day preceding her death, when the nurse, at the request of her patient, took half an hour off. Leah Bunting died shortly after midnight of the next day—coming then it surprised everyone, including the doctor, as in the previous week she had been definitely better. The last and fatal dose of poison must, medical evidence was agreed, have been taken *about* the time Matthew Weir was with her. Further questioning elicited from the nurse that on one occasion, she could not recall which, when Leah Bunting had asked for Weir, she had added, 'I shall have to see him.' The prosecution took this to mean that she was somehow compelled to admit him to her presence, though unwilling to do so. Defense, on the other hand, urged that the words bore a perfectly innocuous meaning—simply that realizing she was extremely ill, Leah Bunting's conscience smote her, and she desired a better understanding with her sister's husband."

"What did Weir say? They put him in the box, didn't they?"

"Yes. Coffin likes an incautious bluff of that sort, and as a matter of fact everybody agreed that in this case it was a brilliant plunge. Weir's manner was his best defense—and say what you like, let the judge say what he likes, more than half the time the jury are influenced more by the prisoner's demeanor than they are by the facts of the case. Anyway, Weir was the gentle, naïf, faintly puzzled scholar to the life. It did him yeoman service, I'm convinced. Even the touch of absentmindedness wasn't overdone. This was borne out by one specially damaging piece the nurse let out. She said that once—not the last time he was there—when she went into Miss Bunting's room after Weir had left it, the patient asked her to throw away a scrap of cardboard on the bedside table. It turned out to be an empty packet that had contained matches, like those Weir used. When she went to toss it into the w.p.b. Leah Bunting—she seems to have had an economical turn of mind—told her to look inside 'in case Matthew has left a match in it.' There was no match there, she said, but when she poked her finger in, *a little white powder*, only a few grains, came out. The accused, questioned about this, readily admitted that the box was probably his. He said all the family knew his habit of leaving odds and ends in various rooms. But he denied all knowledge of any powder."

"Who were 'all the family'?" Salt asked with some emphasis.

"There were a nephew and a niece, orphans, I think, whom Weir schooled and generally looked after. They don't come into the story. The boy was in his first year at Oxford, and in the middle of a term there, and the girl was away at boarding school. A funny thing was that Leah Bunting died in a weekend when Mrs. Weir had gone on a visit to the school to see the girl, and while Weir's brother, who is a writer and lives in London, was staying with them."

"And what did Weir have to say about his visits to the Bunting's bedside?"

"Oh, he openly admitted them, of course, but said that though his sister-in-law had not been actually antagonistic there had been no attempt on her part to patch things up. She seems to have rambled on, at times incoherently, in the pseudo-missionary style peculiar to her, and had impressed him as being even stranger than in the days when she had freely nagged him. He said he attributed this to the effects of her illness and bore with it accordingly."

"Well," said Salt, resigning himself to the incredible, "he got twelve blokes to believe him, anyway."

"Yes. After nearly two hours' absence. It was touch and go. Old Coffin, in fact, was rather nasty about it—he was used to juries endorsing his eloquence in less time than that. The judge—it was Kyte—summed up with what passed for impartiality, but the press undoubtedly detected hostility to the prisoner and some little coercion of the jury. But Weir was lucky in his peers. By Jove, he was lucky. They were an unsentimental, intelligent collection that acquitted him on insufficient evidence and lack of corroboration among the witnesses. One or two of them had made bad impressions, you know, notably Mrs. Kingdom, who didn't stand up well to cross-examination and seemed to have what you might call a universal grudge. And Nurse Geary's manner suggested that she was prejudiced. Coffin pounced on every vulnerable point of their testimony and reduced a good bit of it to absurdity."

Pardoe paused. "So that was the Weir case," he finished quietly.

Salt was pursuing his own train of thought.

"They left Penmarket for good, didn't they?" he remarked.

Pardoe remained silent for a few moments, frowning thoughtfully at the papers on his desk.

"Yes," he said without further comment.

Salt watched him closely. "D'you believe Weir killed her?"

The inspector met his searching gaze squarely. "I don't *believe* on incomplete evidence," he said. "There's the danger of making theory fact. And the full story wasn't told. When is it ever? Well, whatever the truth of *that* business, old man, from now on the open mind is going to be no mere figure of speech for you and me."

"Why—what—?" Salt began.

"The story isn't finished. The Weirs went to live in a manor house in the Cotswolds. Two days ago Mrs. Weir died there, the day after Easter Monday. She died of arsenical poisoning. We're to go down there in the morning."

CHAPTER VI

SCOTLAND YARD TO STEEPLE CLOUDY

You look at these scattered houses, and you are impressed by their beauty. I look at them, and the only thought which comes to me is a feeling of their isolation, and of the impunity with which crime may be committed there.

A. Conan Doyle: *Adventures of Sherlock Holmes.*

"When you say '*a* local doctor diagnosed poisoning,' " Pardoe said, "I take it you mean the family doctor?"

The inspector and Sergeant Salt were in Superintendent Creed's office in Cottlebury. The police station was a fine old Regency house in a forsaken square, its decayed facade in harmony with the forgotten dignity around it. The superintendent was an immensely fat man with a subdued manner. He lived in the perpetual shadow of his own corpulence. An industrious, conscientious officer, he was troubled by the notion that everybody was a prey to the fallacy that stoutness spelt indolence. He had been at some pains to explain to the Yard men that it was only the unfortunate background of the case, so to speak, which had induced the chief constable to hand it over.

"No, no," he answered testily, vexed with himself for not elucidating the point earlier. "Dr. Smollett is the doctor in attendance at Spanwater. He lives in this town, and that's nearly thirteen miles, you understand, from Steeple Cloudy. But there's a village called Steeple two miles from Cloudy, this side of it, and a more sizeable place. I reckon you'd best put up there at the pub. Well, when Mrs. Weir was first taken bad it was on the Easter Monday night, as I was saying. Their first move was to ring up Dr. Smollett, but as luck would be the doctor 'd been called out to another case. So then they phoned the lady doctor living in Steeple—Fisher's the name—and she came pretty soon."

"I see," said Pardoe. "Now when did Dr. Smollett take over?"

"Not till well into the middle of the morning. He couldn't. He had a confinement he couldn't leave. Dr. Fisher did all she could—folk swear by her, you know—but it was hopeless. The poor old lady had had too much of the stuff and her heart couldn't stand up to it. It seems she'd been very middling for a long time, well, since Christmas. She collapsed and died just after five o'clock on Tuesday. Dr. Fisher by then was pretty sure the symptoms were those of poisoning by arsenic, and Dr. Smollett agreed."

"And they found she'd been drinking her herbal mixture on Monday, and confiscated what was left in the jug?"

"That's right. The companion remembered the stuff was still about and suggested some harmful weed may have got in it. Dr. Fisher took charge of it early on. Since then they've got it analyzed, with what result you know. And Sir Lewis Blayne's report this morning says 1.24 grains were found in the body."

"Chiefly," said Pardoe, consulting the report, "in the kidneys and alimentary canal. Hardly anything in the stomach. Yes, I've got all that. I'll want to see Dr. Fisher, Smollett too. Got anything else for me?"

"We searched the place for arsenic—found nothing but the old tins in the potting shed. Then one of our men spotted a thermos flask lying in the shrubbery. It was empty and fairly clean, but there were faint traces of this herbal brew left in it. There wasn't much trouble in finding the owner. Miss Brett said it was hers. She couldn't account for it being there, and said it had never to her knowledge held any of the herbal stuff. It had been in her bedroom. She hadn't missed it till we found it."

"Any traces of arsenic in it?"

"No." The superintendent remarked with sudden irrelevance, "Pity Weir didn't change his name."

"He was acquitted," Pardoe remarked mildly.

Creed reddened and looked almost angry. "I know. And you and I know how much difference it makes to the man in the street. *He* brought in his verdict weeks before the jury got a chance. And look at the talk now. Besides, it would have been 'Not Proven' in Scotland."

"And the axe in Germany most likely," Pardoe finished curtly. "We've got a new job on our hands now."

He and Salt left the station and before going on to Steeple lunched at a recommended place in the High Street. They talked little while they ate.

"Creed's made up his mind anyway," the sergeant said as they came out into the street again. Pardoe's only reply was an eloquent grimace.

A moist wind was blowing from the south, fine rain that was hardly more than mist pricking their faces as they walked briskly along the pavement. At intervals the neutral tint of road and shops was broken by the vivid wares of the flower sellers who stood beside the curb, offering daffodils and violets, mimosa and bunches of bold tulips from the Channel Islands.

"Smollett first," the inspector said. He had a note of the address, and in a few minutes they were crossing the churchyard through which Aurelia Brett had hurried nearly three weeks ago.

But the doctor was out, in attendance at the hospital, the maid explained.

"Elusive sort of chap," was Pardoe's comment as they turned away. It did not matter for the present; he was well informed of the latest medical points, and for immediate purposes Dr. Fisher's testimony was the more important.

Pardoe commonly preferred rail to road travel, relying on a hired car, if such was necessary, when his destination was reached. This time, however, in consideration of the specially rural character of the case, he and Salt had run down in his elderly Morris, an outdated model that more than compensated for its lack of spectacular verve by the cheerful spirit with which it tackled the toughest of secondary roads.

At the parking place the inspector himself took the wheel. To Salt, who belonged to the group of overcautious drivers who are a source of anxiety to others as well as to themselves, it was not a happy responsibility in a strange district.

They took the north road, passing out of Cottlebury in a driving mist that spun a veil over the town behind them. Pardoe was quiet as he drove at a moderate pace past the new villas and clustering council houses with their virgin gardens that a year or two ago had been the rough pastures at the foothills of the Cotswolds. He knew this country and loved it. The towns that were stretching insensitive feelers in all directions might be encroaching a little even here, but their intrusion would never be the violation it had been to the plains and valleys. The hills, like the sea, would always be dominant and uncivilized. It was an invigorating thought. For centuries man might wring a living from their harsh breasts, but it would always be the same living, unmodified by change, progress, invention. They were for ever free from his urban impertinences.

But they were not to climb the heights this journey. The road kept its humble course between acres where only spring seemed alive, and the houses that, on the outskirts of the town, had been an advancing army were here only sentinels. Trees and hedges, shining with the almost invisible rain, looked in full leaf and unbelievably green. A row of elms separated one field from another, and above their bunchy crowns the sky was flaked with cawing rooks that swung and dipped in the falling vapor, drifting at last like a handful of soot on to fallow ground the other side.

Salt, with the privileges of a passenger, was attentive to his surroundings. To him, as to many who spend their working lives in the cities where they are born and bred, the country remained for the most part an ideal vaguely extolled, seldom realized, never understood, and, if truth be told, rarely coveted. But this afternoon his thoughts were quickened more than was usual by an uneasy sense of isolation and secrecy.

Pardoe gave him a sidelong look.

"Like to settle down hereabouts?" he asked.

"Not me," Salt said promptly. "It 'ud give me the jim-jams. I mean to say," he added hastily with a note of apology, "it's lovely fresh air and quiet, and all that—but—well, I dunno."

" 'And all that,' " Pardoe echoed softly. "Yes, it is all that. The world doesn't break in much here, Salt."

"No," said the sergeant, and astonished Pardoe who was inclined to credit him with too little imagination, by adding, "p'r'aps it would be better if it did."

They were silent for a little while after that, until Salt showed where his thoughts were.

"Come to think of it," he said, "he could have had the country without being buried in it."

"It's not as inaccessible as all that," Pardoe replied. "I suppose you're thinking of the doctor? But the doctor at Steeple is a woman, and sex plays a big part in one's preferences in that line."

The sergeant did not answer, but his silence was dissatisfied.

The road they were traveling dodged and twisted with, it seemed, the pointless convolutions of a game, now hiding, now revealing, the stretches they had just traversed. They were running almost parallel to the railway, hugging the embankment with the line a dozen feet and more above them. A little train sped past, and when the smoke cleared, the roof of an immense barn came in sight, a haphazard pattern of houses, and some hens picking at a plat of grass in front.

"Steeple," Salt said, with the short sigh of one revisiting civilization after too long an absence. They bore to the left where the road broadened into a bay, behind them a flight of steps leading up to the halt. Pardoe's first objective was the inn. He had no difficulty in locating it, for it stood facing them on the other side of the tree-shadowed road that curved out of sight behind the village.

It was a modest little limestone house with a frail wisteria climbing over half of it and, projecting over the front door, a weathered sign bearing a fox of doubtful color. An ivy-leaved geranium hung in a wire basket above the entrance where a man with a grave, pleasant face, evidently the innkeeper, stood talking earnestly to a short clergyman.

"The Silver Fox," the sergeant read out carefully. Pardoe slowed down. As he stopped the car the clergyman, who was hatless, moved away from the inn, passing them closely with a courteous glance in their direction. Pardoe saw that he was a small, stout, compact man, like a plump starling, rather bald, with dark eyes and a ruddy complexion.

The Yard men alighted and went in. Rooms were easily secured in Steeple in the middle of April, even at the close of Easter week, and they were quickly satisfied, for the place was clean and quiet if a little damp and closely pressed by trees.

The proprietor's name, as they had observed, was Henry Cox. His incurious acceptance of their own titles impressed Pardoe favorably. While a boy carried up their bags he asked for Dr. Fisher's house.

"Third on the right fronting the road, sir," was Cox's reply. "You'll see the name, Meadowscrown, on the gate. Not many of us here at all, and nobody hard to find."

Pardoe thanked him. "That was your rector, I suppose, who passed me just now?"

"That's right, sir. The Rev. Flood. The rectory is down there, in the hollow." He waved a hand towards the barn, then looked back at the inspector with something uneasy in his mild eyes. "Excuse me, sir, but I take it you've come down to inquire into this sad affair at the manor out at Cloudy. It's a scandalous business—I don't mean the death, for of course the poor old lady was too fond of picking wild stuff from the hedges—but the rotten talk that's going all about. And rector, he's just been to ask me to do what I can in the bar to stop it." His face reddened suddenly. "By *gum*, I will—and so will Walter."

Pardoe looked at him curiously. "In a case in which the police are asked to help, Mr. Cox, you won't find it easy to stop talk. But perhaps it's a special piece of gossip you've got in mind?"

"Well, it is," Cox said in a more unwilling tone. "But I'll be as bad as they if I spread it. I oughtn't to have said anything at all, that's a fact, but with you gentlemen coming in as the rector went away I can't but have it foremost to my mind."

"If you tell me," Pardoe said, "that's not spreading scandal. We're the general clearing house for every kind of tale, you know. In any case if the story's going round I shall be bound to hear it soon."

Cox still looked worried. "I don't even know her," he said, partly to himself.

"You'd better let me have it," the inspector said patiently. "If you think it's false, isn't it better I should hear your version first, before I hear the malicious one from those who think it true?"

His manner persuaded the innkeeper. "It's like this, sir," he plunged into hasty speech. "There's a lady living in Cloudy—Miss Leith is the name. I don't know her, she comes and goes. But she attends church here, and Mr. Flood, he knows her well. It seems as how she's friendly with them at Spanwater." He hesitated. "Too friendly, according to these tales. They're saying as how there've been goings on between her and Mr. Matthew Weir, and that the poor lady dying this way is the best thing can have happened for 'em," he finished bluntly, distaste for his story only too evident.

The sergeant grunted enigmatically, while Pardoe nodded without surprise.

"The usual kind of thing," he said. "Though they might very well correct their story in one respect. A death in circumstances like these can only be the very *worst* thing that can happen for two people misbehaving in the way your scandalmongers suggest. Let 'em put that in their pipes and smoke it." He smiled briefly at Cox. "Carry on the good work as the rector advised. Let them remember the law relating to slander is a pretty active one."

He signed to Salt, and they left the inn in quest of Dr. Fisher. The sergeant looked at Pardoe in some surprise.

"Looks like he didn't know about Weir's past," he said naively.

The implication was so pointed that Pardoe could not help smiling.

"Old fellow," he said indulgently, "he wasn't born yesterday—if you were. And he hasn't been wrapped in cotton wool the last couple of years. Keeping a pub would soon unwrap him anyway. Everybody else knows, so why not Mr. Cox?"

"P'r'aps everybody don't know," was Salt's tentative suggestion.

"What's wrong with you?" the inspector retorted. "Creed's attitude gives me some idea of the feeling about Weir. No, all we happen to have struck first go is a decent chap who won't subscribe to the common twaddle. I thought it was pretty neat too, the way he casually slipped in his opinion of how Mrs. Weir died—he intends to meet their story with his own, that her death was accidental."

"Well, arsenic don't grow under hedges. I should have thought he'd have known that if he wasn't born yesterday," Salt replied triumphantly, getting a little of his own back.

As was obvious at first glance, Meadowscrown was a recent addition to Steeple. Its stone front stared with a primrose freshness that took one aback after the prevailing grays of the cottages by the station. It was the third and last house on the road; the rest of the village appeared to have run down the slope and hidden between road and railway.

A strip of garden lay in front of the house. Against the wall near the door stood a pair of steps, and on them a woman, in a stained overall and wearing gardening gloves, was engaged in fastening up a rambler rose.

Pardoe opened the gate and went in, followed by Salt.

"Is Dr. Fisher in, please?" the inspector asked, as the woman turned her head at sound of the gate.

"I am Dr. Fisher," she replied, adding briskly, "one moment please," as she administered a final rap to her work. Then, placing the hammer on top of the steps, she came down to greet them.

"I am Inspector Pardoe of Scotland Yard," the inspector said, "and this is Detective Sergeant Salt. Can you spare us a few minutes?"

She was a woman of average height, stout in a firm, muscular fashion, with a scrubby Eton crop and clever eyes in a homely red face.

"Why, yes," she said in the clipped tones she had used at first. "Come inside."

She pulled off her gloves, smacked them sharply together, and let them drop at the foot of the steps. Opening the door, she led them into a diminutive hall and thence to a small room, untidy in a mannish fashion, that was clearly the consulting room.

When they were seated, Salt close to a corner of the heavy table that served as centerpiece, so that he might have a place to rest both elbow and notebook, Dr. Fisher spoke first.

"It's about Mrs. Weir, isn't it?" she said. "I gave Superintendent Creed a statement on Wednesday, and shall, of course, be attending tomorrow's inquest. But if there is anything additional I can tell you now—?"

Her manner, which was politely detached, suggested that there wasn't. It struck Pardoe that her qualities were wholly scientific. She probably lacked sympathy in its more human interpretation, and if she had a bedside manner it would not be the type that appealed to elderly ladies permanently occupied with their insides.

"I have your statement, of course, Dr. Fisher," said Pardoe. "Tomorrow's proceedings won't carry us far. As I was in Steeple, what I wanted was to meet you before going on to Spanwater, so that I could hear a few of the facts afresh."

She nodded briefly. "As you like, Inspector."

"You reached the house shortly after midnight?" Pardoe asked.

"To be precise, at twenty minutes to one on Tuesday morning. It was a quarter past twelve when Mr. Terris rang me up. I understand he had been unsuccessfully telephoning Mrs. Weir's doctor. I had gone to bed, so I dressed as quickly as possible and then got the car out of the garage."

"What did you at first think of Mrs. Weir's condition?"

"I diagnosed it then as acute gastritis. My opinion was strengthened when I was told that the patient had been subject to similar attacks of a much milder nature during the past month. There was retching, vomiting, severe abdominal pain. Her temperature was high. I knew nothing, of course, of the history of the case."

That made Salt look up. History was an ambiguous term in *this* case.

"Who was it," the inspector asked, "told you that Mrs. Weir had had these attacks?"

Dr. Fisher frowned. "I am sorry, Inspector, but I don't remember. It was either Mr. Weir or the housekeeper, whose name I have forgotten. But I can't properly recall which, and was unable to tell the superintendent when he asked. Does it matter?"

Pardoe shook his head. "It's not very material. Several members of the family were up and about then when you arrived?"

"All of them, I should think. Their anxiety to help looked like being a nuisance, so I turned them all out except the housekeeper and a maid, I think the cook, who could give a hand when necessary."

"But there's a companion, isn't there? Mrs. Weir's companion, who remembered the herbal drink?"

"Oh yes, but she was quite unable to give any help for some time. You know what happened, don't you?"

"No," Pardoe said, interested. "The only report I have of her is in connection with the infusion Mrs. Weir had been drinking. I understand she drew your attention to it."

"That is correct. No, of course, nothing was said at the time. My fault. But one patient as ill as Mrs. Weir was enough on my hands at once, and I didn't think the matter important at that stage. Afterwards, Dr. Smollett dealt with it. I can tell you what was told to me and what came under my own observation. When I got there, Mr. Weir met me in the hall and went upstairs with me. He said that Miss Brett—that is the companion—had gone to wake him shortly before midnight to tell him of his wife's illness.

He was not in his room, but downstairs reading, so when there was no answer to her knocking she roused first Miss Terris, then her brother. Eventually either the boy or his sister went downstairs and found Mr. Weir. But in the confusion which followed, nobody seems to have wondered where Miss Brett was. I'm afraid I didn't think of her, for I had my hands full with Mrs. Weir, and never having seen Miss Brett, I didn't miss her."

"And where was she?" Pardoe asked.

"In her room, asleep," Dr. Fisher said, adding at Pardoe's look of surprise, "obviously a drugged sleep—I mean she had had a draught to induce it, that was clear. Until a quarter to two, apparently no one missed her, or even thought about her, though her bedroom was next to Mrs. Weir's with a communicating door. There she was eventually found, lying on her bed, not in it, and wearing over her pajamas the dressing-gown she had had on when she went to wake the family."

"Who found her?"

"Miss Terris, I think. She tried to wake her, then called to me. I went in the room, saw what was the matter, and had her put properly to bed with a hot-water bottle. She wasn't ill. The dose must have been a moderate one, and I thought it better to let her sleep it off."

"Did it strike you as peculiar, Doctor?"

"Just for the moment perhaps. But I didn't know any of them, you see. That was the first time I had ever seen Miss Brett, and for all I knew sleeping tablets might have been prescribed for her. I certainly thought it odd that she should have chosen to sleep so soundly that night of all nights, and that she should be doing so in her dressing-gown. It didn't occur to me then that it might not be voluntary on her part."

"And it wasn't?"

"No. But Dr. Smollett knows more about that than I, and of course Miss Brett herself. I had to give my whole attention to Mrs. Weir, with whom I stayed till after five o'clock. Then I left, after telling the housekeeper what to do and promising to come back in a couple of hours."

"How was Mrs. Weir when you left?"

"Very much easier, but extremely weak. The heart was in an enfeebled condition. When I got back here I made up a soothing mixture, the usual chloroform and bicarbonate of potash, to take back with me. Also, I had time to think."

In the grim little silence that followed, Pardoe gave the doctor a keen glance.

"You mean," he suggested, "you were doubtful then of the nature of the illness?"

She nodded, her eyes on his. "Yes. I had never experienced a case of gastritis in which *all* the symptoms were as violent as these. What was perhaps more important I *had* met with a case of acute arsenical poisoning."

"What was that?" the inspector asked, and Salt looked up quickly from his notes.

"A farm laborer in Henford, a village four miles east of this one, drank liquid weedkiller from an unlabeled bottle in mistake for cold tea."

"And his symptoms resembled Mrs. Weir's?"

"They were practically identical. I happened to be in Henford when his illness started, and attended it in every stage. The only difference was that his greater strength helped to prolong his life. He did not die until the fourth day—Mrs. Weir in, roughly, twenty-four hours."

"So you returned to Spanwater with a different opinion of the case, Doctor?" said Pardoe, who suspected that something else had played its part in suggesting arsenic to her.

"I wouldn't say that exactly. It would be nearer the mark to say that I went back with a new idea and was prepared to look at the case from a fresh angle. Gastritis can imitate arsenical poisoning with horrible exactitude, and where it's easy to theorize it's difficult to give a decisive opinion."

"What time did you pay your second visit?"

"At half-past seven that morning. A message was awaiting Dr. Smollett on his return, but he was attending a troublesome maternity case the other side of Cottlebury and up till then knew nothing about it. Mrs. Weir was quiet when I got in, but she had had another attack of vomiting, the housekeeper said, half an hour before, and she was definitely weaker."

"It was on this second occasion that you made some inquiries?" the inspector asked.

"Yes. Well, actually certain information was volunteered by the companion. Miss Brett was awake then, though feeling heavy and seedy. She was drinking black coffee the cook had made. I thought her very excitable and upset, but was not surprised in the circumstances. I wanted her to keep quiet for a time, but my apparent refusal to hear what she had to say only made her more excited, so I let her talk. You will, of course, hear her own story from herself. What was of interest to me was mention of the herbal drink, of which I'd heard nothing till then. I went downstairs with the cook and found what was left of it in a jug on the kitchen sideboard. It was very little, not much more than half a pint. I took charge of it immediately."

"Now, Dr. Fisher," Pardoe leaned forward, "when this infusion was made, was it usual to leave the plants in the jug?"

"I don't know what was usual," the doctor said carefully. "You will have to ask that of Dr. Smollett. On this occasion they were not left. I was told the infusion was made in one jug and after cooling strained off into another ready for drinking. That being so, I wanted to know what had become of the stuff from which it was made. The cook said it would be in the bin ready to be transferred to the incinerator. So I went out to the bin and after a little poking about found it and fished it out. It went to the county analyst with the liquid."

"Prompt work, Doctor," Pardoe said with sincerity. "Can you recall what condition the herbs were in and how far down in the bin?"

"Yes," the doctor said at once. "I remember because there was something queer about the find. The bin was three-parts full and was to have been emptied into the incinerator by the gardener in the morning. The herbs were about halfway down, rather nearer the top perhaps, but before I got to them I found something else—several leaves of the wild arum, which children call lords-and-ladies, still joined at the base, and with the inner sheath that contains the club that later turns to berries. It was bruised and had obviously been in water, but had kept its shape and even its glossy texture. It was resting on a crushed cardboard carton that had held a bar of soap, and immediately *beneath* the carton was the soggy mass from which the infusion had been made."

"And the relative positions struck you as odd?" Pardoe put in.

"Yes. The arum looked like an addition. It seemed to have been placed on the cardboard where it had little chance of slipping down into the bin and so escaping notice."

"I see," was Pardoe's only comment on the doctor's deductions. "Anything else peculiar?"

"Yes, the difference in the appearance of the plants. Boiling water gives a blackened look to herbage. The stuff underneath the carton was of this color. It was matted too, and pulpy, difficult to separate and say what had been what. But the arum was recognizable at first glance and by comparison hardly damaged."

"Did you infer anything from that?"

"That the arum had been in cold or, at most, tepid water," Dr. Fisher said promptly.

Pardoe agreed. "The analyst's report is an extremely interesting one. The cuckoo-pint—I'm sorry, I should say the arum—had not been part of the infusion. But not only was its poison absent from the liquid submitted to the analyst, but arsenic, with which the liquid was heavily charged, was completely absent from the herbs found in the bin."

"Quite so," Dr. Fisher said. "Arsenic got into the infusion *after* it was strained."

"Yes. Now a few minutes ago, Doctor, you spoke of Mrs. Weir's death as taking place approximately within twenty-four hours—did you mean twenty-four hours from the time the poison was first taken?"

The doctor hesitated. "If we had not got the vehicle in which the poison was taken, I could not have made such an assertion. As it is, you will hear that the infusion was made in the middle of the morning and not strained until after lunch. We know Mrs. Weir had not drunk any before two-thirty. She died at five o'clock on Tuesday afternoon, so that the limit of the time in question must be twenty-six and a half hours."

Something slow and less incisive in her voice drew Pardoe's attention. She was frowning, looking absently at the fire.

"And you're puzzled, Doctor?" the inspector asked.

She looked back at him instantly. "I am. Arsenic, as I expect you know, is a puzzling poison. The time at which a dose was taken is rarely predictable unless circumstantial evidence comes to the aid. Its actions through the organs is rapid, especially if it is taken soon after food. The symptoms of poisoning would not appear so quickly in a hungry person. Other factors, of course, like health, age, and so on play their part too."

"Yes, I've heard those facts about arsenic," Pardoe said. "So the time question is unsatisfactory in this case?"

"It is rather. You see, on the evidence of several members of the family, Mrs. Weir had a glass of the mixture in the early afternoon, about three o'clock. She had had a fairly good lunch at one-thirty, tea not much more than an hour after drinking it, and dinner at seven-thirty. She went to bed at nine o'clock. Yet the symptoms don't seem to have begun till about eleven-thirty."

"On the evidence of Miss Brett?"

"Yes. She herself had gone to bed early—I forget why exactly, but you will hear—shortly after Mrs. Weir. She says no sound came from Mrs. Weir's room up to eleven. At about a quarter to, Miss Brett, who could not sleep, had poured some water from her bottle and drunk half a glassful. The sleeping draught—it was medinal—was afterwards found to have been in the bottle. She dozed in about half an hour, and says she was roused from a kind of stupor at about half-past eleven by groans and retching from the next room."

"I see your point, Doctor," Pardoe said. "It means that Mrs. Weir felt no effects of the poison till at least eight hours after taking it."

"In spite of having eaten once before and twice afterwards," was Dr. Fisher's skeptical rejoinder, "and in spite of the fact that the arsenic was taken in liquid form which acts more quickly than the powder. Eight hours is a very long time, Inspector. I believe I am correct in saying that the longest period recorded is ten hours, and in that case the arsenic was taken as powder on an empty stomach. In addition, Mrs. Weir's heart was weak, she was subject to gastric trouble"—there was a slight pause—"and she was getting on in years. The more I think of it the less I understand it."

Pardoe got slowly to his feet without answering. Salt, too, stood up, his thumb keeping the place in his notebook.

"You were present, I think, when Mrs. Weir died, Dr. Fisher?" said the inspector.

"Yes, with Dr. Smollett. After paying my second visit at seven-thirty, I left at nine. I had to get back to my surgery. I came again just after eleven and Dr. Smollett arrived ten minutes later. After consultation with him I left, but at his request called again in the afternoon when he was there, and so was present when she died. She had been unconscious for some hours."

"A nurse wasn't fetched in?"

Dr. Fisher shook her head. "I did not do so at the beginning because, frankly, I didn't know at what minute Dr. Smollett might not come and handle the case himself. Afterwards—well, Mrs. Weir was dying, and compared with what it had been up to the middle of the morning, her condition was a restful one. Miss Terris too had done a V.A.D. course, and the housekeeper was sensible. There was, unfortunately, little anyone could do."

She accompanied them to the door and along the path to the road. At the gate she stopped, looking from inspector to sergeant and back again.

"One other point occurs to me," she said, addressing Pardoe. "Mrs. Weir did not finally lose consciousness till some time about noon, after I had seen Dr. Smollett and gone away. On my first two visits she could speak, though with difficulty, and several times while I was with her she said the name 'Alice,' and looked at me with peculiar concentration. I don't know whether she took me for Alice, or whether she wanted to tell me something about Alice. Once she pointed two or three times in succession. I supposed she wanted Alice to come to her, so as I knew none of their names I asked Miss Terris who she was. She said it was the name of a woman, a Miss Gretton, who had lived in a cottage near their house and had been friendly with her aunt, but who had now gone away. So I supposed she was wandering a little in her mind. This is a trifling thing to report, but later, Dr. Smollett tells me, Mrs. Weir spoke of her again."

"Impossible to say what's trifling," Pardoe replied. "I'm obliged to you for mentioning it, Dr. Fisher."

They took leave of her and returned to the inn preparatory to setting out for Spanwater.

"Wonder if *she* knows who Weir is?" Salt said speculatively.

"Who is he then?" Pardoe asked innocently.

"You know what I mean." The sergeant sounded impatient. "She jumped to arsenic pretty quick."

"Yes. The laborer, poor silly beggar, wasn't alone in her mind. Leah Bunting had a place there too. But Dr. Fisher is discreet, Salt. *And* professional. She has to exclude prejudice, if not from her thoughts, from words and actions. And we'd better do the same."

CHAPTER VII

THE HUSBAND

There's no art
To find the mind's construction in the face.
William Shakespeare: *Macbeth.*

An hour later, after a hasty tea at the Silver Fox, Pardoe sat facing Matthew Weir by a leaping wood fire in the library at Spanwater. Some distance off, in the shadows on the far side of the long table, Salt was trying to make himself as inconspicuous as possible. He felt a little crushed by the lofty beauty of the room that had been assigned to them for the inquiry, its simple lines, the few dark portraits of members of the family that had let it slip from their own into other hands, the heraldic chimney-piece carved in oak displaying their arms, and the proud silence of rank upon rank of books. Funny thing, thought Salt vaguely, scanning them with an alarmed respect that would never persuade him to read one—all that preserved and cherished wisdom, and two men unable to discover the truth of a woman's death. Did the secret lie locked in the mind of the third?

He looked surreptitiously across at Matthew Weir and, seeing that his attention was on Pardoe, let his gaze remain there. He had the uncomfortable feeling that he would be ashamed to be caught staring. But the fact was that though in the years spent in the force he had had the doubtful privilege of looking at more than a dozen convicted murderers without losing a hair of his impassivity, the sight of this man who had achieved notoriety through acquittal was stirring in Salt the frank curiosity of the veriest tyro.

Pardoe too was strongly reluctant to meet Weir's strained, unhappy eyes, but for a different reason. His recoil was not from his own inquisitiveness, but because he was unable to determine whether it was grief or some equally profound emotion of another kind that had put its stamp on Weir, and he despised the necessity for deciding. The man had himself in hand now, but it was plain that he had been through a bad time. Pardoe felt the pull of his personality, and with it a bitter distaste of his own work that he had never before experienced so savagely.

He had covered with casual rapidity the circumstances of the actual illness and death. After all, he excused himself, Matthew Weir had been seldom in the room during that time, and alone with his wife only once, after she had lost consciousness.

Weir was leaning forward a little, with nothing relaxed about his pose, his sensitive, restless hands loosely locked and hanging between his knees. Early evening, loud with blackbirds, lay mild on the meadows in the south, and light from the oriel window fell full upon him. He was unconscious of it. His chin was slightly lifted so that his eyes might search the inspector's face. For what? Pardoe dared not ask himself. Instead he made a penciled note in his book and with head still bent over it put his next question.

"Was it usual, Mr. Weir, for you to stay up reading till after midnight?"

"Quite usual," Weir said after the pause he allowed before every reply. His soft, brusque voice was oddly attractive. "I am bothered with insomnia."

Pardoe looked up at that. "Has the doctor prescribed for it?"

"Oh, yes. I take medinal in tablets. Or did. In fact, they've disappeared."

The sergeant pricked his ears and looked to see what Pardoe thought of it. The inspector had not moved a muscle, but Salt sensed a new alertness in the air.

"Did you report the loss?" Pardoe was asking.

"I didn't miss them until last night. No—not last night," he amended vaguely, and touched his temples with the tips of his fingers. "What day is this?"

"Friday."

"Then it was Wednesday. I don't take them every night. They don't do me much good."

"Do you know that it was medinal Miss Brett drank?"

"Dr. Smollett told me."

"When, Mr. Weir? Before you missed yours or afterwards?"

"Before I think. Yes, it was on Wednesday, too."

"And then you went to see if your tablets were still where you kept them?"

"Oh, no," said Weir in a bewildered tone. "It was when I thought of taking one at night that I couldn't find them. I hadn't thought about it being my medinal that Miss Brett had. It may not have been," he added firmly, with something of the scholar's dislike of supposition.

"Where did you usually keep the tablets?" Pardoe asked, ignoring the last remark.

"Anywhere, I'm afraid. In most ways I am an untidy man, Mr. Pardoe. They were sometimes on top of my dressing table, sometimes inside, in a drawer."

"How many people in the house knew you were taking medinal, Mr. Weir?"

"I couldn't tell you," he said apologetically. "It wasn't a secret."

"And they could be easily got at by anyone here?"

Matthew Weir hesitated longer this time. "I expect anyone could have got at them," he admitted quietly.

"Did you search for them thoroughly?" Pardoe asked. "I mean, were you content to know you couldn't lay hands on them, and leave it at that, or did you go on looking?"

"I didn't look long that night," Weir said nervously. "I suppose I should have. But in the morning—would that be yesterday?—I asked Mond to look again."

"Mond?" the inspector repeated. "Is that the man who let me in, the butler?"

"Is he a butler?" Weir said gently. "Well, perhaps he is. He's done a good many different things."

"And Mond didn't find the tablets?" Pardoe asked while he turned over in his mind the ambiguity of this remark.

"No. He's a very methodical man, and if they had been in my room I think he would have found them."

Weir was looking into the fire now, one hand pressing tightly on his knee, the other elbow heavy on the arm of his chair. His pose was suggestive of something more profound than despondency. Looking at the mournful face that was never entirely free of its puzzled expression, at the hopeless stoop of the shoulders and the nervous fingers, Pardoe reflected that if this man was a murderer, and in that case perhaps twice a murderer, he was a superb actor. He well might be, of course; Palmer had been, Armstrong too, and there were others. But for a poisoner to assume a pose of timidity was rare. Of all methods theirs, judging by results, was the most inclined to breed self-confidence and even assertiveness. Then the inspector remembered Dr. Crippen, and pulled himself up short. But his, he decided, was the exceptional case.

Aloud, he said, "We'll leave the question of the medinal for the moment, Mr. Weir. I want you, if you can, to cast your mind back to Easter Monday, April 10th—that is, last Monday. What did you do that day up to the time your niece came to you in the library to say Mrs. Weir was ill?"

Weir turned his head from the fire and looked at Pardoe. "I have a poor memory for that kind of thing," he said simply, "but I'll try to think of it if it helps you to know."

There was neither resentment nor sarcasm in his voice, merely an indifference that was more revealing than either. Some hope, Salt reflected, that this bloke will remember anything. But after a minute Weir ran his fingers through his hair and met the inspector's eyes.

"I remember," he said more quickly. "In the morning I was in here working on the notes for my book. I am thinking—I mean I had been thinking of writing a history of the Ruffs. They were the owners of Spanwater for three hundred and sixty years. Then it passed to collaterals who finally put it in the market. That was when I bought it, two years ago." He mused for a moment, the purport of his answer forgotten. "You may see their tombs in Steeple church, Mr. Pardoe. I think you would be interested; Thomas, who built the manor, and his wife, and a memorial to their son Philip, who died at Naseby."

"I should like to," Pardoe said. He observed a new composure in Weir's face as he talked, and averted his own eyes to his notebook. "You were in the library until lunch time that day?"

"Oh, yes," Weir said abruptly, as though the question had penetrated through fathoms of intervening thought. "I remember I was undisturbed. It was Easter Monday and people were out."

"And what about the afternoon?"

"I went for a walk with my brother." At Pardoe's look of surprise he added, "My brother is here on a visit. We went only a short way. We intended crossing Pie Wood, but turned back before reaching it."

"Why was that?" Pardoe asked.

"My brother isn't fond of walking. He was anxious, too, to be in time to receive a telephone call he was expecting."

Pardoe made a brief note. "Do you know if the call came?"

"No, it didn't."

Pardoe gave him a keen look. "Who was it from, Mr. Weir?"

"I don't know," Weir said without hesitation.

"Do you mean," the inspector persisted, his tone a little skeptical, "that though your brother mentioned the call to you he didn't say who was to have made it, and you didn't ask?"

"Just that," was the equally firm reply.

Pardoe lifted his brows. "Do you know from what place he expected it?"

"Yes. Cottlebury."

The inspector made no comment, but immediately put his next question. "Were you back much before tea?"

"Yes, some time." Weir stopped, giving the impression that he had been going to say something further, then forestalling Pardoe added more slowly, "I was with my wife until teatime."

"I see," Pardoe said with only casual interest. "Which room were you in, Mr. Weir?"

"In the drawing room. We had tea there afterwards, my wife, my brother and I. The others were out."

"Yes. Now while you were with her did you notice Mrs. Weir drink any of her herbal mixture?"

"No. She had none then. She—I think she knew I thought it was rather foolish," Weir said, locking his fingers together so tightly that the knuckles shone white.

"Did you know that she had been drinking it that day?"

"Not until—afterwards. I didn't know any had been made."

"Did you notice anything unusual about your wife during tea?"

Weir shook his head. "She was a little tired, I think," he said, making an effort to be clear, "but quite happy. She had been to church the day before and stayed there through two services. That was unwise. Then on Monday morning she wanted to go for a walk, so Miss Brett went with her."

Pardoe nodded. "What did you do in the evening, Mr. Weir?"

"I spent it in Cottlebury with Dr. Smollett. My nephew motored me in. I look in on him most weeks, and when he is disengaged we usually have a game of chess."

Pardoe again felt a faint surprise, he could not have said why.

"Can you tell me what time you got there and when you left?" he asked.

"It would have been before six that we reached Cottlebury," Weir said slowly. "Sandy's—that is, Dr. Smollett's evening surgery isn't over until six, and when I got there he didn't come at once. That is quite usual. I'm not sure when I left. I stayed to dinner which was at eight, and for about half an hour afterwards."

"How did you get back?" Pardoe asked.

"Dr. Smollett brought me," Weir said. "There are buses to Cloudy of course, but they don't run after—well, I forget what hour precisely, but the last one was too early for me."

Pardoe made a quick calculation. "Do you think you were back by nine-thirty?"

Weir thought. "It's probable. But I don't know exactly. Perhaps one of the others will remember."

"Had Mrs. Weir gone to bed?"

"Yes."

There was a brief silence which Pardoe broke with some emphasis. "Did you see your wife between then and the time Miss Terris fetched you to her?"

"No," said Weir, in a voice so low it was hardly audible. "I seldom disturbed her. She needed rest"—he gave the word a curious lingering quality—"more rest than she had. Since it has been necessary for us to have separate rooms I rarely saw her after she went upstairs."

Pardoe did not seem to be listening closely. He wrote something quickly in his book, then looked across at Weir and said in a brisker voice, "It will help me if you can give me the names of everyone staying in the house at present, Mr. Weir. I didn't know your brother was here till you mentioned him just now."

"Augustus has been here—several weeks, I think," Weir said with some hesitation. "But he did not know that Kate—that my wife was taken ill until he woke on Tuesday morning at his usual hour. His bedroom is farther off and he heard nothing."

Pardoe nodded. "Now if you will give me the list of names——"

Weir frowned slightly as if he found exactitude in this respect difficult. "Besides my brother and myself, there are my nephew and niece, Nicholas and Dinah Terris. That is all the family. We have another guest, a friend of Nicholas—Andrew Pitt, an Oxford undergraduate."

"When did he come?" Pardoe inquired.

"Let me see—I've a very poor memory for comings and goings. Much of my work is done in solitude, you see, people arrive and go away again, and I am not always aware of their movements. But Andrew has not been here a week, I think."

"And what other people are at Spanwater now?"

"There's Miss Brett, who is—was companion to my wife. She is anxious to leave, Mr. Pardoe, as there is nothing here for her now. Perhaps it could be managed?"

At this Salt permitted himself a modified snort and tried to catch the inspector's eye.

"As soon as my inquiry is finished," Pardoe said, genially noncommittal. He dismissed the point. "What about the staff, indoor and out?"

"Oh, yes," Weir said. "There is my housekeeper, Mrs. Kingdom, the manservant, Mond, the cook"—he hesitated, frowned, then flushed a little—"I'm sorry, I can't remember her name. She's not been here long. There's a maid—Gracie is her first name. There are no more indoor servants, but I think Bessie—that is Mrs. Kingdom—has a woman from Steeple several times in the week to help with the cleaning. We've only one permanent outdoor man, the gardener, Comfort. He's married and lives at the park lodge. In spring and autumn he has jobbing help from the village, a lad and his father who attend to the rectory garden too."

"Thank you. That's quite clear," the inspector said. "There's just one other matter, Mr. Weir—who is Miss Alice Gretton?"

Weir looked disconcerted by the random shot, and flushed again.

"I don't know," he said uncertainly. "She's not here now, of course. She rented a cottage up the lane by the larch wood—they call it Titt's Cote—but I hardly ever saw her. I think I've only set eyes on her twice. I never spoke to her. She left her cottage suddenly, without telling anyone when or where she was going."

"But Mrs. Weir at least was friendly with her?" Pardoe said idly.

"Yes, she was. Titt's Cote is an easy distance from the house, and Miss Gretton appeared to like my wife's company. But no one's besides."

"Are you the landlord of Titt's Cote, Mr. Weir?"

"No. It belongs to Sheeplands, the farm on the other side of the park. Mr. Turk owns it. It's true it was once part of the Spanwater estate, the farm too, but the people who lived here before the last war sold some of the land piecemeal to meet death duties."

"I see. Can you throw any light at all on Miss Gretton's sudden departure, or have you a theory that might explain it?"

"No, none," Weir said hastily. "It was an odd affair at the time, but I didn't know the lady and it seemed to me no business of ours. She was averse to all company except my wife's, and would talk to no one. So it's not remarkable that she should go away without a word beforehand."

"Though you'd think," Pardoe suggested, "that she would have told Mrs. Weir."

"Well, perhaps," Weir said doubtfully. "But as she was peculiarly reticent in some ways, why not in others? Besides, we haven't proof, you know, that Miss Gretton didn't tell my wife she was going away. Kate forgot—my wife forgot very easily," he finished in a low voice.

Pardoe, who did not consider Miss Gretton's vagaries of sufficient importance to take up any more time, assented absently.

"I needn't trouble you any longer just now, Mr. Weir," he said. "May I ring for Mond if I want him?"

"Please do." Matthew Weir stood up self-consciously, and Pardoe rose too. "The servants have their orders to give you what help they can."

He looked from inspector to sergeant in a hesitating manner, loth to stay, reluctant to go. As he moved away Pardoe went quietly to the door and held it open for him.

When he came back Salt was watching him guardedly, tapping his pencil against his teeth. Pardoe stood on the hearth rug, his back to the fire, head and shoulders outlined against the carved chimney-piece.

"He's not obstructive," he said, and wondered at the faintly defensive note in his own voice.

"Nor helpful," Salt rejoined laconically. "*He's* giving nothing away. Most fellows in a rummy position like this 'ud be primed with some theory of how the stuff got in her drink. He never said a thing."

"A point in his favor," the inspector retorted. "Proffering no explanation isn't necessarily a sign of guilt—far from it, often. He wasn't asked to suggest what might have happened, and a man who's experienced police examination before, remember, is chary of volunteering information."

"Well, the medinal business is queer," Salt said, unmollified, "look at it any way you like. And this Dr. Smollett, now. He was back here that night—late too. And what's Weir calling him Sandy for? Seems like they're on pretty intimate terms."

" 'Trifles light as air.' " Pardoe nodded, faintly amused at the sergeant's suspicious face. "No, I'm not laughing at you, old man. Smaller matters than the doctor's Christian name have been before now proof of—well, shall we say, unholy writ?"

He turned and gave the bellrope at the side of the hearth a strong pull.

CHAPTER VIII

THE SERVANTS

Twit me with the authority of the kitchen!
PHILIP MASSINGER: *A New Way to Pay Old Debts.*

AT MOND'S ENTRY Pardoe was standing by the south window, looking out thoughtfully across the bowling green. The sergeant had pushed his chair from the table and was leaning back in it, legs stretched out, thumbs in the armholes of his waistcoat.

The silence and nonchalance of the scene seemed to deny that an urgent inquiry was in hand, and was more disconcerting to the man who came in than activity and conversation would have been. He sidled through with a queerly crablike gait as if to ward off attack from whatever quarter it might be made. Salt got the impression that he was resolute not to turn his back wholly on any part of the room. He favored the sergeant with a flickering look from his light-lashed eyes in which Salt detected a distaste that was mutual. Then he turned his head to watch the inspector walk slowly back from the window to the hearth.

"You rang, sir?"

The voice betrayed how little sure of himself he was. Its effort to turn uncertainty into jauntiness was not successful.

Pardoe leaned an elbow on the mantelpiece and passed his fingers through his hair while he regarded the man in front of him. Not a prepossessing specimen, he thought, and with a lot to learn if he means to perfect his job. Pale, blotched skin, untrustworthy eyes and mouth, hands he doesn't know what to do with. He was in the middle thirties, he judged, and probably stronger than a first glance suggested, if those long, bony wrists and coarse fingers were anything to go by.

"What's your full name?" he asked him.

"William Mond, sir." There was again the wrong inflection in the voice that came near to impertinence, and a covert glance at Salt to see how the announcement was received.

"How long have you been in Mr. Weir's service?"

"Since last November." The darting eyes scanned each face in turn before he added with assumed carelessness, "And not much of a place, it isn't."

The sergeant, lounging in his chair, was going through the leaves of his notebook one by one, the picture of boredom. Pardoe ignored the embellishment and, taking his arm from the mantelpiece and thrusting both hands in his trousers pockets, stood up straight and said sharply, "And where did you work before?"

Mond shifted his feet a little. "Different places."

"What place before this?"

At the insistence the man's face grew sullen "I worked in my brother-in-law's roadhouse outside Rochester for a year or so, if you must know," he said with bare civility.

"And where before that?"

Mond reddened suddenly. "What you getting at?" he demanded. His tone and the out-thrust chin held the truculence of a man who has no reserves of courage. "You got nothing on me—you got to look 'igher for the party as done this job."

"That's enough," Pardoe said sharply. "Keep your tongue clean if you want to steer clear of trouble. What you're doing now is accusing yourself—of what you're the best judge."

Mond flinched at the menace in the words. He still looked sulky, but held himself more quietly, muttering something to the effect that this place was getting on his nerves and he was damn sorry he'd ever come to it.

"What was your job and who employed you before you went to the roadhouse?" Pardoe repeated unhurriedly.

"Butler to Colonel Mason, at the Valley House in Wiltshire," he mumbled, his shifty gaze roving the carpet. "I left when he died."

"And was it on his reference you got the post here?"

"That's right." As self-confidence returned his tone was more eager. "Not but what there wasn't much looking at papers *'ere*." A small sneering smile added unpleasantness to the weak mouth. "Servants aren't easy to get everywhere, and that's a fact."

"Only too obvious," Pardoe agreed smoothly. Salt grinned, and Mond flashed a suddenly suspicious glance at them.

"So they jumped at you, eh?" The inspector advanced a step or two towards him. "Were you here all day Easter Monday?"

The fellow cringed a little without shifting his ground. "No—no, I wasn't, sir. I had time off after lunch, to seven. I was at a footer match in Cottlebury."

"From—when, two o'clock till seven?" Pardoe said skeptically.

"No." He sounded sullen again. "I did a pub or two. An' I didn't get away at two, neither—nearer three it was."

"Who called at the house that day before you went off duty?"

Mond looked up, resentment giving place to surprise. "Nobody," he said slowly, his tone inquisitive. "Well, I mean, I didn't see 'em if they did." All at once, however, he snapped his fingers and flushed a little. "Wait a minute, though," he added huskily. "Somebody did come, after lunch. It was just before I went out. I was having a cup of tea in the kitchen when there was a knock at the back door. Miles answered it—that's the girl—an' I could hear her shilly-shallyin' out there, wanting to shut the door and not doing it, so I went out to see. It was that dam' gypsy from over the hill. Had the blasted cheek to ask to see Mrs. Weir. Seemed excited-like. I thought she was drunk." His face wore a look of contempt. "I pitched 'er out right enough. Told 'er it was a bit o' luck for 'er she 'adn't run into old Kingdom. The rough side of 'er tongue's worse than mine."

The inspector was bending such a meditative look upon him that Mond was elated at what he thought a successful bit of evidence. The truth was Pardoe felt puzzled at the man's palpable pleasure in detailing a commonplace incident. Probably done to divert questions from more personal issues, he reflected; it was an old dodge.

"The woman had called before?" he asked.

"Yeah. She was always coming, trying to sell things she'd pinched. The old lady was kind of partial to 'er. The whole boiling, 'er and 'er son an' the kids up there, wants clearing out, the dirty robbers." He spoke with the vigor proper to the persecutor whose malice wants no motive.

"And leave more room for the honest folk like you and me," Pardoe supplemented quietly. His voice sharpened. "What d'you know of a Miss Gretton living here in Cloudy?"

Mond barely moved, but the suddenly launched question had pierced his guard and Pardoe noted the slow clenching of the hands at his sides. "Nothing," he said with slick promptitude. "Who was she? Oh, the old dame over at the cottage. No, I don't know nothing about *'er*." He shook his head, his wandering eyes at last attentive to the inspector's face. Something he saw there must have disquieted him, for he suddenly broke out with, "What's the game? Can't a woman go or stay as she pleases? I tell you I don't know her. I swear I don't!"

"Shut up," Pardoe said briefly at the shrill note rising in the fellow's voice. "You told me so just now. I'm not deaf. You'd be a bit more convincing if you had less to say. You can clear out now, and ask cook if she will step this way. And my advice to you, Mond, if you're disposed to take it, is to clamp your tongue and not look for trouble before it finds you."

The man withdrew, with the same sly repugnance to turning his back on the Yard men as he had displayed on entering.

"Nasty piece of work," the inspector remarked as the door closed.

"Eyes like a bloomin' lizard," Salt grunted.

"Oh, no. Rather nice little brutes, lizards. But he's a bad egg all right."

"Bad egg? Faugh, I'd say so. Like as if a skunk had been in here whisking his tail round the table legs."

Pardoe grinned. "Metaphorical mixture yielding no fragrance."

"Well, he's got the jumps, anyway," Salt said with satisfaction. "Unless, o' course, they're natural to him. If you ask me, scuttling's more in my gentleman's line than buttling any day."

Pardoe tossed a little wood on the fire and watched a fountain of sparks vanish up the chimney.

" 'What do you know of Miss Gretton?' " he repeated softly. " 'Nothing. Who *was* she?' " He wheeled and looked smilingly at the sergeant. "And I hadn't given her a past, Salt."

Before he had finished speaking there was a timid rap on the door, followed by a much louder one, a sequence a psychologist might have found interesting. To Pardoe's "Come in," there entered a hefty young woman in a print dress a shade too tight for her. Her natural cheerfulness was subdued to the rather blank expression incurable optimists are compelled to adopt in face of a crisis. Nothing, however, seemed likely to dim the apple-cheeked complexion which, together with the dark bobbed hair sleeked smoothly each side her face, reminded Pardoe irresistibly of the wooden Dutch dolls that had enjoyed some popularity with the little girls of his generation.

It was plain to both men that the library was strange ground to the cook. Her large, heifer-like eyes were drinking it in.

"Won't you sit down?" Pardoe said, and turned the chair Weir had occupied an inch or two closer to the fire.

"Thank you, I'm sure," the girl said, sparing him a look, and sat down cautiously.

Pardoe smiled at her and seated himself on the arm of the opposite chair. Now that she had torn her gaze from the room she seemed unable to divert it from the inspector, but sat well forward with her rather shapely hands planted firmly on her knees and her placidly astonished eyes on his.

"This has been a trying time for you, I know, Cook," Pardoe said. "And there's not a lot I have to trouble you with. But I can see you're sensible and will understand that we have to talk to everybody in an inquiry of this sort."

"Oh, that's all right. I'll tell you what I can—no need of the blarney," she said without asperity, to the amusement of Salt who winked at his notebook. "And I don't know as I *am* all that sensible or I wouldn't have taken a job here. Cooks as 'ave been where folk's took poison are not over-welcome elsewhere, I may tell you."

"You think Mrs. Weir herself responsible for taking it?" Pardoe said quickly.

"Oh, *no*. I never said that. I'm sure I wouldn't be the one to say 'ow it got there. But if the poor old dear drank it, she took it, like, didn't she?"

"Quite right," Pardoe said gravely, marking at once the sympathetic note for the dead woman and the caution in apportioning blame. "Please tell me your full name. It's only ordinary procedure, having all the names handy," he added, observing the doubt on her face.

"Oh, well. All me names, you said? Louisa Adeline Mary Blessitt, spells 'lamb' it does," she pronounced happily.

"Very nice," Pardoe replied. "Now, Miss Blessitt—it is miss, isn't it?—I don't mean to bother you with a string of questions. I think it will be very much better if you tell me yourself all you can remember about Easter Monday, and especially anything unusual that you noticed that day."

The cook wrinkled her good-tempered brow in a portentous frown, but produced nothing startling. The day, of course, had not run a quite normal course, because being a Bank Holiday everybody, including the servants if they had wanted it, had had an outing of sorts at one time or another. Lunch had been a cold one, and she herself had been free immediately afterwards and had gone into Cottlebury on the bus, returning just after six o'clock in time to prepare dinner. Mr. Weir and Miss Brett were the only people absent from dinner. Five sat down to table, Mrs. Weir, Mr. Augustus Weir, Miss Terris, Mr. Terris, and Mr. Pitt. Mond waited. No, there'd been nothing unusual that she'd heard tell of, and Mrs. Weir had drunk water at dinner, which was quite the ordinary thing. She herself had gone up to bed at nine-thirty, and was disturbed about three hours later by Mrs. Kingdom, who told her the mistress was dying.

Pardoe caught her up quickly. "You are sure she used the word 'dying'?"

"Positive," Lou Blessitt said calmly.

"Did Mrs. Kingdom wake you before or after Dr. Fisher's arrival?"

"Oh, before. Mr. Terris had rung up the doctor, but she hadn't come when I first went into Mrs. Weir's room."

"I see." The inspector sounded thoughtful. "You're doing well, Miss Blessitt. Now about this herbal mixture Mrs. Weir liked drinking—what did she call it?"

" 'Erb tea. Though what there was of *tea* in such a nasty mess—well, there, don't ask me."

"No. Was the infusion always made in the kitchen?"

"That I couldn't say. I've been a month in this situation, and that a month too long, and this was only the second time any of the stuff was brought into *my* kitchen."

"When was the first time?"

"About a fortnight ago. It was only a drop then, though, and soon cleared away."

"Who made it?"

"The old lady. Both times. I see her with my own eyes. There was nothing to it, but she wouldn't have no one else to meddle."

"What do you mean, 'there was nothing to it'?"

"Well, there wasn't, neither," Lou Blessitt said with a disarmingly indulgent smile. "I mean she only put the weeds into a big jug and poured boiling water over 'em. But *she* 'ad to do it, nobody else."

"Oh, yes, a whim of Mrs. Weir's to make it herself. I see. What time did she do that on Easter Monday?"

"As soon as ever they got in from the walk, 'er and Miss Brett. It was about eleven o'clock, I know, because I reckons to have a snack jes' then," she explained with a giggle, "an' I'd jes' got a biscuit out of the tin when in walks Mrs. Weir to know if a kettle was on the boil. It was—I was going to make me a cup of tea, proper tea, I mean."

"Did Miss Brett come into the kitchen with Mrs. Weir?"

The cook shook her head. "No. If I 'adn't found 'er making the stuff once before, you could have knocked me flat when I see 'er come in with the bunch in 'er hand. But of course I knew what was on. She wasn't—*quite*, you know," she said inoffensively, and tapped her forehead.

"And the herb tea remained in the kitchen?"

"That's right. Mrs. Weir came in to strain it off a minute before I left to catch me bus. I'd been upstairs to get ready, and popped into the kitchen for a sec, and there she was, messing about with it."

"By herself?"

"Yes."

"Do you remember other occasions, Miss Blessitt, when Mrs. Weir was sick and in pain?"

The cook nodded vigorously. "Oh, yes. One other. About a week after I came here. Mrs. Kingdom said it was all through going to tea with that Miss Gretton in the cold weather. But the old cat would say anything—she hated her like poison."

"Who? She hated Mrs. Weir?"

"No, Miss Gretton."

"Why?"

The cook gave the perfect impression of a shrug without shrugging. "Jealousy," she said briefly. "Same as she's jealous of Miss Brett. She wanted the old lady all to herself. I tell you," she added with a sudden flash, "this place 'ud be twice as good as it is if it wasn't for that interferin' old besom, with her long nose an' her pious prayers an' her, 'Now, Blessitt,' an' 'That's enough, Blessitt,' an' her jangling old keys. A wardress she ought to've been."

Salt chuckled, and Pardoe scribbled a line or two. He put a few more questions, but apart from this entertaining sidelight on the kind of impact the housekeeper had made on her associates elicited nothing fresh. Asked about the maid, Gracie Miles, the cook said that she had had the whole afternoon and evening free and was away from the house during that time. No, she herself knew next to nothing about the gypsies, had only heard tell of them, and whatever differences Mrs. Kingdom had had with Esther O'Malley were before she came to the house.

"Yes, I knew it was her come in the afternoon," she said, "but I didn't see her. I was changing to go out. Gracie 'adn't gone upstairs though. She told me about it, an' said as 'ow you'd have thought Mond was driving pigs out of the 'ouse. I suppose gypsies are 'uman after all. *'E's* a dirty blighter if ever there was one."

Miss Blessitt was allowed to leave on this Parthian estimate of her fellow-servant, promising (with considerable gusto, Salt thought) to dispatch Mrs. Kingdom with the message that Inspector Pardoe would be obliged if she would come to the library.

"And be thankful Louisa Adeline Mary's prepared the way," Pardoe remarked, strolling over to a shelf and taking from it a folio Beaumont and Fletcher. "Wonder if the library went with the house, or whether these are Weir's own books."

A sharp rat-tat on the door disturbed his speculations. He replaced the book and invited entry. Mrs. Kingdom came in, a small, belligerent figure in a black dress whose forbidding aspect was emphasized by its boned muslin collar. As soon as she had closed the door she stood silently with her hands folded in front of her, though a less submissive figure it would have been hard to imagine. Pardoe, seeing her for the first time, was unprepared for so tiny a person, and realized all at once that her stunted stature united to the fighting spirit that was in evidence before she spoke only made her the more formidable.

He indicated a chair, and with a smile said, "Please be seated, Mrs. Kingdom."

"Thank you, young man. I prefer to stand."

Pardoe, whose white hairs had more often earned him another epithet, was amused, and as she showed no sign of budging from her decision compromised by leaning against the table. The first glance had shown him that a tactful approach would be only wasted, so he went direct to the point.

"How long have you been with Mr. and Mrs. Weir, Mrs. Kingdom?"

"Ever since they were married, and that's fourteen years ago. And that's nothing to the time I was with the Buntings before Miss Catherine took the silly notion to change her name for another. I was maid to Tim Bunting and his wife rising fifty-year ago, Mr. Policeman, and never been out of the family since. And now the Lord's seen fit to take them all, and spare me."

And put that in your pipe and smoke it, Pardoe added silently. Aloud he remarked, "That's a long time indeed, Mrs. Kingdom. I'm sure you know more of the family history than anybody else. Tell me, when did Mrs. Weir first get the habit of making herb tea?"

"Not till she came to this place forsaken of the Lord," was the housekeeper's surprising answer. She clamped her pale lips together, unsealing them again to add, "She'd the notion she'd do as her mama done all they years ago when they were poor cottagers. But that didn't make it the proper thing to do, none the less. The Lord never put those nasty weeds for folk to make into a stew. What's *he* doing?" She finished so suddenly that for the moment Pardoe was unable to place the pronoun correctly. Then he turned his head to where Salt was engaged in the innocuous task of writing in his notebook. At being caught thus red-handed the sergeant looked quite abashed, and only just checked the schoolboy instinct to hide the offending pencil behind his back.

"Nothing serious," Pardoe said solemnly. "He has to note down a few things for us to remember——"

"And I wonder how much he gets right," Mrs. Kingdom interrupted acidly, hooding her sharp little eyes for a moment. "Oh, yes, I know, young man. I've been in a police inquiry before now, and a poor job they made of it. You know exactly what you're told, but it's what you're not told that matters."

"Is that so?" Pardoe said softly, with a glint of interest in his eyes. "Well, Mrs. Kingdom, I'm inclined to agree with you. And I've always been uncommonly inquisitive about the things I wasn't told."

The bright gaze met his without flinching. Her very attitude as she confronted him, the folded hands mocking humility, the shoulders rigid, seemed to Pardoe a challenge. He looked away, glanced at the clock, and resumed an easy flow of questions.

Mrs. Kingdom's testimony was at least revealing in a personal sense. The range and degree of jealous hatred possessing her made an unquiet narrative, told as it was without passion or gesture by the small, relentless figure. Dr. Smollett, Miss Gretton, Miss Leith, Aurelia Brett, the servants, Augustus Weir, Matthew himself, the gypsies (who had apparently not left Comfort a chicken to pluck), and the Rev. Flood—she held them all in contempt or abhorrence. The implication was of a vast conspiracy, not so much a popish as an Anglo-Catholic plot, to discredit Mrs. Kingdom in the eyes of her mistress and encompass her downfall by getting her turned out of Spanwater, a project only circumvented by an extremely protestant Providence. It struck Pardoe at once that the housekeeper was less concerned with the fate which had overtaken Mrs. Weir than she was with the one she imagined had just failed to destroy herself.

"But what has Miss Leith to do with Spanwater?" Pardoe managed to slip in at the end of this lengthy vituperation. He saw immediately that he had worded the question unfortunately.

"You may well ask, young man," she flashed. "She a spinster and he a married man. Many's the time I've watched the pair of them together, in the garden, in the lane, by her own house, while *she*"—Pardoe had learned that this was Mrs. Weir—"could be left moping on her own. Is it to be wondered that she should go picking the rubbish from the ditches? I've prayed to the Lord to bring down fire on their godless heads."

Pardoe, after deciding that the last remark must refer to Matthew and Miss Leith, was puzzled for a moment as to why the plants Mrs. Weir had been fond of gathering should be judged an adequate substitute for Mr. Weir. After sorting this out, he remarked, "But I understand Miss Leith is away in Oxford most of her time?"

"And spends nearly every weekend in her cottage here," Mrs. Kingdom replied with bitterness, as if such diversion in itself smacked of immorality. "Though there wasn't one that she came back on last term—that I know of," she added darkly. "The house was shut up."

"What's that?" said Pardoe quickly. He had been idly drawing his pencil up and down the middle groove of his notebook, but now he looked up, then down to meet the housekeeper's eyes. "You mean Miss Leith didn't come down to Steeple Cloudy all the spring?"

"Not that I *know* of." Clandestine meetings were clearly not outside the scope of Mrs. Kingdom's suspicions.

Pardoe felt something, he could not have said what, stirring vaguely in his mind, and with it a slightly intensified interest in Miss Leith. However, since the housekeeper appeared only too ready to concentrate her entire attention on this point, he did not press the matter further.

As for Miss Gretton, the subject had needed no introduction from Pardoe. Indeed, it was only the odium in which this absent lady had been held by Mrs. Kingdom that gave, he was sure, such precision to her evidence of Mrs. Weir's recurrent sickness. In most cases when this had occurred she had no hesitation in supplying the exact dates, since they all, she averred, immediately followed or coincided with those on which her mistress had had tea at Titt's Cote.

Pardoe was interested, believing he could discern here something more dependable than jealousy. There was a new earnestness in her manner as she described the course of each bout of illness and the pains Mrs. Weir had complained of on other occasions when there had been no sickness and no doctor had been called in. She was possibly speaking the truth when she related the attacks to the days when Mrs. Weir had visited Miss Gretton; but that need not be proof of anything other than coincidence. There was nothing to dispute the fact that Mrs. Weir's fatal illness had occurred when Miss Gretton had been gone away about three weeks. He would have to get corroboration of the housekeeper's story. Meantime, he could not afford wholly to ignore the Gretton factor.

"By the way, Mrs. Kingdom," he remarked abruptly, "I am told you woke the cook on Monday night with the announcement that Mrs. Weir was dying. Had you any reason for supposing that she was dying as early as twelve-thirty?"

Though she made no immediate reply the unfaltering look did not change.

"Well, she was, wasn't she?" she said at last.

"Yes, but that was not confirmed until much later, Tuesday morning, by the doctor."

"The *doctor!*" She spat the word with such malignance that Pardoe had a quick mental vision of the whole faculty of medicine blenching before it. "Don't think I want a doctor to show me death's at hand. I've seen it before, let me tell you, and no different to this, neither!"

"Very well," the inspector said, though he was not satisfied. "We'll take it you have a remarkably quick eye for the gravity of an illness."

It was after seven o'clock now and growing dusky. He himself preferred the tall room in the shadows it had been used to for three centuries, and was reluctant to dispel them at once. Salt, however, found nothing friendly in a gloom that turned Mrs. Kingdom into a small, glimmering white face above the denser shadow of her frock.

With unspoken condemnation of the frivolities that had taken the rest away, she was telling Pardoe that she had stayed at home the whole of Easter Monday. She had herself brought in tea, had remarked nothing strange about Mrs. Weir, and from personal observation knew only of the one glass of herb tea she had had early in the afternoon.

"Though by what was left in the jug when that there Miss Fisher went to look," she said, evidently thinking doctor an improper title for a woman, "somebody must have drunk it."

Pardoe made a note, then slipped the book into his pocket.

"Thank you, Mrs. Kingdom. Now you can do me one more service—be so good as to show me the way to Mrs. Weir's bedroom."

CHAPTER IX

THE COMPANION

But men may construe things after their fashion,
Clean from the purpose of the things themselves.
WILLIAM SHAKESPEARE: *Julius Caesar.*

MRS. KINGDOM felt none of the inspector's compunction for the twilight. Under her direction the house snapped into brilliance. All the shadows seemed suddenly to dive into the central well of the staircase, only to look out again through the pierced balustrade with its bold convolutions of carved grapes and vine leaves. By the time Pardoe and Salt had gone up two short flights, Mrs. Kingdom was already waiting for them in a narrow, lofty corridor lit dimly by a single light. At the far end a tall leaded window shone.

Standing there motionless and silent, with the feeble light behind and the unpredictable shadows of an old house swooping down upon her, the housekeeper was an uncomfortable little figure. She looked like the tiny warden of some unguessable region, so dwarfed, yet so clearly mistress of the situation. Rather like an illustration to Poe, Pardoe reflected.

She led them to a door on the left of the passage, passing a closed one on the same side beneath which a thread of light shone. Opening the door, she switched on the light and stood aside for the men to pass in. The inspector noticed that she did not aim to enter.

"Who sleeps in the rooms opposite?" he asked, pausing on the threshold.

"Mr. Weir down there," she said, pointing an accusing finger at a room close to the terminal window of the passage, "and this here is a guest chamber. Not in use at present."

"I see. Thank you for your help," Pardoe said. "That will be all now." He closed the door quietly as, without a glance at either, she slipped mutely away.

Salt heaved a sigh and shook himself like a clumsy terrier. "Enough and to spare," he pronounced. "Bar the Blessitt lamb I don't much like what we've seen so far."

Pardoe did not reply. He was examining the room from his vantage point just inside the door, and was struck by the contrast between the dignity and contemporary furnishing of the rest of the house he had so far seen and the bad taste displayed here. That was the first impression. The second was that taste after all was perhaps of secondary moment, and that what really mattered, especially from the detective's point of view, was the fulfillment of personality. Catherine Weir's room must, he thought, have been the perfect expression of Catherine Weir, at any rate in her later years, comfortable, vague, aimless, irresponsible, unnecessarily cluttered. He moved over to the windows, noticing as he pulled the curtains across that though most of the ground floor ones had been replaced sometime in the Georgian era by the sash variety, here they still had leaded lights. In crossing the floor he had seen the door which presumably led to Miss Brett's room, in the wall on the left.

Everything was tidy without appearing to have received immediate attention. A film of dust covered an oak bureau, a wardrobe door stood ajar, and though the bed had been stripped of its linen, a dressing-gown still hung over its foot. Pardoe noticed the position of the bed in relation to the rest of the room, its head between the windows so that whoever lay there faced the corridor door, with Miss Brett's room on the right and on the left a washstand and massive wardrobe. Then he crossed to the right where Salt, without touching them, was looking closely at the crowded array of photographs on the dressing table.

"All the family," the sergeant said, eying a large one prominently displayed of Matthew Weir at a day when fear and disillusionment were still strangers. Snapshots, unframed and curling at the corners, showed him again in the manor garden with somebody who was presumably his wife; another depicted a pair who might be the Terris boy and girl, while behind was one of cabinet size without a frame, the mount blotchy, showing a girl of fifteen or so dressed as an Elizabethan page. She was fair and slender, with a forceful quality developing in the fragile features. Pardoe did not think this one was Dinah Terris, if indeed it were Dinah in the snap.

He had opened his lips to address Salt on the subject when a sound close at hand made both men turn. The door between the two rooms was standing wide and a tall girl in a well-cut dark blue frock, pale-cheeked and with light, misty hair, stood watching them.

"I beg your pardon," she said. "I heard somebody moving in here and wondered who it could be. You are the police, I think? My name is Brett."

"Please come in, Miss Brett, and shut the door," Pardoe said without moving.

She came close to the table, after a cursory glance ignoring Salt and meeting Pardoe's eyes with a look at once authoritative and reserved.

"I wanted to see you, Inspector," she said, with the faintest query on the last word.

"Inspector Pardoe—and this is Detective Sergeant Salt. A mutual want then, Miss Brett. I wonder if you can tell me if this lady is Mrs. Weir?"

He passed her the snapshot of the two in the garden.

"Yes. Mr. and Mrs. Weir." She handed it back.

"And these?"

"Mr. Terris and his sister."

"Then this is not Miss Terris?" He picked up the photograph of the child in theatrical dress.

"No," she said, bending her gaze upon it, "I have heard Mrs. Weir say that this is her sister's granddaughter."

"Oh, yes?" Pardoe replaced it and added, "Now you are here, Miss Brett, I'll be glad if you will show me where the other bedrooms lie. I understand you went to rouse Mr. Weir first, then Mr. Terris, on Monday night?"

"Yes," she said. "Come with me."

In the passage she turned to Pardoe. "It's nearly dinnertime, but if you would prefer to interview me now, Inspector, I can excuse myself and have something to eat later."

There was a hint of eagerness in the suggestion that did not escape Pardoe. Salt too, more used to the evasive type of witness, thought her a trifle anxious to oblige and promptly put it down to self-interest. Means to get it over early and then see if she's let leave the place, he decided.

"That will be best," Pardoe agreed, and followed her along another passage and down two worn oak steps into a wider corridor with a slender, deep-seated window at each end. Here the bedrooms were ranged along one side only. Having indicated to the inspector those occupied by Nicholas Terris, his sister, and the guest, Andrew Pitt, she pointed to the corner of the guest room where another short passage formed an L with the main corridor.

"Mr. Augustus Weir sleeps down there," she said briefly, before leaving them to attend to the matter of dinner, promising at Pardoe's suggestion to wait for them in the library.

When they arrived there, however, the inspector was surprised to find two people instead of one. In the now lighted room, where the old calf and vellum bindings took kindly to the glitter after all, Aurelia Brett was seated in a deep leather chair opposite the door facing a tall young man who, hands in pockets, was scowling down at her, one shoulder hunched against the bookshelves. That they had been having words was plain to the inspector as soon as he and Salt were in the room. Two bright spots of color burned in Aurelia's cheeks and something of her cool restraint had vanished.

"I've explained, Inspector," she said, getting up from her chair, "that you want to talk to me in here"—she glanced defiantly at the equally ruffled youth.

"Oh, all right, I'm going," he said with angry resignation, then removing his hands from his pockets gave Pardoe an apologetic smile. He was a pleasing specimen, the inspector thought, straight and fair with long, candid features and an air of repentance for the ill-temper he was displaying.

Aurelia introduced him as Mr. Andrew Pitt. "And he has something to tell you, I think, Inspector," she added with a noticeable touch of spite.

The young man blushed a fiery red. "Rot," he said instantly. "Nothing of the sort. I mean"—he looked appealingly at Pardoe—"there's nothing I have to say, nothing at all. We—we were only—well, I mean to say, I simply don't see eye to eye with Miss Brett. That's all—purely a private matter."

Pardoe diagnosed his agitation as the unsmooth course of true love, though the boy was obviously some years the younger and the girl's remark had been odd.

"Well, Mr. Pitt, I'll be seeing you later on," he said, "but if there's anything urgent you'd really like to tell me now's the time."

Andrew Pitt shook his head and looking thoroughly miserable made his way to the door without a glance at Aurelia. She, on the other hand, had kept her gaze steadily upon him since effecting the introduction—a curious look compounded of anger and some other emotion it was hard to define.

She took a deep breath as he left the room, then turned it not very successfully into a mock sigh.

"Won't you come over by the fire, Miss Brett?" Pardoe said. "This is a cold spot."

She consented readily, remarking as she sat down, "I'm afraid I'd hoped to put an end to the argument by retreating over there, but Mr. Pitt is very persistent."

Her laugh did not altogether conceal the tremble in her voice. She was making a strenuous effort to control herself but was still angry, it was plain. Pardoe, seated opposite, ran through his notes to give her time to pull herself together. Salt took a chair at the end of the table where he could observe without being observed.

After a minute she met Pardoe's eyes, favoring him with a faintly rueful smile and a surprising remark.

"I'm not really anxious to have my neck broken," she said quietly.

Pardoe frowned his astonishment. "I beg your pardon?"

Aurelia Brett laughed.

"Mr. Pitt has one of those uncomfortable racing cars of which he's very proud. He's given me more than once a pressing invitation to be a passenger in it, but he's a notoriously reckless driver and I'm not disposed to end my days in that fashion."

Pardoe smiled, but his expression was thoughtful. "I see. Your refusal hurts his pride, no doubt. Well, Miss Brett, I understood you to say you wanted to see us. That being so, I'd prefer you to take the initiative and tell me first whatever it is you want to tell. Then I can question you. It's the most economical way to conduct an inquiry, as your own statement will no doubt eliminate some of my questions by answering them."

"Very well, Inspector. I'd like that best too. But first can you tell me, please, if there's any chance of my being allowed to leave Spanwater in the next day or two?"

It was a frank question untinged by anxiety, and Pardoe treated it as such.

"Your choice of words makes it a little difficult for me, Miss Brett. I'm not detaining you here, but as a material witness you'd have to give me full particulars of your whereabouts, and as I should want to be in constant touch with you the arrangement for both of us would be very much more inconvenient than the present one. Is there a special reason why you should be somewhere else soon, or has Mr. Weir pointed out that he would prefer you to leave?"

"No—to both questions," she admitted, obviously disappointed. "Well, it's not to be helped, and I see your point about convenience. I certainly shouldn't enjoy being pursued by the police when I'd once left this place—where I ought never to have come."

As she was the third person tonight to express the regret, it was to Pardoe by now a familiar lamentation.

"Try to stick it a little longer," he said, "until we've cleared things up."

"Yes. But when it's perfectly certain I was drugged in this house four nights ago, I think you will agree that it's natural I should want to be well away from the place."

With that she began what she had evidently intended saying ever since the case had been turned over to the police. Now that she had recovered from her passage-at-arms with young Pitt the inspector saw what he had suspected from the first encounter, that here was the perfect witness. She gave, in concise and unmistakable terms, a simple account of her engagement as companion to Mrs. Weir, stressing no superfluities and omitting nothing cogent. Innuendo and hedging were absent from her exemplary narrative, and where suspicion had been entertained it was directly voiced. Even in an account which was careful to confine itself as far as possible to facts, Pardoe was surprised at the scope of the girl's shrewd deductions and the extent of her suspicions. He was impressed too by the objective handling of her statement. No issue was confused by prejudice. If she felt sympathy, resentment or dislike for her employers, these sentiments were rigidly excluded from the story she gave to Pardoe. To him, at least, it was almost unpleasantly scientific, for it seemed now and again as if Matthew Weir and Dr. Smollett were regarded much as might be black beetles beneath the microscope.

The preliminary recital done, Pardoe seized the opportunity of inserting some questions of his own before tackling Monday's crisis. Certain parts of her story had been treated with such admirable brevity that he felt them to be rather too bald a prelude.

"Before we pass to more immediate events," he said, "there are several points in what you've just told me which I should like to hear in greater detail. For instance, you've once or twice mentioned that you were engaged for this post *although* you have no qualifications as a nurse. Why do you attach importance to that?"

"I thought it peculiar, and still think so," Aurelia replied promptly, "that the doctor should have insisted that a properly qualified person wasn't necessary when he knew that Mrs. Weir had had several bouts of painful sickness only recently. They were not trying to cut down expenses either, because they readily paid me on their own suggestion three guineas a week, for which they could have got a trained nurse."

"Then will you tell me exactly what you think about their choice of yourself?"

Aurelia was silent for a minute. "Am I privileged to voice *any* suspicion?" she inquired.

"To us, yes," Pardoe replied. "But not to anybody else. In fact, it goes further than privilege, for though you are not bound to answer my questions, the only sensible course is to keep nothing back."

"I never talk to other people about these matters," she said. "Very well. I think I was chosen to come to Spanwater because I was unqualified, because they thought, and correctly, that I should be more easily hoodwinked than a nurse."

Pardoe, expecting something of the sort, showed no surprise. Salt breathed heavily and turned his chair round a little in an access of interest.

"That implies," the inspector said, "that something was planned which was not intended to be observed."

"Yes."

"But why should it have been necessary to have anyone extra in the house that could be 'hoodwinked'? Why engage you at all?"

"I think that's obvious," the girl said. "It could always be urged later on, with apparent truth, that nobody at Spanwater could have intended harm to Mrs. Weir since they had taken the precaution of getting a companion for her a few weeks before her death. In short, Inspector, they must have wanted everyone to think what your question to me shows you thought."

Pardoe wondered if he ought to look crushed. He was silent for a few moments while he considered her thoughtfully.

"I don't know, Miss Brett," he said, "whether this is shrewd of you or fanciful. But whichever it is we can't leave it at that. I should like to hear more fully what things besides your own ignorance of nursing gave you suspicions as grave as these. What did you mean just now when you were telling me about your first week at the house when you said that you thought the family were upsetting Mrs. Weir?"

She hesitated. "It's hard to pin anything down definitely," she said slowly, "especially as I asked no questions. But she didn't seem comfortable in their presence, and it is true that I came upon her one day in tears when Mr. Terris, her nephew, was in the room with her."

As she described the incident Pardoe raised his brows. "But didn't you question Mr. Terris?"

"Yes. He said he didn't know what was wrong. Then he slipped away. Mrs. Weir soon cheered up—emotionally she was quite unstable, and it was worse than useless to bother her with the matter, as a reminder of that sort was only liable to bring back her distress. So I had to leave it at that."

"Did you speak to Mr. Weir about it?"

"Oh, no." She shook her head with decision. "That is another thing I found—well, puzzling. On the occasion of my first interview with him, Dr. Smollett made a point of asking me not to trouble Mr. Weir with anything relating to Mrs. Weir's health, but to refer it to him."

Salt looked across to see how the chief took this. Pardoe's eyes were bright, but otherwise he betrayed no special interest.

"And what did you think of that?" he asked quietly.

Aurelia Brett looked him straight in the eye. "I thought it meant that Dr. Smollett was in command of the situation," she said bluntly.

"What situation?" the inspector took her up quickly.

She flushed a little at the peremptory note, but answered readily enough, though with more moderation.

"Whatever might have been intended here, I mean."

"As that remark was made at your first interview," Pardoe said dryly, "you were quick to feel suspicious."

She was clearly disappointed at his lack of enthusiasm.

"I was," she said, with no effort at evasion and in a colder tone, "but it was the very last thing said to me that afternoon, and I'd already been wondering why they were so keen to have me."

Pardoe nodded. "And was there any other evidence of keenness besides their satisfaction in the qualifications you could offer?"

"In the qualifications I couldn't offer, you mean, Inspector," she flashed. "Yes, there was. I was paid my first week's salary there and then in advance. I thought it most unusual."

"Who paid you?"

"Mr. Weir. I told you I saw him for a few minutes at the end of the interview. But I had the idea that Dr. Smollett suggested it to him."

He let that pass. "And what did you think of receiving your salary so early?"

"I thought it was because they wanted to make sure of me."

"I see," he said noncommittally. "Now can you think of anything else to support your belief that something was wrong at Spanwater?"

"Several things," said Aurelia coolly. "But they will probably only appear uninteresting trifles in your eyes, Inspector."

Pardoe inferred that she was still sore at his indifferent response a minute ago, and put her down as acutely sensitive to even indirect censure.

"On the contrary, Miss Brett," he replied, "trifles are never uninteresting. And I've been deeply interested in all you've told me"—in which the inspector was speaking nothing more than the truth.

The girl shrugged. "All right," she said shortly, and gave him, with the same rare selective power she had displayed before, her reasons for doubting the *bona fide* nature of the case. The cumulative character of the suspicious circumstances certainly bore weight, as Salt, thumbing his notebook, had to admit. The fact that she had always been, as she said, a light sleeper until coming to Spanwater, when she had slept heavily on successive nights, began to assume sinister proportions in the light of her drugged sleep on the night of Mrs. Weir's fatal illness. She confessed too that she had been very puzzled why the doctor had not forbidden the herb tea altogether. It would not have been hard to do so, yet he had seemed anxious, she thought, to indulge Mrs. Weir in the fad. What was more, she had not been able to dismiss from her mind Mrs. Kingdom's remark that it was "funny" that Mrs. Weir had not once been sick since a companion had been engaged for her; and the housekeeper too had been the first to acquaint her with news of that sickness.

"I didn't like that at all," she added. "I think Dr. Smollett should have told me in the first place."

She waited for Pardoe's comment, but all he said was, "Thank you, Miss Brett, that covers the ground well up to last Monday. Now I want you to tell me as much as you remember of that day, especially anything, however slight, that struck you as odd."

The girl complied, though Pardoe again got the impression that she was not too pleased with his reception of what she had said. When, on resuming, she forsook theory for fact, both men felt that her manner lacked something of its old spirit. Though she was clear enough her mind seemed to be on something else.

She described the walk she had had with Mrs. Weir in the morning. It was usual for them to have a daily walk after breakfast on fine days, and there had been nothing to distinguish this from any other recent one except that Mrs. Weir had picked a great many herbs for the tea she intended making. They had gone across Mr. Turk's meadows, as, Aurelia explained, she avoided Pie Wood as much as possible and kept to the other direction.

"Why?" Pardoe asked.

"Because of the gypsies. I know nothing of them myself, but they were discouraged at Spanwater, only Mrs. Weir being friendly to them, and I thought it best to meet their wishes in that respect. Besides, that way was more of a climb, and a strain on Mrs. Weir's heart."

Pardoe nodded. "Did you notice what it was Mrs. Weir picked?"

"Yes, but as I told Dr. Smollett when I first met him I don't really know what's good and what's harmful. I don't know a thing about wild flowers. There was a quantity of stinging nettles, I know, and dandelion leaves, and some trailing sticky stuff, and a tiny blue flower Mrs. Weir said was jill."

"Any wild arum?" the inspector asked.

"Oh, no. Nothing like that," she said absently.

There was a short silence which Pardoe broke by asking, "What time did you come home?"

"From the walk? I didn't come back to the house. You see," she explained, "it had been arranged that I was to have most of the day off. I had had very little free time in the fortnight I'd been there, and Mr. Weir suggested that if I liked I could take most of that day. So as there was a bus for Cottlebury which passed Spanwater lane at eleven-twenty, I saw Mrs. Weir as far as the gates and then went down to catch it."

"You spent the day in Cottlebury?"

"Yes. I suppose you want to know what I did with myself? I had an early lunch at the Shanty in Edinburgh Square, then went to the opening of the Lido in the Park—there were a lot of people there, though it was cold. After that—it must have been about two-thirty—I went to the Town Hall and heard some music. There's a car park outside, and when I came out about an hour later I ran into Mr. Pitt and Miss Terris. It turned out they'd been in Cottlebury since lunch time and he'd just returned to the car to fetch something. They asked me to join them for tea. I didn't want to, but I couldn't invent an excuse and it would have been churlish to decline. So we all went to the Lantern Café. After tea they said they were going for a run before returning home, and wanted me to join them. But I didn't feel inclined to cram into that awful car, and I wasn't ready either to go back just yet. When they left me I went to the first house at the Arcadia Cinema—it was a murder picture called 'The Second Key.' When it was over I had only to wait five minutes for the last bus out to Steeple Cloudy. I was in the house again soon after nine o'clock."

Pardoe was a little surprised at this unsolicited recital, but merely said, “What time did you go to bed, Miss Brett?”

“Almost directly. I had a headache. The housekeeper told me Mrs. Weir had already gone up. I just looked in at the kitchen to see if cook was there.”

“Why did you want her?”

“She would have made me a cup of tea. But the kitchen was empty and in darkness, so I didn’t bother but went straight to bed.”

“Did you see Mrs. Weir that night before you were roused by her groans?”

“Yes. I went into her room before going to my own to see if she wanted anything. She was asleep.”

“Now,” said Pardoe, leaning forward a little, “about this medinal in your drinking water. Was there anything unusual about your room when you went in that night, or was anything out of its usual place?”

Aurelia Brett shook her head. “If there was I didn’t notice,” she said. “I don’t think there could have been anything.”

“You drank nothing immediately? Took no aspirins, for instance?”

“No. I found I hadn’t any left. I didn’t want to disturb anybody then.”

“I see. Please tell me as carefully as you can just what happened up to the time you roused the household.”

“Well, to be frank I don’t recall anything later than knocking on Mr. Weir’s door. But Miss Terris and her brother say that I roused them. It’s all hazy now, I’m afraid, but I can remember what I told Dr. Fisher and the superintendent. I lay in bed about an hour and couldn’t sleep. My headache was better but by then I was feeling thirsty. So I turned on the light, looked at my watch—it was a quarter to eleven—and poured out half a glass of water. After drinking it I turned out the light and lay down again. I don’t remember anything else till I was standing in Mrs. Weir’s room, but I’m sure I had slept a little. The others know what time I went to their rooms, so it must have been about half-past eleven when her groaning woke me.”

“And what do you remember after that?”

“Nothing. Not till I was drinking coffee in the morning. I suppose that feeling dreadfully sleepy I must have struggled back to my room after waking the family. Dr. Fisher and Dr. Smollett know the rest. I’m told it was nearly two when I was found on my bed.”

“That’s quite clear,” Pardoe said. “I shan’t keep you much longer, Miss Brett. Tell me this—were you in the habit of locking your door when you left the room for any length of time?”

Aurelia looked surprised. “No. Why ever should I have been? But I may tell you that I never sleep with it unfastened now. The communicating door too—I asked for the key of that after Monday. And I fetch my own drinking water at night from the bathroom.”

"A precaution easily understood," the inspector admitted, "though I don't think there's anything more to be feared in that line. By the way, did you ever hear talk of a Miss Gretton?"

If he had expected the suddenly posed question to catch her off her guard, he was not successful. Aurelia laughed.

"Who didn't? Yes, many times. Mrs. Weir was always speaking of her and wondering when she was coming back. She showed me the cottage she lived in. It seemed to me rather unkind that Miss Gretton should have left without a word to her."

"Did Mrs. Weir ever confide in you that she had felt ill after taking tea with Miss Gretton?"

"Good gracious, no," the girl said emphatically. "Oh, I see, you've been talking to Mrs. Kingdom." There was a touch of contempt in her voice. "Mrs. Weir had nothing but good to say of Miss Gretton. Her name was often on her lips, and because she was always a little muddled she was apt to call various people 'Alice'—Miss Leith, for instance. In fact, she's used the name for me."

Pardoe frowned at his notebook. "Did you reach the house that night before or after Mr. Weir got back?"

"A few minutes after. Mrs. Kingdom told me that he and Dr. Smollett had just come in. As I was going upstairs I saw Dr. Smollett come out of the library into the hall. I was carrying my little lunch case, and he made a joking remark about picnicking on my day off."

CHAPTER X

THE DOCTOR

O, mickle is the powerful grace that lies
In herbs, plants, stones, and their true qualities.
William Shakespeare: *Romeo and Juliet.*

The next day, which was Saturday, was a busy one for Pardoe. To this he had relegated his examination of the rest of the household, as well as his visits to Dr. Smollett and the lawyers who were handling the dead woman's estate.

Before leaving Spanwater on Friday night he had gone in quest of Comfort, the gardener, who could show him where the weedkiller was normally kept. A light was burning behind the drawn curtains of the lodge, and when the man came out to them he seemed ill-pleased at the interruption. He was a gaunt, stringy fellow who belied the agreeable prospect of his name, and though not dull of comprehension appeared too ready to take as a personal affront any activity of the police in his own domain. Something of this was made clear to Pardoe when the gardener explained that Superintendent Creed had had a padlock fixed on the hitherto unlocked shed containing what was left of the commercial arsenic, that he, Comfort, had been asked to remove from the building any tools in immediate use, and that a Cottlebury police sergeant had then locked it up and gone off with the key. There was an undertone of triumph in the man's voice as he hinted that Pardoe would have to go away unsatisfied; and when the inspector, who had received it from Creed in the morning together with the reports of the case, was able to produce the key, he looked crestfallen. However, he led them without more ado down the lane to the shrubbery door set in the wall.

Once inside they found themselves in what seemed a damp tunnel between looming bushes, the more mysterious because at night they were incognito. The toolshed, with its red wooden walls and tin roof, was on the far side of a tiny stone footbridge beneath which they caught the fugitive gleam of water. The gardener pointed out two empty tins of Slayweed that had contained the supply for the previous season. None had yet been bought for use this spring. Near them stood a large watering can with nozzle attached that had served for spraying the paths.

Pardoe looked closely at all three by the light of his torch. The tins were rusted and practically empty save for a crust of deposit round the inside rim at the bottom. They showed no signs of having been tampered with. The watering can received a more meticulous examination, and the inspector drew Salt's attention to the thick coating of white sediment choking the rose and crusting the screw of the spout. While they were thus engaged Comfort looked on aloofly without apparent interest, admitting when questioned that the door had never been locked and was accessible to anyone and everyone. Bearing in mind the natural hiding places afforded round here by the dense growth of bush and tree, it was easy to imagine an unauthorized person slipping in and out of the shed, perhaps finally emerging by the door into the lane, with nobody the wiser.

"That coating from the can could have been scraped," Pardoe said, after they had locked up and, dismissing the gardener, were making for their car. "The report states that Slayweed is sixty percent arsenic. That is, three grains of the powder contain two grains of arsenic, and two grains of arsenic are soluble in ten drops of water and constitute the minimum fatal dose. Now that deposit on the spray is largely arsenical and if dissolved in sufficient quantity would prove as poisonous as the powder from which it is formed. I didn't see any evidence of scraping, but we'll have another look in the daylight."

The inquest which opened in the morning at ten-thirty and occupied only a quarter of an hour was completely formal in character. Adjournment was to that day fortnight. When they came out Dr. Smollett, whom Pardoe had waylaid for a minute before the proceedings began, ran the inspector and Salt in his car to his house. To Pardoe, meeting him for the first time, he seemed an edgy, mercurial fellow, so quick of eye as to appear shifty, and full of irrelevant remarks that were effective in preventing the inspector from making one of his own till they had reached the house.

In the study, however, where Aurelia Brett had been interviewed a few weeks earlier, the doctor's loquacity deserted him. What Salt privately dubbed a do-or-die expression came over his pale features, and the look which he gave the Yard men had in it a touch of hostility that made an uncomfortable prelude to the business in hand. Though he gave them chairs he would not be seated himself, but fidgeted in the confined space between table and fire as if movement upon his feet gave him some superiority over his questioners. Like a bloomin' water wagtail, thought Salt irritably; purposeless activity always rubbed him up the wrong way.

Once he had taken the plunge, however, Dr. Smollett gave a more straightforward account of things than might have been expected. He corroborated Dr. Fisher's evidence as to his own absence on the night of Mrs. Weir's final illness, and was even careful, to Pardoe's surprise, to furnish them with the name and address of the patient whom he had been attending till well on into the next morning. He had arrived at Spanwater about eleven-twenty and had been in attendance until Mrs. Weir's death late in the afternoon. He had nothing illuminating to add to Dr. Fisher's story of the course the illness had taken, but mentioned of his own accord that before sinking into the coma which remained unbroken until she died Mrs. Weir had several times uttered the name "Alice" and had tried once to struggle into a sitting posture and point.

"Which way?" Pardoe asked.

"Towards the photographs on her dressing table," said Smollett, "which seemed to me significant. I know it was thought that she meant Miss Gretton, a woman who's lately been living over at Titt's Cote. But I'm not so sure. My own idea is that the poor woman wanted somebody sent for, some relative, perhaps, before she died."

"Do you know if she has any relative of that name?"

The doctor admitted, rather acidly, that he didn't, adding that he had had more important things to think about than this one half-conscious utterance. Pardoe refrained from pointing out that he had thought enough about it to volunteer a statement.

"What I've been anxious to see you about, Doctor," he said, "is the matter of Mrs. Weir's previous attacks of sickness—also this herb tea she was in the habit of drinking. To take the herb tea first—what exactly were the medicinal properties of the stuff she put in it?"

Before he had finished speaking the doctor had taken two nervous turns to his desk and back, looking out for a moment at the garden.

"In two words, perfectly harmless," he said snappily. "But I suppose you won't take that for an answer. Very well—the whole concoction when properly brewed is mainly diuretic in action."

He shot the inspector an impish look.

"You're quite right," Pardoe remarked mildly, "I don't know what it means. D'you mind explaining the term diuretic, please?"

Dr. Smollett flushed a little. "Plants which are diuretic," he said in a less offhand manner, "increase the action of the kidneys. The greater bedstraw, which is sometimes called cleavers, is one of those. Mrs. Weir called it 'hayriff,' the name she knew in Herefordshire when she was a child."

Pardoe nodded. "And what's jill?"

"Eh?" The doctor frowned. "Oh, that's another of her words for ground ivy—*you* know," he added as the inspector made a sound expressive of recognition, "nepeta, cat's mint, is the garden variety. The wild one is a useful little plant, and should be picked in flower for making into a tonic. It's one of the first things to come out, soon after the poisonous dog's mercury. Ground ivy's diuretic too, a stimulant and very appetizing."

"And what about the nettles and dandelions she used to gather? They any good?"

"Both good. Dandelion's a laxative as well as good for the kidneys, and stinging nettle gathered young is a wholesome thing either as an infusion or not. The very tender shoots are edible and a substitute for spinach."

He stopped and looked curiously at Pardoe. "But look here, she died of arsenical poisoning, didn't she? What's all this about the herbs she used? There wasn't a scrap of harm in them. Not one, nor all combined, could have produced the symptoms she had."

"I believe you," Pardoe said, "but I like to satisfy myself on every point. And though I'm a countryman and can put a name to most of the commoner flowers, to my shame I'll confess I don't know their virtues. Was there anything else she used?"

"Not that I know of," Smollett replied. "I warned her against one or two things, dog's mercury, for instance, and spotted arum, but mind you, she knew more about that sort of thing than any of the rest of us, and I'll stake my all she never herself included a poisonous thing."

Pardoe was impressed a little in spite of himself by the emphasis with which the doctor weighted his assurance. He passed smoothly on to the question of Mrs. Weir's previous sickness, but here the doctor was not at first so forthcoming. He looked uncomfortable and could only reiterate that he had regarded it as gastric trouble of a more or less mild nature, aggravated by the cold, and by Mrs. Weir's rashness in wandering about in inclement weather, and had treated it as such.

"Of course I know," he added bitterly, "that wisdom after the event can say she was taking arsenic then. Well, what doctor in my position was going to jump to that conclusion?"

Something in the inflection of the voice, a faint stressing of the possessive, gave peculiar force to his last remark. At Pardoe's request he consulted his book and jotted down for the inspector's use the dates on which he had treated Mrs. Weir for sickness.

Pardoe considered them. "You didn't make it your business, I suppose, to find out every time what Mrs. Weir's movements had been that day, Doctor?"

"Not every time, of course," was the reply testily given. "I naturally inquired what she'd been eating and drinking, and I may say it was too early on for her to have made any of this year's herb tea. As I said, she'd been out in bad weather on one or two occasions before the onsets."

"Exactly. It might have been worthwhile finding out where she'd been. How was it," Pardoe went on, ignoring the doctor's glare, "that Miss Brett was told nothing of these illnesses at the time she was engaged as companion?"

"She wasn't a nurse," the doctor said lamely, after hesitating a fraction of a second too long.

"Surely that's beside the point," the inspector returned. "She was going to look after her, and there was at least a fair chance that Mrs. Weir would have another attack while Miss Brett was in the house. Had she known the state of Mrs. Weir's health she might not have accepted the post."

"That was just it," Smollett said with a rush, then caught himself up sharply. "Anyway it's your argument that's beside the point now, since Mrs. Weir's sickness never did recur after Miss Brett came."

"No. A very interesting point," Pardoe agreed. He added quietly, "Will you explain, Doctor, what you mean by 'That's just it,' to my suggestion that Miss Brett might have turned down your offer if she had known beforehand the full truth about Mrs. Weir's health?"

The doctor looked still more uncomfortable. "Aren't you treating me rather as a hostile witness?" he retorted. "To be asked to account for every casual phrase—well, I see no necessity for explanation."

"All right," Pardoe said. "Then you can't object if I draw my own conclusions."

"Damn your own conclusions," said Dr. Smollett vigorously. He took his hands from his trousers pockets, sighed sharply, then thrust them back again.

"Look here, Inspector," he went on suddenly, "I don't care for this beating about the bush any more than you do. But I've tried to keep the past out of this for Weir's sake, for all our sakes. It's going to be hellish for us all if the muckrakes get to work on the Bunting case as well as this one. But as you know all about that it's pretty pointless playing mum any longer. And if I do you'll only turn your suspicions in God knows what direction. It's like this—at the interview I had with Miss Brett I was waiting all the time for her reactions to the name Weir. The Bunting trial isn't such ancient history as all that, and when I even went so far as to explain Mrs. Weir's mental trouble in the light of a great shock through a relative's death, entailing a complete change of residence for the family, I took it for granted she would respond to the test and either refuse the job on the spot or show her indifference to the past by accepting in spite of it. I was astonished when she showed no sign of remembering."

"Might have done so, though," Pardoe remarked. "And what about not mentioning the sick bouts to her?"

"I was coming to that. Miss Brett was insistent on her inability to do sick nursing. She started off by reminding me of it—she'd already stated it emphatically in her written application—and she hammered it home at intervals that afternoon. She didn't realize it was in her favor, and I wasn't able to point that out to her fully. So I said nothing about the sickness, which frankly I didn't think serious, in case she shied at taking the job, and in case mention of gastric trouble woke memories of the Bunting woman. If she had forgotten, all to the good. I happen to be a friend of Mat Weir's," the doctor added with defiant inconsequence.

At that moment Pardoe liked him better than he had at all.

"Well, that lets a bit of fresh air in," he said. "Now, do you mind explaining yet another remark—why was Miss Brett's ignorance of nursing a point in her favor?"

"If you remember the Bunting case," Smollett replied, "you'll recall Nurse Geary and her prejudicial evidence. Since then Mat—Mr. Weir's attitude has been that he won't have a nurse at any cost, and as I didn't consider a trained person in the least necessary in his wife's case, I set about finding somebody who hadn't qualified. I naturally couldn't let Miss Brett know that what she thought was a snag in the way of her employment was actually an asset—not, that is, without dragging the past into light."

"I see," the inspector said. "Whose idea was it in the first place to get a companion for Mrs. Weir?"

Dr. Smollett flushed, and hesitated a moment as if he were looking for the catch in this. "Well—we—we discussed it, as the poor woman grew mentally less responsible. I—it was really I who suggested somebody ought to be got, but Weir agreed with me directly," he finished on a firmer note.

Pardoe looked at him steadily for a few moments in silence. "Dr. Smollett," he said at last in a kindly tone, "are you sure that knowing all you knew about the Bunting murder trial you never felt the least anxiety about Mrs. Weir's recurrent illness? Wasn't that why you suggested a companion for her?"

The doctor's first look of anger melted to a rather rueful amusement. "I don't know what about 'Ask a policeman,' " he said, "but 'Tell a policeman' seems more in order here. You're right. I was a bit uneasy now and again. Yet I couldn't find anything inconsistent with gastritis when I examined her, and I was heartily relieved when a companion was agreed upon because I hoped that if everything wasn't quite as it should be the sickness would stop when a person in that capacity was brought in."

"And it did," Pardoe said, "—until the last attack."

"Yes, it did."

All at once Smollett caught his eye and broke out savagely, "This all looks dam' suspicious, and I must make it clear that I was always convinced Weir had nothing to do——"

"We're not apportioning guilt," Pardoe said quickly, putting out his hand to check him. "The Bunting case had to be introduced into this talk, but my own inquiry is an independent one. To change the subject, Doctor, why was Miss Brett paid her first week's salary in advance?"

The doctor looked surprised. "Great Scott, what's that to do with it? If you must know, I was pretty sorry for the girl. She'd been out of work five months and was very nearly all in. I thought she was going to faint when I offered her the post. I had an idea she'd spent her last dollar on coming from London to friends in Gloucester on the chance of being favored with an interview—so I hinted to Mr. Weir to let her have the wherewithal to carry on."

Pardoe accepted this without comment. "And why was it Mr. Weir didn't interview her himself instead of coming into the room at the last minute?"

"He never intended coming at all," Smollett said candidly. "We were pretty sure she'd recall the past, and he naturally preferred to keep in the background. When it appeared she didn't know I went and fetched him. That's all there was to it."

That was nearly all there was to Pardoe's business with the doctor that morning. He was due at the lawyers' immediately after lunch and would have to be moving on. But first he satisfied himself that Smollett's evidence confirmed Matthew Weir's as to the manner in which they had spent Monday evening; the doctor thought they had got back about nine-fifteen.

"Mr. Weir could have caught the last bus to Cloudy then?" Pardoe said, remembering Aurelia's statement.

"He didn't care about buses," the doctor said shortly. "Too many people. He thinks they stare."

"About the sleeping draught in Miss Brett's bottle," Pardoe remarked at a tangent. "How did you get on to that, Doctor?"

"The girl herself. It was obvious she'd taken something of the sort, and all she'd had to drink the night before was the water in her room. The bottle was still half-full when I took charge of it, and a little was left in the glass she'd used."

"And you found—?"

"Medinal," the doctor admitted in a tone in which Salt, who was looking for it, detected reluctance. "An ordinary dose. Creed went over it for prints, as you know, but there were only the girl's."

"You never prescribed it for her?"

"Who—for Miss Brett? No, never mentioned the stuff to her. She wasn't an insomnia victim. In fact, according to her she slept too heavily after coming to Spanwater. Country air and decent food taking effect."

He accompanied them to the door and in the little front hall stopped and gave the inspector a shrewd glance.

"Weir and I weren't the only ones who thought a companion would be suitable for Mrs. Weir," he remarked. "We thought she herself would oppose it, in which case it would have been unwise to urge it, but instead, after a day or two, she was the one who pressed it. Dinah—that's Miss Terris, told me later that the woman at Titt's Cote had been persuading her aunt to fall in with the plan. By the way," he went on rapidly, "don't bother Dinah Terris too much. She's the apple of Weir's eye, and this business has been pretty tough on her."

As though regretting his impulse the doctor shut the door on them more hastily than he had intended.

"Funny thing," Salt grumbled as they took the short cut under the sparse new green of the pollard ash, "how that Gretton dame pops up every time."

"Bit of a gatecrasher, isn't she?" Pardoe said with cheerful unconcern.

CHAPTER XI

SOMEWHAT BELLICOSE

Full of strange oaths.
William Shakespeare: *As You Like It.*

The offices of Messrs Wilbury and Kirk were situated between a florist's and a hat shop, their narrow, somber front resembling a staid old gentleman struggling to retain his ancient dignity in the company of two giddy girls. Pardoe, after dispatching Salt on the first tentative inquiry for any recent sales of Slayweed, mounted the dark stairs at two o'clock precisely and found the junior partner awaiting him. Junior was a questionable term, thought the inspector, noting the shriveled skin and gleaming pate, and could not help wondering how Mr. Wilbury wore his seniority.

"How was it," he said, the preliminaries over, "that Mrs. Weir's affairs did not remain in the hands of the Sheffield firm whose client she was for years?"

Mr. Kirk looked a little shocked and lifted his thin brows in reproach of such indelicate phrasing.

"My dear sir," he said, "you are, I take it, only too well acquainted" (rather good, that, thought Pardoe) "with the unfortunate history of the Weir family. The Sheffield solicitors who looked after the Bunting estate had a branch in Penmarket, and—I understand"—he faltered a little as plain speaking seemed imperative—"well, there was some slight difference of opinion, I gathered, arising out of the—the trial, which the late Mrs. Weir resented, and when she left Penmarket for good she was particularly anxious that no interests of hers should remain in that town. So she transferred her business to Cottlebury, to our hands."

"Oh, yes, that's all right," Pardoe said genially. "I was merely wondering. As a matter of fact, I'm congratulating myself I haven't to go farther afield for the information I want."

After that they got down to business, Mr. Kirk proving, in spite of a certain fussiness and oblique method of approach to even the most innocent features of the affair, a sound lawyer with all the essentials at his fingertips. As Pardoe himself was not entirely ignorant of the provisions of Tim Bunting's will, the matter was quickly dealt with.

"So it amounts to this," the inspector said. "Hannah Bunting, who married a clergyman named Murray, was the first of the three sisters to die. Her share of the inheritance passed to her own son, while Leah, who was a spinster, predeceased Catherine, that is, Mrs. Weir, who inherited all Leah had."

"Quite correct," Mr. Kirk replied. "Had Hannah, Mrs. Murray, been living at the time Miss Leah Bunting—er—died, the latter's estate would, of course, have been equally divided between her surviving sisters. As it was, Mrs. Weir was the reversionary legatee of the whole of Leah's."

"Naturally," Pardoe said impatiently, having grasped this perfectly well beforehand. "And you say that when the death duties and so on are cleared that should amount to something like £90,000? Now—"

"Excuse me," the lawyer interrupted hastily, "£95,000 would approach more closely to the truth. And I should mention that in addition to that sum in which she had only a life interest, Mrs. Weir had a little more than £6,000 of her own to dispose of as she wished. She was always, you understand, a very frugal liver—not miserly, but with such few wants that she could hardly help being economical and saving on her income."

"And who gets the six thousand?" Pardoe asked bluntly.

Mr. Kirk gave a deprecatory cough. "Mr. Matthew Weir—unreservedly."

The inspector made a note of this in silence.

"Now," he said briskly, "what I was going to ask you a minute ago—who is the heir to Mrs. Weir's fortune?"

The lawyer rubbed the palms of his hands against one another with a slow rasping movement, and tucked his chin down in a gesture which said plainly, "Ha-ha."

"That raises an interesting and—yes, a very troublesome question, Inspector. The heiress to the combined Bunting fortune is a grandchild of Mrs. Hannah Murray. Unfortunately the family have been out of touch with her for some years, and we're trying to ascertain where she is, providing she is still living."

The inspector looked thoughtful. "Since she inherits I take it her father is dead?"

"Both parents were killed in a car crash during Christmas week, 1937. That is partly what I meant by the troublesomeness of the present situation. The legal advisers of the dead couple have tried through the usual channels to trace the whereabouts of Joyce Murray who left her home seven years ago. So far their efforts have been unavailing. We, of course, shall now renew the attempt to discover this girl, but we frankly don't expect much response."

"She cut herself off completely then?"

"Oh, quite. I'm afraid I know very little of the personal side of it, but Mr. Weir may be able to enlighten you. There was a serious family quarrel, I understand, the upshot of which was that Miss Joyce, then nearly eighteen years old, left home for good and all. That was in 1932. It was rumored that she had obtained work as a—er—chorus girl in London. It was a sad affair, a very sad affair, for she was the only child, and her father was Mrs. Hannah Murray's only son."

"Did Hannah have any other children?"

"A daughter who died childless many years ago. The Buntings had very few relatives, and none now traceable."

"Supposing Joyce Murray is found to have died, who then inherits the Bunting fortune?"

"Providing she died without leaving legitimate issue, the next of kin—in this case, Mr. Matthew Weir."

"Well, it's up to us to find out whether the girl's dead or alive," Pardoe said more cheerfully than he felt, shutting his notebook and picking up his hat. "I'm much obliged to you, Mr. Kirk. I'll be seeing you again. If you want to get in touch a message at the police station will find me."

On his way there himself the lawyer's information gave him something to think about.

The money at stake provided, as experience only too plainly indicated, a more than adequate motive for murdering Mrs. Weir. People had been poisoned, or done to death in other ways, for a good deal less than £90,000. That raised the question, who benefited most in the financial sense by Mrs. Weir's death? The answer was Joyce Murray. But suppose, as was quite probable, that Joyce Murray were dead? Then Matthew Weir stepped into her shoes. But if the husband were the murderer it seemed conclusive that he had already known Joyce Murray was dead, else the sole result of his crime would be to enrich a distant relative who had herself lightly regarded family ties.

"For Banquo's issue have I fil'd my mind," came as an unbidden corollary to the inspector's thoughts—surely the most tragic, because the most hopeless line in Shakespeare. It could not be that, unless indeed Weir's motive had been the lesser sum, the six thousand. If he had killed his wife it was either that or he knew that Joyce Murray would never come forward to claim her inheritance. In that case why could he not have proclaimed the fact and so expedited matters? The shadow of something sinister crept across Pardoe's mind. He shook it off and tried to think of a possible motive that excluded money, though that was unlikely. There was this rumor about Miss Leith, of course. It was possible that an ailing wife had been considered an obstacle to her marriage with Weir. Besides, there was still the six thousand whichever way it was. That wasn't to be sneezed at. Perhaps Weir was short of ready cash. He must find out. Where Miss Leith was concerned some sort of inquiry too seemed necessary, for she interested Pardoe on her own account ever since he had been told of her absence from Cloudy in the spring. Much as he disliked fantastic notions, always plumping if possible for the plainer view, the more reasonable explanation, he could not rid his mind of a queer picture that was forming there. Titt's Cote . . . Miss Gretton . . . Miss Leith's cottage in the spring—what was it Mrs. Kingdom had said?—"The house was shut up."

Pardoe was still trying to fit these odd aspects of the case into a rational whole when he walked into the police station. Here he had arranged with Salt to receive the sergeant's first reports, if there were any, of the weed-killer sold in Cottlebury. He had little hope, however, of tripping the murderer on that score.

Salt was not there, but Pardoe was greeted by Superintendent Creed with such a mixture of irritability, fluster, excitement, and relief at the sight of him that it was rather overwhelming. A word in private before he was led into the office explained this emotional disturbance.

"You've turned up just pat," the superintendent said, breathing noisily. "I've had all I can do to keep him quiet. It's old Sir Jacob—old Borth, you know, reg'lar holy terror. *You* know," he went on with an impatient jerk of his head at Pardoe's bewilderment, "the old johnny that's pocketed most of the plums in this part of the world—Borth's Chemicals, and all that. Why, he's one of the country's war lords—he could turn up his nose at the Mint itself. He's worn himself out a bit now, but a while ago he was breathing *that* fire and slaughter you never see."

"But what's it all *about?*" put in the inspector.

"His kid got smashed up this morning in one of the Weirs' cars. Gone to hospital, and we've got the car. I can't make out how bad he is. But it doesn't seem to be that that's troubling the old man so much as the malice aforethought of the Weirs. But come and see for yourself."

Pardoe's first impression of Sir Jacob Borth was of an immense toad sunk in an immobility that might become venomous at any moment. He rejected the simile instantly, however; toads in reality were gentle, fragile creatures, not the mountain of malignity this old man looked. Yet in the yellow, pouchy skin and physical lethargy there was something of the amphibian. He sat ponderously and well forward in the superintendent's most comfortable chair, a stout ash stick clutched in his formidable old hand. The little black, greedy eyes gave Pardoe what Salt would have called the once-over.

"Perhaps we'll get some sense out of you," was his acknowledgment of the superintendent's introduction, his voice hoarse with asthma and outraged pride. "If you're in charge of this (adjectival) case out at Spanwater you'll need to look no further for your man. You've got 'im. Hear what I said, you've *got* 'im! *I'll* tell you who killed the woman and tried to kill my son—and that's that (adjectival) Nick Terris, blast 'im, the (adjectival) devil!"

"Dear me, this is interesting," Pardoe said mildly. "D'you mind explaining yourself, Sir Jacob? And I fancy I'd take it in better if you could forget the violence and let me have a straightforward account."

The murderous eyes, unable at once to determine what this meekness meant, lost something of their glare, and a rather less vitriolic version of what the old man termed a planned attack upon his son was given to Pardoe than had assaulted the ears of Superintendent Creed.

It appeared that Sir Jacob had a son Freddy, who was at present living at home with his father in Ebro House, Cottlebury, engaged in diligent study which would one day give him the privilege of becoming a member of

Oxford University—a very doubtful privilege in his father's eyes, judging by tone and glance. But as this innocuous occupation evidently failed to afford sufficient scope for Freddy's youthful exuberance, what must the damned idiot of a boy do but pick up with such vicious company as that of Nick Terris and his friends. He'd sneaked off to Cloudy that morning, borrowed that (trebly adjectival) racing car, and promptly gone and smashed it and himself to smithereens.

Pardoe pricked his ears. "Are you quite sure that Mr. Terris has a racing car?" he asked.

"Of course I'm dam' well not, sir!" the old maniac roared, the apparently harmless question applying the spark to gunpowder. "But if his (adjectival) friends have got 'em where's the (adjectival) difference!" He trembled visibly, and with labored breathing got himself under some sort of control. "Fellow named Pitt—staying in the house—brought the dam' thing with him. They know Freddy's not got the guts to drive anything faster than a milk float—so they put him up to it. Saw to it that the (adjectival) car would buckle up. Put him up to it, I say, to get him (adjectivally well) killed!" He was off again.

"Look here, sir," Pardoe said sternly, "making every excuse for the shock this accident's been to you, you can't go on flinging wild accusation left and right like this. Either you'll have to close down in your own interests as well as other people's, or you must substantiate what you say. Why should anybody want to kill your son?"

The black eyes were peculiarly sly and unwinking. "He knew too much for them."

"In what way?"

Old Borth leaned forward and jabbed his stick at Pardoe. "He paid a visit to the house last Christmas," he said, gutturally confidential, "the first time he ever set foot in the place. He saw somebody there pretending to be what he wasn't. And when he recognized 'em for what they was, he wasn't believed. See? And ever since then Nick Terris has never left him alone. See?"

Pardoe was not sure that he did. "Who was this person he saw?"

But the old man either could not or would not say. "Find out for yourself," he finished rudely.

"Putting that aside for the moment," Pardoe went on, "why do you accuse Mr. Terris of these designs on your son when Mr. Borth was driving Mr. Pitt's car at the time of the accident?"

"Because he never knew this Pitt fellow in his life before," Jacob Borth said savagely. "That's why. *He* wasn't in the house last Christmas. And he's known Terris a year or so—knew him at Oxford before they sent my boy down." He added with a sneer, "Terris soon followed him. *And* Terris on his own admission wouldn't mind doing a bit of murder on the q.t."

As a description of a plot violent enough to have involved the smashing to smithereens of a high-powered car, the inspector felt that this was something of an understatement. Old Borth seemed to divine his thoughts.

"And I ain't only referring to my boy," he said with a deliberation that was even uglier than his rage. "I take it you're not down here on holiday. Weir's wife is dead, ain't she?"

He thrust his stick out at Pardoe again and opened his mouth in what was meant for a grin, disclosing dirty fangs.

"Keep your hair on. I'll bring no charges in that direction. But it's my opinion that anybody standing for euthanasia" (he called it "uthanasia") "is a (adjectival) murderer before the (adjectival) deed's done—let it be arsenic or the loan of a car."

Creed looked puzzled, but the inspector nodded. "We don't need any additional information as to the principles held by Mr. Terris," he said in a cold voice, hoping to take the wind out of Borth's sails by an assumption of knowledge. "I'm only surprised, Sir Jacob, that he should have thought it worthwhile to expound them to you."

Sir Jacob, impervious to snubs, chuckled grossly.

"Proud of it," he said. "Proud as Lucifer of being expelled for preaching it. Said that if he had his way he'd snuff out the unfit, physically—and mentally. D'you hear? *And mentally*."

"I hear you," Pardoe said. "In fact I've heard plenty. There's just one thing I'd like to ask you, Sir Jacob."

He met the malevolent gaze of the small, pouchy eyes.

"Do you know," he said quietly, "the meaning of the term euthanasia?"

Sir Jacob Borth stared at the inspector as if he actually thought that the Yard man was seeking instruction on the point. Pardoe wondered, not for the first time, whether he was really a shrewd old man or only a very stupid one.

"Doing the hangman's job for him," he wheezed, enjoying his own joke.

Pardoe ignored him. "It means the easy way to death. Passing out of life with as little pain and unrest as possible. Would you say, Sir Jacob, that death by arsenical poisoning or death in a splintered, perhaps burning, car fulfilled those conditions?"

Old Borth did not answer. A nerve in his upper lip kept twitching, and the knuckles of the hand grasping his ash shone white. But he had not done yet.

"Bad blood will out," he said hoarsely. "The old man cheated the gallows once, didn't he?"

All at once, like a whale coming to the surface, he heaved himself out of the chair. "And if you poor fools can work it you'll see that the young one slips out of the noose too. Well, you got your pick—the devil won't mind which he gets, Weir, or Terris, or his brother."

"Whose brother?" Pardoe's tone was sharp. "Mr. Terris has no brother."

"He's got two uncles, ain't he? I'm talking about that japey, lah-di-dah, jumped up peacock from London"—he made the gesture of spitting aside, then favored Pardoe with a crafty look—"his affairs won't stand looking into."

"We will decide that, Sir Jacob."

The old man came a step nearer, the veins on his temple swollen ridges. "Then why did he come pumping me for a loan, eh? Called it buying shares in his paper—his *paper*, the dirty rag—*pah!*" He spat in earnest under the furious eye of the superintendent, and leering at them both shambled towards the door. "He don't know where to turn for a dime, I tell you. But mebbe that's for you to decide too."

In the passage outside Salt was waiting. He received the full force of Sir Jacob's valedictory glare, but watched with stolidity unshaken the departure of the ogre.

"Apoplexy'll be the end of 'im," he announced phlegmatically, and evincing no curiosity went straight on to give the inspector a summary of his tour of the shops. He had so far inquired at seven establishments that sold weedkiller of one make or another. Of these one had made a recent sale of Slayweed and two others of Aypresto; in the case of Slayweed and one of the others the purchasers had been local nursery men, the third being a man living out at Wick's End, a village between Cottlebury and Gloucester.

"So it don't look too good," the sergeant finished. "But there's one or two more places I can try."

"Yes," Creed put in, "there's a little place in Foley Street that stocks it or did, as well as Byfleet in the Gloucester Road. Been there?"

"No, but I will," said Salt doggedly. "See here," he turned to Pardoe, "do we know for cert, the stuff was Slayweed? Couldn't it ha' been some other brand?"

"Oh, yes. One or two others with the same percentage of arsenic. Only Slayweed happens to be the one in most general use, has been bought for Spanwater, and agrees with the relative amount of arsenic remaining in the jug of herb tea. Your Aypresto—what names they get for the stuff—is a weaker mixture altogether, only about forty percent arsenic."

Before leaving Cottlebury Pardoe thought a visit to the bedside of the prostrate Freddy might not be amiss. He therefore outlined for Salt's benefit what they had learned from Sir Jacob, with the choicer epithets omitted, and leaving the superintendent to recover in solitude from his lurid experience, took the sergeant first to review the remains of the car.

"I only hope there's a bit more left of young Borth," Pardoe said grimly as they gazed at the crushed chassis and fragmentary bonnet and mud-guards. It had been brought on a lorry from the scene of the accident less than half a mile out of Cloudy, and reposed now in mangled misery in the station yard. A young constable who had been early on the scene came forward to point out to them the worst features of the wreckage. Such whole-sale destruction seemed to puzzle him.

"What did he do?" the inspector asked idly. "Run into a flotilla of lorries or what?"

"Oh, no, sir," the p.c. explained earnestly. "A lucky thing for him there was no other traffic on the road at the time. He hit the bank on a corner of the road, and a five-barred gate beyond. It's funny how he managed it. We've examined the place—conditions this morning make an ordinary skid out of the question. Of course he was going hell-for-leather—it's a wonder he wasn't mutton when we picked him up. It tossed him clear, right *through* the gate. Now, this here is very funny—" He stooped and with gingerly care took up the steering wheel, still intact, and then its snapped rod, and handed them in silence to Pardoe.

The inspector whistled, and Salt drew in his breath quickly. The clean exactitude of the break was unmistakable. Mr. Freddy Borth suddenly became in the inspector's eyes a subject ten times more acutely interesting than his father had tried to make him.

At the hospital they were at first short and inclined to be uncommunicative about anything relating to the invalid. Pardoe's card, however, worked wonders, and after an appeal to the matron he and Salt were permitted ten minutes at the bedside.

Freddy's adventure had left him with a fractured rib, a broken collar-bone, a badly wrenched shoulder and numerous cuts and abrasions chiefly in the region of the head, which was swathed in alarmingly turbanwise fashion. He had, it seemed, miraculously escaped graver internal injury, though he would be under observation for some time.

He lay mute and long and gruesomely corpse-like in the private ward Sir Jacob had secured for him, bearing the pain of his shoulder with as much fortitude as his infantile mind could muster.

As the nurse explained his visitors to him, then drifted out silently, he turned his only visible eye on them and whispered cheerfully, "Sit down, do."

Pardoe, conscious of the meager time at their disposal, led off immediately. He eyed all he could see of the boy's face, the weak chin, the scared eye, the rather pathetic mouth. There was nothing physically of the old block in this chip.

"How old are you, Mr. Borth?" he asked quietly.

"Twenty."

"You feeling up to telling me a bit about this car drive of yours? In your own words, anything you like. And only if you want to."

The flatness of Pardoe's tone, the lack of urgency in it, had its desired effect upon Freddy, who took them for local police on the routine job of inquiry into an accident.

"I'd like to. But I don't remember much. I went to see Nick—Andy Pitt showed me the Lagonda—I wanted to try it. Pitt said I couldn't handle it. But then he let me. I forget the rest. It happened—just as soon as I started, I think. I remember the car—seemed to leave me. I—I don't remember any more," he finished abruptly.

"All right," said Pardoe. "That's fine." He leaned forward a little. "Mr. Borth, who is living at Spanwater under a different name?"

There was a short silence in which Freddy closed his eye. His lips trembled faintly. Just as Pardoe was sure that they would get nothing more out of him, he opened his eye and said irrelevantly:

"I shall be here a long time, shan't I?"

"A few weeks, I'm afraid," Pardoe said soothingly, "but—"

"That's O.K. then," was the lighthearted rejoinder, delivered in a stronger key. "This morgue's pretty safe, I expect. Because I wouldn't put much past him if he knew I told. I'll tell you, though. It's the butler. Listen, how I know is this—I can't pass in to Oxford. And when I'm there I can't stay in. I don't want to. A year ago I went to Benny's—the crammer's place—old Benedict, you know, in Somerset. This chap was house porter there—name of Bill Fennick. I went to Spanwater at Christmas—said, 'howdy, Fennick,' to Mond—recognized him on the spot."

The nurse stuck her head round the door and warned them that they had only one more minute.

"The sands are running out," said Freddy, grinning weakly. "Well, that's all. Fennick looked as if he could kill me—I never liked the bounder. We used to think he pinched things. He denied it flatly. Threatened me afterwards with a slander action if I called him by the wrong name again. All rot, I expect—but to be on the safe side I didn't tell even the pater who it was I'd seen—he might have blown up or done something drastic. Likes interferin' with people, you know. That's all. But I know he's Fennick," Freddy whispered with simple conviction.

Pardoe got up. "Thanks, son. You've helped a lot. Did you tell anybody about Mond being Fennick?"

"Only Nick. He was with me when I hailed him."

"I see. And this Mr. Benedict—is he still living in those parts?"

"Rather. Dad's got the address. I say, keep me out of it, won't you?"

"That's all right," Pardoe said, catching a glimpse of the nurse's uniform out of the tail of his eye. He patted the boy's arm lightly, and went out followed by Salt, after bestowing on the nurse a smile calculated to win access to Freddy's ward on a later occasion if need arose.

"The skunk," said Salt, as they left the hospital. "Him and his brother-in-law's roadhouse at Rochester."

" 'Mm. A word with Mr. Mond seems to be in season."

Neither of them could have guessed at this juncture that that was something they would never have.

CHAPTER XII

FRIENDS AND RELATIONS

I do affirm and always shall . . . that murder is an improper line of conduct.

De Quincey: *Murder as One of the Fine Arts.*

When it was all over Pardoe was inclined to date the solution of the case from the event of Freddy Borth's accident.

At Sir Jacob's mansion, a building as ostentatiously ugly as its master, they were met at the door by a skeptical footman who, his doubts overcome, admitted them to the presence of an equally disdainful secretary. Sir Jacob himself was providentially out still (probably expatiating at his club, Pardoe surmised, on the iniquity of paying taxes to keep the police force going) and when the secretary was at last convinced that Scotland Yard was exerting itself on behalf of Mr. Freddy Borth, he managed to produce, after a rummaging that did small credit to his efficiency, the address of Mr. Benedict. Pardoe took it down, noting that it was in the Mendips that this gentleman carried on the good work for which Freddy and his like were so little grateful.

The connection with Mrs. Weir's death was at the moment obscure, however, and when inspector and sergeant returned to Spanwater after tea, thought of it was not uppermost in Pardoe's mind. What he wanted now was a talk with those he had not seen the night before, particularly with Augustus Weir, and to get some amplification of what the lawyer had told him about Joyce Murray. Inquiry into Mond's alias he put off to another day. If the fellow really had some game on hand which the alleged false name suggested, and there was of course still the faint possibility that young Borth had made a genuine mistake in the matter, the more rope he was allowed the worse for him. Up to a point, that was. They didn't want him taking the alarm and clearing out before the time was ripe. The best thing was to watch him quietly for a day or two. Pardoe at this stage was pretty sure that his part in the mischief afoot would prove independent of the main issue—a nuisance, in a way, if it were so, as it would involve two separate lines of inquiry.

So when Mound admitted them Pardoe apparently ignored him, while observing with satisfaction that his hands as he took their hats were trembling and that the brazen look had gone from his mean features.

Matthew Weir came to them with the embarrassing touch of apology in his manner that suggested he had engaged them for this task and was sorry to be troubling them. The rather prominent eyes had such a strained look, and the man's general appearance was so worn, that Pardoe once for all shelved the idea that he might be acting. Whatever his responsibility for the present catastrophe, he was a genuinely sick man.

His weariness gave way to surprise when the inspector raised the question of Joyce Murray.

"Does it really help you to inquire along that line?" he asked, puzzled. "Of course we've known for a long time that she would inherit if she were alive. Wilbury and Kirk have had little to do with the matter till now—they didn't tell you she went overseas?"

Pardoe shook his head. "Where did she go?"

"To Australia. She sent one letter to her parents from Wollongong, I think it was. Very short, very uninformative. They passed it on to Kate, and we both read it."

"When was that, sir?" Pardoe's voice was eager.

Matthew made an effort at concentration. "Two—no, it must be three years ago now. The autumn of 1936, I think it was. She was with a touring theatrical company that had been doing the southeastern coast of New South Wales that winter—during our summer, of course."

"Did she go out to Australia directly after leaving home?"

"N-no. But it's hard to say how soon after. I think the first time she wrote to her parents was from London." His husky voice changed abruptly to a less vague tone. "You know she relinquished her name Murray as soon as she ran away?"

"Oh. What did she call herself?"

"Fenella Pagan."

" 'Mm. Rather arresting," Pardoe remarked. "Though I shouldn't have said she was the kind that was reluctant to carry on to the stage the name she was born with."

"Oh, it wasn't that. It couldn't have been. I think she wanted to shake the old life off completely. The kind of idea that makes you think with a fresh name you will start a fresh history. We are not all so wise. Joyce has all my sympathy, Inspector. Her mother had a touch of religious mania that showed alarming signs of developing, and her father was the sort of waster an indulgent mother with plenty of money can make out of an only son if she wants to. He lived on credit, as far as I can gather, and was ready to sacrifice everything, including his own family, to personal comfort. The girl had the grit few of us are blessed with, and refused to stand for it any longer."

Matthew Weir seemed to have forgotten his diffidence, and Pardoe looked at him curiously, surprised at the length and lucidity of his statement.

"Was she heard of again after that?"

"Not that we knew. I remember the letter said they hoped to move on to Sydney in the spring. That was all."

It was more than Pardoe had expected.

"Do you happen to know where she was in London—with what company, I mean?" he asked doubtfully.

Matthew shook his head. "I don't. If the early news of her ever reached us I've forgotten now."

The inspector gave him a thoughtful look. "Would you know Joyce Murray, Mr. Weir, if you were to see her again?"

"I'm afraid not. I only saw her once, a year or two before she left home. She was a little fair girl then, very bright and talented. There's a photograph—upstairs, if it's any good to you. But it was taken years ago."

"Thank you," Pardoe said, "I should like to borrow it."

Matthew Weir promised to let them have it before they left. To Pardoe's inquiry he said that his brother was in the drawing room. At the door he turned back for a moment.

"I hope," he said in his hurried, gentle way, "that you will succeed where the Murray solicitors have failed. Find Joyce, I mean. But somehow I don't think you will."

When they were alone Salt slowly lifted his eyebrows, giving to his comfortable features a popeyed, slightly ludicrous air.

"P'r'aps it's a case of 'I know you won't,' " he said.

Pardoe did not reply.

The windows of the drawing room looked south and west. The small morning room lay between it and the library, and Pardoe, who had the knack of becoming quickly cognizant of the plan of a house, found his way there without difficulty.

They came into a room full of charm and conventional personality, furnished in the brittle delicacy of the eighteenth century. In the midst of this graceful display Augustus Weir was, oddly enough, not an incongruous centerpiece.

When they came in he was writing at a frail little table, his bulk miraculously sustained by a Hepplewhite chair. His greeting struck the correct note of affability, and he put his pen aside with a leisurely dignity that Pardoe took for the result of well-controlled nerves. He wondered what it was that reminded him instantly of Matthew. Apparent likeness there was none. This man was huge, stout, black as a raven; Matthew was slight, with reddish hair and wary, mistrustful eyes, light blue in color. He had, too, a gentleness of manner that was even awkward and disconcerting, totally unrelated to his brother's self-possessed courtesy. Yet in spite of contrasts a subtle common denominator made itself felt, sufficiently potent to make it unthinkable to question the relationship. Perhaps it lay in the smiles, or the voices, Pardoe reflected, though Matthew's shy, hasty speech had little in common with his brother's deliberately rich cadences; but a fleeting undertone in each marked the resemblance.

To the casual observer Augustus Weir looked like a *poseur* who had strayed forty years out of his proper picture: the nineties were his domain. But Pardoe who from time to time had seen *The Archon*, the journal he edited with such consistent brilliance, and had read his poetry that made little concession to the traditionalists of any age, recognized that in this man the senses would always be subordinated to the intellect. Before he had been five minutes in the room he knew too, by that sixth sense which functions between two people who constantly work together, that Salt was vaguely disgusted and thought Augustus a fool.

The big man laughed softly, with a note that struck uncomfortably on his hearers, as he described his ignorance of the happenings of Monday night.

"I sleep deeply," he explained, "a gift more likely to be bestowed upon the unjust than the just—as my brother, to whom it is a stranger, and I can testify. It's no sign of innocence. Only the unjust are ever able to lull their consciences sufficiently to enjoy the balm of sleep."

Pardoe passed over this persiflage and went quietly on to the events of the day.

"There I'm afraid I can't help you," Augustus said regretfully. "I live only in and for the present. My memory is so rarely exercised it has grown to resemble me—fat, old and idle." He smiled winningly at the inspector.

Reminded of his walk with Matthew, however, he certainly remembered that they had gone out, though chiefly, he admitted, because of his abhorrence of walking in which he indulged only because his brother liked it.

"You returned early to see if a telephone message had arrived for you?" Pardoe prompted.

"Oh, yes. It hadn't. It still hasn't." He sighed.

"Would you mind telling me who the message was from, Mr. Weir?"

Augustus studiously lowered his eyes and examined his nails one by one. His hands, which one expected to be pudgy, were extraordinarily handsome.

"No—I don't think I mind," he said, picking his words with exasperating care. He lifted his eyes to Pardoe who saw, for all their blackness, how coldly they looked at him. "Mr. James Gow, a Cottlebury—merchant, shall we say, has been gracious enough to display some interest in my literary adventures. I had hoped that the interest would become financial. The telephone call would have decided that."

"In short, you wanted a loan from him?"

Augustus bowed. "The crudity of expression is your own, Inspector."

"And he didn't make it?"

"Alas, for the frailty of human hopes—and human health. Mr. Gow has been stricken with bronchial pneumonia ever since Easter day. I telephone daily to learn what progress he makes."

"Have you rung them up today?"

"Not yet. Night calls are less expensive." He smiled again, his eyes cynical.

"Then if you will give the sergeant the number, he can do so now," Pardoe said evenly, watching him. "The telephone's in the hall, Salt."

If he had expected hesitation he noticed none. Augustus supplied the number with airy unconcern, and when Salt had gone out sat regarding Pardoe with a faint mockery that, to his annoyance, put the inspector a little out of countenance.

It was Pardoe only who turned his head as Salt opened the door. The sergeant's stolid gaze met his.

"Mr. Gow died at two o'clock this afternoon," he said.

Pardoe looked quickly back at Augustus, though not quickly enough. The eyes were veiled again, the hands playing with a little ivory paper-knife, but the heavy lips still curved to a derisive smile.

"So there *was* a Mr. Gow after all," he said caressingly. "In more senses—and tenses—than one. I'm so glad I was right, Inspector. Too bad, isn't it? Especially as I don't suppose the executors will stand by an unwritten contract. And I, alas, have no proof that he agreed to—what was it?—make me a loan."

A subtle emphasis was perceptible on the word "proof." His voice was as controlled as ever. But all at once the paperknife snapped.

"Very unfortunate," Pardoe agreed dryly. "Sir Jacob Borth too—he wasn't willing to negotiate?"

Augustus was fitting the edges of the knife neatly together. His only visible reaction to that was a momentary stillness. Then he looked up.

"Your turn to be right, Inspector," he said, inclining his head. "Sir Jacob Borth—dear me, how titularly generous England is—is a—er—child of nature. I should have known better than to suppose we might have mutual interests. Besides which, his prejudicial attitude to my nephew Nicholas has made, perhaps, rather a Montague-Capulet business of it—and *toujours la politesse* was never Sir Jacob's motto, I fear."

Pardoe consulted his notes, feeling uncommonly hot and bothered as he did so at the amusement with which the other was regarding this move.

"Sir Jacob then," the inspector remarked curtly, "gave as a reason for withholding a loan his dislike of Mr. Terris?"

Augustus gave him a searching look. "Sir Jacob was rarely so explicit," he said softly. His tone changed. "Mr. Pardoe, it was thoughtless of me to have mentioned Nicholas. He has nothing at all to do with this catechism which, I own, seems to me far from the proper field of your inquiry."

"I must be the judge of that," was the reply. "And if Mr. Terris wants to be outside the scope of this inquiry, he should be more careful of what he talks about. Euthanasian principles are not to be shouted from the housetops."

Augustus was silent for a minute, looking, Pardoe thought, a little at a loss.

"But why?" he insisted at last. "If one has the principles, why not proclaim them?"

Pardoe shrugged. "Because unscrupulous people may take advantage of one, perhaps."

Augustus looked interested, though his eyes were hard. He nodded briefly.

"I think I understand you," he said. "I shan't take the trouble to explain how it is that Nicholas, who dislikes me heartily, is no catspaw of mine." He laughed richly. "There were no chestnuts belonging to me for him to pull from the fire. I'm much afraid, Inspector, that I am what you call a suspect?"

The tone was light, but so steady, almost hypnotic was his stare that Pardoe had the unquiet feeling that eyes and voice belonged to different men.

"You misunderstand me, Mr. Weir," he said. "I was not particularizing."

But Augustus took no notice. "I ought perhaps to disillusion you," he mocked, shaking his head playfully. "Well, I've no principles—euthanasian or otherwise. Only a few prejudices. And one of them—this is confidential, Inspector—is against murder. But don't, I beg you, let that get abroad. Some people might think it old-fashioned of me, or even"—he shuddered—"wholesome."

"Luckily it's an aversion most of us share," Pardoe said. He looked at him thoughtfully. In spite of himself the man could not help sincerity breaking through the affectation.

"Since we've aired the dangerous subject of murder," Augustus went on, "there are one or two things I would remind you of, Mr. Pardoe. After that, perhaps I may be left in peace to finish the octave of my sonnet. The first thing," he placed one elegant forefinger against the other, "is that with the death of Mrs. Weir my brother becomes a poor man and will undoubtedly be compelled to leave Spanwater. Therefore his dependents also become poor. Secondly, it might be both humane and expedient to discover why my nephew is a passionate upholder of euthanasia. He is an orphan. His mother died when he was a child, and seven years ago his father was involved in a hideous train disaster which maimed without killing him. He had been a painter of watercolors—you may remember a few private exhibitions of Lee Terris's work in the late nineteen-twenties. He would never paint again. He lost both arms, and his other agonies were untellable. Nicholas was just in his teens when it happened. He adored his father. He watched him—perhaps not always literally—suffer like that for nearly four years, finding no one with what he thought would be the moral courage to help death have his way."

He stopped. Nobody said anything, and after a minute he added:

"I tell you this in the hope that you won't make Nick tell it. The ordinary garden variety of person cultivates an innate sensitiveness, but one doesn't know whether one ought to exempt dons and policemen."

Pardoe flushed hotly, and wished himself as invulnerable as Salt who went on writing composedly. He checked his first words. "I'm glad you told me," he said simply. "But please realize, Mr. Weir, that your explanation is a voluntary one. I'm not responsible for the assumptions you care to make from the line of inquiry I have to follow. About the money—Mr. Matthew Weir and his dependents are only likely to be poor in the event of Miss Murray's being still alive."

Augustus seemed to be struggling out of a morass of private thoughts. He looked politely astonished.

"Oh. Ah, the heiress. I had forgotten her. This seems to be a case of where there's life there's no hope. But she is surely not dead?"

Pardoe did not answer. He stood up, opening his notebook. "Will you give me the address of your editorial office, Mr. Weir?"

Augustus laughed in his disturbing fashion. "I do believe he's going to pump Ronnie! Why, of course." He drew a card from his pocket, glanced at it, replaced it, and then pulled out another which he handed to Pardoe. "Sir Ronald Edwy is my sub-editor, charming and very much at everyone's service. If you do extract anything from him, Inspector, do let me know, won't you? I've often wondered what Ronnie really thought of me *sub rosa*. But you're not going? No, please stay. Pardon me, but you've quite destroyed the atmosphere of this room. Mount Helicon's very remote. I'll have to seek it elsewhere. I beg of you to stay and replace poetry with policing."

He stood up with more grace than his corpulence suggested. He ought to have looked like a bull in a china shop, and unaccountably didn't. Taking his writing materials with him, he bowed to Pardoe and Salt in turn and moved fastidiously to the door.

"I had better compose a note of condolence to the late Mr. Gow's relict," was his suave farewell. "It might possibly soften the hearts of the executors."

As the door closed, Salt let out a mighty breath and tapped his forehead.

"Not a bit," said Pardoe. "Clever as a bagful of monkeys. I like him."

At that the sergeant looked as if the head-tapping should more properly relate to his superior.

"Did you see," Pardoe went on, "what his octave was?"

"No," said Salt, all at sea on the subject. He vaguely surmised an octave to be something out of a geometry set.

"A sheet of paper covered in £ s. d. for varying amounts, in addition and subtraction—mainly subtraction, I fancy."

He turned away to ring the bell.

Dinah Terris stood at the window of her bedroom and looked south across road and meadowland to where a mile or two away the climbing trees made a clearly defined horizon. Over there, somewhere beyond the grim guardianship of Pie Wood and all the fields and spinneys on its far side, Oxford lay, shining like a jewel one must admire but dared not covet. Now that it was irrevocably gone from her, it had suddenly become more desirable. That was the crooked way of things. She felt miserable, though assuring herself indignantly that it was the cowardly misery of fear that filled one with vague depression and made one's hands cold and damp. It had been a wretched day with that poor silly little Freddy Borth smashing himself up like that. And now she would have to tell this new man they had fetched from London what she had kept to herself all the week. Not that she'd be telling him now if she hadn't told Matthew first; Matthew, who had urged her to say what she knew and keep nothing back, but Matthew, also, whom she'd die to protect.

A sound at the door made her spin sharply on her heel, her heart at her throat. Everything frightened her these days. Even the house, once so eloquent, had turned traitor, closed in upon itself, offended at the baseness it had unwittingly sheltered.

It was only old Bessie. But why should she stand there a full minute without speaking? She felt inclined to giggle hysterically at the brand-new mourning Mrs. Kingdom was flaunting, so unrelieved that anybody who hadn't got any felt themselves wearing gala dress.

"Yes, what is it, Bessie?" Her mouth felt dry, too small for her tongue.

"The policemen are asking for you," the housekeeper said baldly. "They're in the drawing room if you please. And if they think *you* can tell 'em anything they must be worse 'n I thought."

The remark was accompanied by such a searching look from the old woman's bright little eyes that for the moment Dinah fancied she was trying to discover what indeed she did know. Then, after a disapproving glance at the girl's leaf-brown frock, Mrs. Kingdom moved away and went down the passage towards Mrs. Weir's room. Dinah hesitated a moment, then made her way downstairs.

It was not so bad as she had expected. For a minute or two she was left to her own devices, while Pardoe, after acknowledging her presence, continued a casual conversation he had been having with Salt.

She sat down to wait, hoping earnestly that the thumping of her heart was not audible. Pardoe turned to her with a smile. In that artificial room she looked like something fresh and honest blown in out of the woods.

Her evidence of the Monday night did little but corroborate the statements of Dr. Fisher and Aurelia Brett.

"Yes," she replied to one of the inspector's questions, "I certainly thought Miss Brett looked queer when I opened my door to her. Not ill exactly, but strange. I said to her, 'Aren't you well?' or something like that, but she didn't answer. Afterwards I though it was finding Auntie in that awful state had made her look funny. Then I'm afraid we forgot all about her, till I thought ages after how odd it was that she wasn't anywhere about helping."

Pardoe nodded. He took her through the incidents of the day. She had not seen her aunt with the herbs, nor making the infusion. Her account of the afternoon tallied with that of Aurelia, with whom she and Andy Pitt had had tea. Afterwards they drove round the hills for nearly an hour and came home about six-thirty. Something increasingly distrait in her manner as she reached this point made Pardoe say:

"Something else you've remembered, Miss Terris?"

Dinah swallowed hard, gripped the arms of her chair, and tried to look resolute.

"Well, yes, there is. I mean I've remembered it all along. I'm afraid I ought to have told you before, but I was very stupid—I couldn't see how it was going to affect people, so I kept quiet."

"Better late than never," Pardoe found himself saying sententiously to this astonishing candor. "It's usually better for everybody if things are told," he lied.

His phlegmatic response made Dinah less fearful.

"Of course. It was silly of me. But I was afraid for myself too. I thought I might have dreadful pains—and die, like Auntie."

She moistened her lips and went on rapidly, "I drank some of the herb tea myself—in the evening. Auntie told me when I got back that it was extra good—she was proud of it, poor dear—and begged me to sample it. I was the only one who ever drank it. It wasn't very nice, you know. But I didn't like only pretending I'd had some, so before dinner on Monday I went to the kitchen and took a cupful."

Both men were so visibly interested that even in her dismay at telling her story Dinah felt secretly flattered. She gained confidence from the thought that they were obviously too intent to feel annoyance with her.

"What time was this?" Pardoe asked, leaning forward.

"About seven. I changed for dinner just after."

"Then how was it the cook didn't see you?"

"The kitchen's shaped like an L. Blessitt was in the shorter piece by the electric cooker. The dresser where the herb tea was standing was at the top of the L. She wouldn't have seen me, nor heard me because of the sound of the cooking. And she was talking—I think Gracie was peeling potatoes down there."

"I see. Now why didn't you tell Dr. Fisher this on Monday night, or at any rate the next morning, if you thought you'd drunk poison?"

"Oh," Dinah cried, "but don't you see? None of us thought of the herb tea till Miss Brett mentioned it in the morning. Nobody thought Aunt Kate's illness had anything to do with it. It was only the second time she'd made the stuff *this* spring, and she'd been sick—oh, many times before, only never so bad as this time, of course. But it certainly didn't seem to be the herb tea."

"No. That's reasonable," Pardoe said. "But why didn't you say something on the Tuesday?"

Dinah hesitated. "Well, at first, you see, I thought I was poisoned. And I thought speaking about it would make it more real. I felt I must wait and see in silence—you know how it is."

She was so solemn that Pardoe had to laugh. "Yes, I know. A sort of playing possum to oneself. Well, when nothing happened to you, why did you go on keeping it secret?"

"I don't really know," she said, not enjoying this interrogation. "I suppose I'd got used to saying nothing. And I was afraid—I thought—I mean," she faltered, "I thought it would make you suspect."

"Who?"

"Me."

Pardoe looked skeptical at the pat answer, then smiled. "All right, Miss Terris. You read detective fiction, don't you? So do I. The police don't do half as much suspecting as you think. Not of uncles or nieces. Not till they've got the facts. Tell me, how much herb tea was in the jug when you had a drink?"

Dinah, relieved at the change of subject, frowned. "It was more than halfway up. Yes, of course, that was a funny thing. There was only a drop when Dr. Fisher went to look. Auntie must have drunk a lot that night."

"It looks like it," said Pardoe, who did not think so. He tacked swiftly. "Miss Terris, what do you know of a woman called Esther O'Malley?"

"The old gypsy?" The girl looked startled. "Not much, I'm afraid. She lives in a cottage in Pie Wood with her son, and the son's children. He does odd jobs for Mr. Birchall, the farmer who owns the land over there. Some parts of the year he's a woodman. The children run wild, and they're always getting into trouble with the school inspector. They keep fowls and goats, and Esther goes about selling eggs and mushrooms and blackberries, things like that. They're awful cadgers, of course, they just can't help it, and it's said she sells poultry and eggs to the same people she steals them off. I don't like her much. The only people who were really kind to the O'Malleys were Aunt Kate and Mr. Flood, the rector—and they were kind to everyone."

"And Mr. Birchall, I suppose? He tolerates them?"

"Oh, yes. But that's different. Years ago when the gypsies were camping on his land, old Esther saved his children from a fire in the barn. The little boy and girl had gone in there to play. They had matches, and in no time the chaff had caught fire and the place was ablaze. There was hardly anybody about, only old Esther dozing near by in the caravan. It's a miracle she ever got them out. She tied something damp round her face, but the bodice of her dress was burned right off. After that Birchall let her and her son have the cottage rent free."

"She was a plucky old thing," Pardoe commented. "Did your aunt ever visit the gypsies in their cottage?"

Dinah stared frankly. "I don't think so. Not lately, at any rate. You see, a very funny change came over old Esther after Christmas. She'd always been attached to my aunt, and then all at once she started shunning her and behaving oddly. Auntie met her once when she was out walking with Miss Brett, and told me that Esther got off the path and pointed her fingers at her like this."

Dinah thrust them out crossed towards the inspector.

"Protection against the evil eye—or against some other form of evil," Pardoe said softly. "Why—has anybody been harsh to her?"

"Not Auntie Kate. Mrs. Kingdom told her off, I know. Bessie's a sort of Bible-puncher, you see—she goes off to queer meetings in a tin shed in Steeple, and she hates Esther because the rector's been good to her. It might have been that, but I don't see why she turned against my aunt." Dinah mused for a minute, and added illogically, "Esther told fortunes—awfully true ones too. She said she could see into the future. Bessie Kingdom declared she was a witch that would have been burnt in the old days. I said, perhaps so, but these were not the old days."

Pardoe smiled. "Exactly. And she'd been burnt enough these days, I should have thought."

"Rather. Poor old thing, it must be awful to feel an outcast, and yet it isn't easy to be friendly with people who are so secretive and have such odd customs. Miss Gretton didn't like her either. She told Auntie she wouldn't have folk like that scrounging round her house."

Pardoe gave her a shrewd look. "Did you know Miss Gretton well, Miss Terris?"

"Never spoke to her," Dinah said. "She wouldn't see anybody but Auntie. I took her some fruit one day when Aunt Kate couldn't go up to see her. She didn't come to the door. I could see her moving about inside, but I had to leave the basket on the step and come away."

"Not a hospitable lady," Pardoe commented. "Yes, what were you going to say?"

Dinah was looking eager. "Only, I think—well, I mean she was Auntie's friend, and I think—it would be better—I think we ought to do something about finding out where she is."

"I agree with you," Pardoe said firmly. "I should like to have a talk with Miss Gretton."

"So would Mr. Turk."

"The landlord?"

"Yes. I met him yesterday. He says she paid him the quarter's rent up to March 25th. But she never said a word about giving the cottage up, and she hasn't written."

"Is it known precisely which day she left?"

"Well, no. At least," Dinah added shyly, "I think I know. It was the snow made me wonder. I can remember the dates because of Cottlebury steeple-chases on March 22nd. That was a Wednesday. The night before my aunt had had a bad sick turn. Then in the night the snow came. It started just after midnight and didn't stop till noon on Wednesday. The doctor came that day, and Auntie was in bed, but on Thursday afternoon when nobody saw her she slipped out and went up to Titt's Cote with all that snow lying on the ground. She might have died. I happened to be talking to Mrs. Comfort by the lodge when I saw the old shepherd from Sheeplands hurrying across the park. He told me Auntie was up at the cottage with only slippers on her feet. I raced up there and brought her back home. The place was locked up. It was then I noticed a funny thing."

"Yes?" Both Pardoe and Salt were hanging on her words.

"There were only Auntie's footsteps, and mine, in the snow."

The inspector broke the short silence by saying, "And the shepherd?"

"Old Daniels was looking for lambs in the meadow by the park. If you go along there you will see how easy it is to see Titt's Cote from that corner. He didn't come into the lane at all except up at the top by the park gate."

"But you're telling me, Miss Terris, that the lane wasn't used all day Wednesday and Thursday morning. What about the baker, the milkman?"

"But this is the country," Dinah protested. "The baker calls twice a week, on Tuesday and Saturday. And our milk—I mean for Spanwater—is brought from the farm across the park. Miss Gretton bought condensed milk when she went into Cottlebury on the bus. She didn't want any callers. Even the baker put the bread in a basket she hung outside, and never saw her. Sometimes the piece of lane to Titt's Cote wasn't used all the week except by the baker and Auntie."

"Didn't the people from Sheeplands come down that way?"

"Practically never. They have a far shorter cut to the Cottlebury road at the other end. And if they wanted us they came across the park."

Pardoe looked at her with genuine admiration. "You've got the makings of a sound detective, Miss Terris," he said. "So it looks as if Miss Gretton went away before the snow fell, or while it was falling?"

"She must have," said Dinah, flushing at the praise. "I went round the cottage, but back and front the snow was unbroken except for our prints. And in the lane itself there were only Aunt Kate's because I used the park."

"Are you sure of the hour at which the snow began to fall on the Tuesday night?"

"You can ask Mr. Turk's shepherds. They were sitting up with the ewes. They said it was clear at midnight, and snowing just afterwards."

Pardoe was satisfied. "And what time did Mrs. Weir leave Titt's Cote on the Tuesday?"

Dinah thought. "It must have been soon after five o'clock. She used to stay talking after tea."

He nodded. "You've told us something really useful, Miss Terris. Unless you can think of anything else you'd like me to know I won't keep you any longer."

"There's nothing else," Dinah said, getting up. She had had an overwhelming sensation of freedom since the revelation about the herb tea.

Pardoe rose too and moved over to the door with her. "What date did Mr. Augustus Weir arrive?" he asked casually.

She stopped and looked at him quickly. "The same day as Miss Brett—same train too. But they didn't know each other. March 28th—just a week after Miss Gretton disappeared." She broke off, then added with a rush, "But what does it matter? You mustn't think anything about Uncle Weir. It's only his manner. I know he keeps on saying things he doesn't mean in a voice like thick honey spread on farmhouse butter. But he's a dear really.

He was awfully kind to Aunt Kate. Only when people are dead he doesn't bother about them any longer, and so other people think he's callous."

"All right," Pardoe interrupted her speech for the defense, repressing a smile in face of such earnestness. "Like everybody else, Miss Terris, you give fearful significance to my most innocent questions. Quite often, you know, they're every bit as harmless as they sound."

"I'm sorry," she said, managing a smile. "But so many people are unreasonable about Augustus. I'm always trying to change their point of view."

"Well, I won't be unreasonable," Pardoe promised.

"No, you wouldn't," she said, and added, "I've just remembered something. A letter came for Miss Gretton after she'd gone away."

"What? Here?"

"Oh, no. To Titt's Cote. Auntie told me about it. The day she was out with the companion and old Esther crossed her fingers—only a day or two after Miss Brett came—they saw a letter sticking out of the slit in the door. They pushed it in, to be safe. So it will be there still. It might help you to know where she is."

"It might very well," Pardoe said heartily, opening the door wide. "Don't worry, Miss Terris. I'll find Miss Gretton for you."

An electric chandelier inadequately lit the center of the hall. Beyond the pool of light indistinct shadows were grouped. From them came an audible breath, then the unmistakably stealthy sound of one who wishes to move unseen. Pardoe took one stride into the hall behind Dinah; but there were too many doors, and only silence, the busy silence of an old house, fell upon his ears.

The girl looked back at him in some surprise.

"Thank you, Miss Terris," he said. "Will you please ask your brother if he will come here?"

Salt raised his eyes from his notebook as the inspector closed the door.

"This Gretton dame," he said, as one might speak of the Old Man of the Sea. "What say she's dead inside the cottage?"

It put into brutal words a thought which had occurred to Pardoe. If it were true it revolutionized the first theory he had reluctantly formed.

"Maybe," he said curtly. "We'll have a look tomorrow. Somebody else in this house is interested in the fate of Miss Gretton."

CHAPTER XIII

DESIGN FOR AN ACCIDENT

Suspicion grave I see, but no clear proof.
MATTHEW ARNOLD: *Merope*.

BEFORE Nicholas Terris had been ten minutes in the room Pardoe had introduced the subject of young Borth. Nick's own activities on Easter Monday were soon dealt with; and anyway, as Pardoe had now become aware, household alibis were of small account in this affair. Dinah's belated evidence had negatived the importance of the time factor before dinner on Monday. Whoever had poisoned the herb tea had done so at night, when there was equal opportunity for all, since everyone, including Dr. Smollett, had been in the house at some time between seven o'clock and midnight. The police would have to concentrate on motive, in which Freddy Borth's accident might well play a pertinent part.

"No, I don't think he had any special reason for calling this morning," Nick said in a careless voice. He was very like Dinah, except that he had matured far more quickly. There was the same dark honesty of feature, wide cheekbones and direct gaze, but the mouth was bitter and the face set in stubborn lines. "He was just kicking his heels as usual, and pretty well bored with the old man, I expect, so he blew in on us."

"Was he in the habit of turning up at Spanwater?"

"There was no habit about it. Nobody had invited him this morning, if that's what you mean. He was just mooning about as he always did, poor kid—at a completely loose end."

"So you said just now," Pardoe answered. "It doesn't tell me what I asked though. Was Mr. Borth often at Spanwater?"

"No, he wasn't." Nick flushed a little. "I can't really say why. He and I haven't much in common, I suppose. And his father isn't a very come-hithery gent, you know. Freddy might have jibbed a bit at coming when he couldn't ask us there. Silly, of course, but it may have struck him like that."

"I see. You don't think Mr. Borth had any reason for avoiding the house, Mr. Terris?"

"He didn't avoid us," Nick retorted indignantly. "Gosh, what are you driving at? I've been away all the term—he had nothing to come here for except in the vacs."

"No," said Pardoe. "But I didn't suggest he was avoiding *you*, but the house. Did he come indoors this morning?"

Nick shook his head. "He was too much taken up with the car. He hadn't been with us many minutes before he'd taken it out to try it."

"He saw you and Mr. Pitt in the grounds?"

"Yes."

"Now which of you two suggested he should try the car?"

Nick gave him a look that was curiously calculating. In the silence that followed Salt watched the conflict on the boy's face as he tried to keep his temper in hand.

"Your suspicions are pretty patent, Inspector," he said at last. "Neither of us suggested Freddy should handle the car—and neither of us hoped he'd get killed in the attempt. A pity we can't confess and make things easy for you, isn't it? Though what Freddy Borth's smash has to do with my aunt's death I'm afraid I don't know."

"Neither do I," said Pardoe. "But I mean to find out. Don't lose your temper, Mr. Terris. And don't leap to conclusions. So it was Mr. Borth himself who proposed he should drive it?"

"He insisted," Nick said more quietly. "Andy was against it. He was thrilled about the Lagonda—his father who's in India gave it him for his birthday. And now he's mad with Freddy for making matchwood of it."

"Freddy's quite possibly mad with himself," the inspector said grimly. The unfortunate youth seemed to be evoking little sympathy. "Tell me all that you know happened from the time he drove out of Spanwater."

It proved more than Pardoe had anticipated, thanks to Nick's curiosity and Andrew Pitt's infatuation for his car. They had gone to the brick wall below the bowling green and there waited, their eyes glued to the road far beneath them, for Freddy's emergence into view. Presently he came, driving, Nick said, with the kind of unskillful caution and lack of confidence you might expect. By prearrangement he had glanced up to where they were leaning on the wall, and they had waved to him and cheered him on. At that moment he had accelerated, either out of bravado and to spread himself in the eyes of spectators, or because he really didn't know what he was doing. Whichever it was he shot away at amazing speed, much to the dismay of Andy who didn't care to see a tyro putting the Lagonda through her best paces. Just out of range of their watch-out the road turned on a steep corner.

"Not exactly a hairpin bend," Nick explained, "but bad enough, with a bank on the off side and a gate a bit below the turn. I could have sworn that before he reached the corner Freddy waved back at us, but Andy, who has longer sight than I've got, says he didn't see him do that. I don't know—

but he started to wobble anyway and then he vanished out of sight. Andy said he did the corner on two wheels. He was positive something would happen. We didn't stop to go down by the lane, but got over the wall and tore down the meadow and saved about ten minutes. A lorry was picking him out of it by the time we got there. It was they who took me on to the nearest kiosk where I could phone the police."

"You didn't actually see the accident happen?" Pardoe put in.

"No. But he was curvetting about to such an extent that Andy knew something was wrong. He said he couldn't have taken the corner properly like that."

"If young Borth had killed himself," the inspector said sternly, "I'm not at all sure it wouldn't have been manslaughter for you and your friend. You knew he was inexpert, to say the least of it, yet under your very noses you watched him take control of a powerful engine like that. Not a sportsman-like joke, Mr. Terris."

"I'm not proud of it," Nick admitted more readily than Pardoe expected. "But it wasn't a joke, I swear. Stopping him wasn't as easy as you might think. I couldn't very well put my foot down when it wasn't my car. And Andy's a guest here, and I know he didn't want to be in a dog-in-the-manger and squash Freddy, who was also a sort of guest, if you like to look at it that way."

Pardoe was not sure that he did. It was plausible enough, but there was a touch of casuistry in the reasoning. How was it too that young Pitt's better eyesight had failed to discern the hand-wave which might be supposed to have engineered a genuine accident? Had Nick invented that bit to protect himself? On the other hand, it appeared to have been Andy who had immediately jumped to the idea that an accident had happened. The best Pardoe could think of both was that reaction from a week of strain that might well have been unbearable had made them only too ready to watch Freddy Borth make an ass of himself. The worst he put aside for the moment.

"You were sent down from Oxford at one time, Mr. Terris?" he asked abruptly.

There was a short pause. "Not for inducing greenhorns to break their necks in racing cars," Nick said. "Yes, I was. Highly suspicious, what?"

"When were you down?"

"All Michaelmas. I organized a public meeting in the summer for discussion of euthanasia." His tone invited argument.

"Quite so," the inspector remarked mildly, as if the purpose of the meeting had been to propose means of increasing the export trade. To Nick's further astonishment he said nothing more on the subject.

"About Miss Gretton," he went on. "When Titt's Cote was found closed, didn't it occur to any of you that she might have been taken ill indoors?"

Nick adjusted himself to this fresh viewpoint rather ungraciously. "Why the devil should it? There was her notice on the dovecote, wasn't there?"

"What notice?"

"A piece of cardboard stuck over a nail with 'No Bread' scrawled on it. If it's not there now the wind fetched it down."

Dinah had forgotten to mention that. It looked then as if Alice Gretton had really gone away, from every point of view a preferable theory. If there had been foul play it was, of course, conceivable that its perpetrator had been astute enough to gage the value of just such a message. Well, they would soon see.

He had no further business with Nick. But he was taking no risks. It was easy to prevent young Terris from passing on to his friend a hint of what line the inquiry was taking, and when he rang for Mond to fetch Mr. Pitt he did not release Nick until Andy appeared in the doorway. One significant detail Pardoe observed, and to his misinterpretation of it attributed afterwards his slowness in disentangling the case. Mond had returned to the room with Andy, to bring the inspector a small, oblong parcel wrapped in paper, which, he mumbled, was from Mrs. Kingdom. Pardoe, guessing it was the photograph of Joyce Murray he had been promised, put it down unopened. His attention was wholly on the manservant, who had none for him. Nick Terris had already gone out, and the fellow's gaze was all for young Pitt. In it there was such a mingling of fear and baffled fury that Pardoe, who had intercepted too many looks to experience more than an objective interest in most, felt a momentary chill as if he and not Andy had evoked the malignity.

Andrew Pitt seemed not to have noticed. With the closing of the door he took the chair Pardoe indicated, gratification and anxiety struggling in his expression. He was obviously extracting what enjoyment he could from the circumstance that had brought him into contact with Scotland Yard, while prepared to regret the personal discomfort it might entail. A spoilt type, Pardoe reflected, egotistical in the charming way that was rarely found out, intelligent, more impulsive than Nick Terris.

"Where is your home, Mr. Pitt?" he began.

"Well, it's here and there," Andy confessed surprisingly. "My people are in India, and when I'm not up at Oxford I spend most of my time with relatives either in Bath or Brighton. I was there—in Brighton, I mean—with my sister, when Nick invited me here for Easter."

"When did you get the invitation?"

Andy looked pleased. "Gosh, is that important? It came early last week, I forget which day. I came down on Saturday, I know." He added awkwardly, "I don't seem to have brought them any luck."

While he put to him questions about the Easter weekend, one half of

Pardoe's mind was fretting at the problem of the boy's presence at Spanwater forty-eight hours before the murder. Had his arrival precipitated action?

Though there was little he could tell that narrowed the range of suspicion, Andy brought a welcome freshness to bear on the inquiry. For one thing, he had met none of the family before except Dinah, who had visited Oxford in Eights Week of last year. Neither prejudice nor preconceived notions cramped his style, though to Pardoe's regret the duties of a guest made him tongue-tied now and again; and the inspector was left to infer from silence or from a flagging in the narrative the distrust he might be entertaining for certain individuals. Among these was Augustus Weir and Mrs. Kingdom, neither of them surprising inclusions. The little he had seen of Catherine Weir had made a good impression; he thought her kindly, if vague, and to Pardoe's surprise added that she had shown a lively interest in his own affairs and had been singularly cheerful on Sunday. This was a more illuminating contribution to their knowledge of the dead woman than might appear, for it seemed to Pardoe to discount still further the idea of suicide. That possibility had had to be considered, but the presence of arsenic in the jug itself had prevented it from becoming a serious one: unless, of course, Mrs. Weir had planted the evidence of murder before taking her own life, a sinister view inconsistent with what they knew of her.

Of Matthew Weir himself Andrew Pitt spoke with diffidence.

"He's had a hard knock," he said hotly, eyeing the inspector with a look that suggested Pardoe had delivered it. "Several hard knocks. And he's stood up to them marvelously. How many men wouldn't have changed their names and let the whole ghastly business drag them down completely?"

He drew in his breath as if conscious all at once of an audience, and went on hastily: "I mean, he's frightfully decent to everyone—Nick and Dinah and—and everyone. Nick has the chance of doing a fourth year, but he doesn't like to, in a way, because it will be pretty expensive for his uncle, and he's been so mighty good to them as it is. And now Miss Terris has got an entrance to Oxford, and Mr. Weir's frightfully bucked and all that, but she's not sure either if she ought to take it because of the cost."

Pardoe's reception of this confidence betrayed nothing to the ingenuous Andy, who had been resolute to speak a good word for Matthew if he had to drag it in by the hair of its head. He was mercifully unaware of the train of thought it started in the brain of the quiet man seated opposite. Salt, too, who arrived at his theories by an equally sure if more devious route, frowned at his lazy pencil and glanced across at the chief. Pardoe was looking at the boy with a misleadingly benign eye.

"So Mr. Weir educated Mr. Terris and his sister?" he prompted.

"Oh, rather," Andy said, though with more reserve. He was a little doubtful of the good taste of his outburst. "They're orphans, you see."

"And you'd say he was very devoted to them, and they to him?"

"Of course." But this time the tone was unmistakably cold.

Pardoe took the hint, with the mental reservation that he had learned something which made it at least reasonable to assume that even £6,000 would have been a timely sum for Weir to get his hands on. He cut the subject clean adrift, as was his disconcerting habit, and turned straight to that of Freddy Borth.

It did not catch young Pitt off his guard. A more wary expression came over his candid face. He leaned forward a little.

"Look here, sir," he said earnestly. "Here's something I've kept to myself—I've told nobody, not even Nick. They've got enough hanging over their heads with this awful arsenic business. But the Lagonda was tampered with—I know it was."

"That's possible, Mr. Pitt," Pardoe said, remaining disappointingly calm. "What are your reasons for saying so?"

"Just this. You know a lorry came along and took Nick on to the nearest telephone? Well, they would have taken Borth too, but they were loaded to capacity and—well, we thought it might be risky. We couldn't tell how bad he was. So we put him on the bank as well as we could with a coat rolled under his head and another over him—he wasn't bleeding much—and decided we'd better wait for the proper ambulance. I stayed behind with him, and of course I had the chance to snoop round a bit."

The devil you did, thought Pardoe.

"I found the steering," Andy went on, "snapped clean through. In a funny way too—no splintering, but the wheel lifted clear. Worse than that, I had a look at the hub caps. Three of them were still intact, but the fourth, belonging to the near front wheel, was picked up yards farther along the road. Two of the screws were gone altogether, and the others picked up at good distances from the accident."

"And what did you think?"

"That somebody removed two of the screws, loosened the others and the hub cap, and damaged the wheel sufficiently for it to come off as soon as the driver accelerated."

"Pretty drastic," Pardoe said, watching him closely. "Was Mr. Borth's call this morning unexpected?"

"Quite. Oh, it wasn't meant for him, the poor little fish," Andy said good-naturedly.

"No?"

"No. It was meant for me."

Pardoe received this quietly. "Why do you think that?"

Andrew Pitt looked less sure of himself. "There's nothing else to think.

The car was wilfully damaged, I'm certain. And since I came here a week ago nobody else has driven her."

"Do you suspect anyone?"

"Good Lor', no," the boy said, but the hesitation had been a shade too long and his face was oddly flushed.

"Was the car kept locked up?"

"I'm afraid it wasn't—the garage doors were just closed."

"Now, Mr. Pitt," Pardoe said suddenly, "wasn't there something you had to tell me yesterday?"

Andy made an impatient gesture and looked embarrassed. "No, there wasn't," he said miserably. "There never was. I thought we'd had that out before."

Pardoe made a guess. "Hasn't there been something here since your visit that you were surprised to find?" he persisted, undefeated.

"I wouldn't put it like that," the boy muttered, his face redder. "You can say if you like that I thought—I'd seen a ghost."

"That's better. Whose ghost?"

But Andy had gone as far as he intended going. His lips were obstinately clamped to stop his tongue from committing further indiscretion.

"I was mistaken," he said unconvincingly.

Pardoe glanced down at his notes. "Where you ever coached by a Mr. Paul Benedict, of Maple House, in Somerset?"

Andy looked from him to Salt, who was thoughtfully scratching his face and kicking one toe against the other, and decided he might answer without risk.

"No. The crammer, you mean? But I know plenty of chaps who've been to him. Borth was there at one time—but he's tried everybody, poor beggar."

Pardoe raised his eyes to the clock. It was getting on for dinner time, and he had something to do in Cottlebury before returning to carry out a piece of work allotted to the night hours.

"I won't detain you any longer, Mr. Pitt," he said. As Andy stood up he looked at the boy gravely. "You may or may not be right in thinking that somebody has had designs upon you. We must first prove wilful damage to the car. Meantime I'd advise you to watch your step. Confide in nobody, and remember that you can easily get in touch with us day or night if you need us. We're staying at the Silver Fox—it's on the telephone."

He noticed that Andy received his warning without incredulity.

"I've been thinking much the same," he said simply. "I mean, that somebody wouldn't be sorry if I wasn't here. The worst of it is I've no idea why I'm considered superfluous. Whatever I know, I jolly well don't know that I know it. Only I can't tell 'em so. Well, I don't want medinal in my drink, that's sure. I'll play for safety. Good-night, sir."

Pardoe turned to Salt as the door closed. "Come on, my lad—it's Cottlebury for us, then a bite of supper at the Fox, then a spot of burglary. I'll put you wise to it on the way back."

Before leaving, however, they went round to have a look at the garage. Pardoe had noticed it the night before when Comfort had taken them to the shed. It stood clear of the north side of the house, overlooked by the servants' quarters and fringed by the shrubbery. The doors were furnished with a padlock, but the Weirs were either careless or indifferent to the possibility of car thieves, for by its rusty condition it was seldom used.

As they drove back through Steeple Pardoe confided to Salt his plan for entering Titt's Cote that night. Daylight, as the sergeant was not slow to point out, had its advantages, of course, for an examination of the cottage, but the inspector was reluctant to postpone it since suspecting an eavesdropper was aware of his interest in Miss Gretton. Procrastination could be fatal, he knew by experience, as in the Minsterbridge case last year when he had failed to provide for the housemaid on her way home the protection his private judgment had urged. His plan of campaign was simple. After clearing up the day's business in Cottlebury, not likely to occupy more than half an hour or so, they would return to Steeple for supper, then push on to Sheeplands to see Turk and get his permission to go over Titt's Cote.

"May as well do it with the landlord's blessing," Pardoe added. "And if I'm not mistaken he'll be as pleased as anybody to have the thing cleared up."

"She'll've been there more 'n three weeks if she's dead," Salt remarked, reckoning ghoulishly. He got no reply. In practice he might be a cheerful enough colleague, but his fashion of expressing himself at times lacked stimulation.

In Cottlebury Pardoe dropped him at the police station to glean what he could on the subject of Mr. James Gow, deceased. He himself drove on to the post office. It was lighting-up time by now, and he spared a moment's admiration for the famous promenade, above it the strip of cold sky pricked with a few stars, the glittering lights, the tall trees in first leaf, age in their boles, youth in their branches, and on the road and pavement the brisk throngs of cars and shoppers, each intent upon his own business of life or death. The word gave an ultimate grimness to Pardoe's thoughts, so that he got out of the car with some impatience and, turning his back on the leafy boulevard, ran up the post office steps.

He spent about ten minutes inside, composing a long, carefully worded cable to police headquarters in Sydney, Australia. That done, he drove to Mr. Kirk's office, only to find, as might have been expected, that it was closed, and returned to the post office to ring up the lawyer on his private number.

"And see that 'Fenella Pagan' goes in this time, won't you? We've got to remember that a good many folk in the last seven years probably never knew her as Joyce Murray at all. What? Yes. Something of this sort——"

There followed a slow recital of what the inspector thought might jog the interest, if not of the girl herself, then perhaps of her onetime associates. He grinned amiably into the tube as he visualized Mr. Kirk's disapproval of the mounting expense, then replacing the receiver left the building for the second time.

At the station he picked up Salt, who was standing on the steps with a uniformed officer deep in argument about the relative merits of Peckham and Cottlebury. The sergeant fitted his bulk unhurriedly into the car, grunted and settled back before divulging his news.

"Mr. Augustus is sure hard up," he said. "The late lamented Gow was a moneylender."

"You *don't* surprise me," Pardoe answered, letting in the clutch.

CHAPTER XIV

TITT'S COTE

Through this house give glimmering light,
By the dead and drowsy fire.
William Shakespeare:
A Midsummer Night's Dream.

It had started raining before they reached Steeple, and by the time supper was over had developed into an unpromising downpour. To Salt's disgust, however, the inspector was in favor of walking. Sheeplands, he argued, was too near Steeple to justify the use of a car, and after that part of the business was over he had his own reasons for wanting to approach the cottage on foot.

What to Salt was a mild form of purgatory was to Pardoe a rare pleasure. The cool, damp air that blew in their faces, the sting of the rain, the swish of it on trees and hedges, and the thin chime of water in unseen ditches turned his thoughts momentarily to sweeter things than the work in hand. It was easier to walk in the darkness of the countryside than to guess at what lay beneath the darkness of Spanwater.

After arriving at Sheeplands by way of a stony track down which the slipping water seemed to Salt to be gurgling satirically at their plight, it was not surprising that they knocked, and knocked again, at the wrong door. The rain grew quieter, but their mackintoshes were still streaming when presently a stout woman, after the first cautious look, admitted them, commiserating on their condition and the mistake that had kept them waiting. Mrs. Turk fulfilled all that the sergeant had ever dreamed should be the womanly aim of a farmer's wife, and the country which a minute ago had seemed to him sadly overrated began to redeem something of its lost character. Their wet raincoats taken firmly away from them, they were conducted across the stone floor of a dimly lit dairy, down a passage from which came the merry clatter of crockery, and into a cozy parlor at the end of it where the master of the house was enjoying a pipe, at his feet an aged sheepdog that thumped its tail in welcome as they came in.

Turk was a lanky man with a face like a winter apple and the long-sighted eyes of a shepherd. Intelligence, the slow, fruitful variety that mellows in the country, looked out of them too, and when Mrs. Turk, showing no perturbation at this nocturnal visit of the police, had left them together, he soon grasped the significance of Titt's Cote to the more important investigation.

"Ay, I've heard tell she was friendly with the lady at the manor," he said. He shook his head slowly. "I ain't liked this flit of hers, and that's a fact. 'Tisn't so much the rent—though I don't want to lose it—but I wouldn't like to think anything had happened as didn't ought to. I would have said a word to the police mysel' before now, but that the card she hung out for the baker seemed like as if she might be coming back any day."

Pardoe agreed, and led him neatly to tell of his first acquaintance with his tenant. After a little thought he said he had received a typewritten letter early in December saying that the writer understood the cottage was to be let furnished, and that she would like to look over it. It had carried a London address and was signed "Alice Gretton," but he had since destroyed it and could not recall the address. The writer arrived just before Christmas, looked at the cottage, liked what she saw and moved in on December 27th. She sent him the first quarter's rent through the post with no accompanying letter.

"How?" Pardoe asked. "I mean in what form was the money?"

"In cash," Turk said. "Notes in a registered envelope."

Pardoe sighed. "What was she like?"

"I never saw her above twice," Turk replied, leaning forward to knock the ashes from his pipe. "Once when she came down from London to look at the place, and the next time a day or two after she moved in—New Year's Eve, 'twould be. I was passing along the meadows by the park, an' I see her in the garden. I thought mebbe I'd ask her if she was comfortable like, but those was early days, an' after knowing as how she did whisk inside when people went by I didn't intrude again. She was short with me, turned her back soon and pretended to be busy 'tother side of house."

He peered into the bowl of his pipe with an interested expression, then looked up at Pardoe with a frown.

"What was she like, you're asking? A tall 'ooman, well-built, wrapped herself up a lot. Cold weather, o' course. I always say she come in the snow and she went in the snow. Darkish hair turning gray. She wore glasses, the least bit smoky like. P'r'aps she was sixty—but she did seem lissome."

The inspector nodded. "Did she have much to say when you showed her the cottage?"

"No," Turk said, tapping the pipe stem against his hard palm. "No. It was funny, that. She only just popped her head inside the downstairs rooms, never looked at anything properly nor asked questions before she said she'd take it. *And* here's something else puzzled me proper at the time"—he bent towards Pardoe—"when she wrote to me from London I hadn't been advertising the Cote as a 'let.' "

"What?" the inspector cut in, and Salt sat up straighter.

"It's true, sir. She wrote more'n a fortnight before Christmas to say she'd like to look over the furnished cottage, an' I hadn't advertised it nowhere since April. It was let all summer to artists, man and wife. I didn't think nobody would be wanting it for the winter."

"Did you ask her how she got to hear of it?"

"Ay. I did that." He wrinkled his sky-blue eyes in a smile. "Bein' natural curious. She was short about it, said a friend had give her to know it was vacant. I didn't say no more, but if that were so, 'twas a friend in Cloudy, or else Steeple, for none else would know."

Pardoe, who now and again had wondered irritably if his interest in Alice Gretton were sheer waste of time, felt renewed respect for his earlier intuition.

"I'm much obliged to you, Mr. Turk," he said as they rose to go.

The farmer stood up, looking a little worried. "There's no key," he said. "I mean to say, there's only the one, an' that the lady herself has."

Pardoe smiled. "That's all right. We'll have to do a bit of forcible entry. The sergeant is a useful chap—he comes provided. We'll take the responsibility, and I can promise the minimum of damage."

Turk chuckled wholeheartedly. The notion of the very arm militant of the law burglariously engaged was often to recur in the months to come and provide a perennial joke for his simple telling. As he pointed out to Mrs. Turk, right on your doorstep like that it was better 'n the pictures. That wasn't saying much, though. He had, when all was done, found a greater thrill in the lambing season at Sheeplands than in any of his rare visits to Cottlebury cinemas.

Pardoe decided on the shorter cut to the cottage, across the pastures and over the stile by the park. He declined Turk's offer to come with them, feeling that the fewer the better. He and Salt both had their torches and were unlikely to blunder from the direct eastward walk across the meadows. The farmer took them through a back door into a yard, smelling of straw, where a pony clinked in its stall, some sleepy hens made faint complaint, and an old hound stalked out into the beam shed by their torches; thence to a small paddock, and from there watched them on their way over the sloping turf.

The rain had stopped now and the upland air was full of wholesome scent. The closely nibbled grass made easy walking, and the line of the larch spinney on the right kept them from straying out too far. Here and there a sheep got up at their approach and moved off, a shapeless form in the darkness. Once an old ewe blundered up at their very feet, shook her wet wool and spattered them with the drops. Salt breathed a mild imprecation.

"This is the country of the sheep," Pardoe said in a low voice. "We are of no account here."

From every side came the cry of lambs and the deep, responsive notes of their mothers. Far away a cockerel sent his shivering challenge to the night, and listened to the night flinging it back from the still lonelier hill farms. There was no other sound except the occasional tap of water, or the rustle, the sigh, the faint scurry that is the prerogative of the night people. The trees of Spanwater park loomed up, and through them and below dim lights picked out the windows in the manor. To their left and at the foot of the land that lay behind the lodge, a yellow square shone out.

"That the gardener's place?" Salt muttered.

"Too far along the lane," said Pardoe. "It must be Miss Leith's house."

As he spoke the light went out.

Salt spoke with irrelevance. "Chap at the farm didn't have much to say about the poisoning down there." He jerked his thumb at Spanwater.

"No," said Pardoe. "Countryfolk like that wouldn't. Their manners are too good. Like old Cox in Steeple. They don't get a kick out of that kind of thing."

They climbed the stile, went down the path past the park, and came to Titt's Cote.

As Pardoe pushed open the gate the cottage was only discernible as a darker mass against the back-cloth of the larch wood. Their footsteps on the uneven flags seemed curiously out of place in the motionless presence of the night. The inspector shone his light on the front door while Salt's blunt fingers delicately manipulated the spring. But even when the catch was thrust back and the latch lifted, the door did not yield to pressure.

Pardoe pushed, the sergeant shoved, still it stuck. After a minute of vain grunting, in the middle of which Salt callously suggested that Miss Gretton's body was obstructing entry, Pardoe discovered that one of the hinges was sagging from the post. The door merely wanted lifting back; when that was done, it went wide.

They found themselves on the threshold of the main living room, the front window on their right, a door in the center of the dividing wall on the left, and opposite the wan square of a window on the garden. Pardoe turned the torch on to the bare floor at his feet, then up at the letter-slit. He said nothing, but followed Salt into the room. A small oil lamp stood on an otherwise empty table. After examining it, Pardoe turned up the dirty wick and lit it. The soft, feeble glow, that sent the monstrous shadows of himself and Salt leaping up wall and ceiling, only emphasized the desolation of the vacant room. It was clean, bare, with a minimum of old-fashioned furniture, featureless save for a jar of shriveled flowers in the far window. A few yards below, in the left-hand corner, narrow oak stairs, black and shiny and scooped with the years, vanished into the blackness overhead. Not a picture graced the walls, nor an ornament the tiny, leaning mantelpiece. If there had ever been anything personal to her in this room, Alice Gretton must have smuggled it away with her.

Salt opened the door into the second room. Pardoe could hear him moving about inside. He himself flashed the light into every corner and across the dusty boards their feet had scuffed. The grate, with a hearth rug spread in front, was quite empty, and though Pardoe knelt to examine it, there was nothing to reward him for his pains.

As he got to his feet he heard the sergeant shout. The body, he thought in one grim instant, and made for the dividing door. The other room was tiny, equally scant as to furnishing, though with a square of carpet on the floor and full of the cold, fusty odor of neglected habitation. The sergeant was not there, and Pardoe hurried to a doorway under the stairs. It led to the kitchen, a box of a room with a stone floor and the most primitive of cooking arrangements.

Pardoe had no eye for these. Salt, his stolid form looking as if it would burst the meager dimensions of the place, was staring at the floor. He pointed as the inspector joined him, and, following his gaze, Pardoe saw on the stone flag at their feet two dirty splotches a few inches apart. He stooped to test them with his finger. They were still damp.

"Somebody was in here—just now," Salt whispered.

Pardoe said nothing. He stretched a hand to the back door and tried it softly. It was locked. Then he stooped over the moist patches on the floor. They were roughly egg-shaped, and behind one of them at a distance of an inch or so was a smaller dirty mark. The light picked out here and there a faintly discernible diamond pattern.

"Galoshes," said the inspector, straightening himself. "Sole and heel."

When they turned to look at the floor of the room behind them no tracks were visible; and though they subjected it to a minute scrutiny there was no evidence to show that the intruder had advanced farther than the couple of square yards that served for kitchen.

"Not in galoshes," said Pardoe in a low voice. "Look at the way they're pointing. Our visitor isn't likely to have stood with her back to the room behind and facing a blank wall. She took 'em off outside or just in the doorway, and put them down there."

Salt made no comment on the gender given to the unknown. He watched Pardoe kneel again by the marks and take a measure from his pocket, which he stretched from the tip of the larger patch to the outer edge of the small bit of dirt that represented the heel.

"Toe probably didn't touch the floor," Salt grunted.

"No. Or evaporation's taken place where the pressure was least." Pardoe made a note in his book, then got to his feet again. "Come on—if there's nothing down here we'll try upstairs."

First they had a careful look round the confined space of the kitchen, but nothing seemed likely to be more sinister than its blameless appearance suggested. The grate in the adjoining room contained a few cinders which yielded nothing to poking and were probably, as the sergeant pointed out, the remains of the last fire Miss Gretton had had before her disappearance.

On the way to the stairs, Pardoe turned out the exhausted lamp in the larger room. When they were feeling their way up the unfamiliar steps, their sleeves brushing the wall on either side, Salt in the rear was quick to realize how easily they might be plugged by a determined marksman on the top landing. If indeed there was a landing. There wasn't; a closed door almost hit Pardoe on the nose. He shut his light off, motioning Salt to do the same, before he raised the latch and pushed the door back gently to its full extent.

They were in a little room that extended over the smaller and some way over the larger downstairs. Once inside with the door shut and the torches throwing bright rays on every object, they could see the heavy roof beams slanting down from ceiling almost to floor on the outer side. The oak boards under their feet were full of little ruts and holes. A narrow bed, unused since it had last been made, stood along the wall the open door concealed. There was a fireplace in the center wall, and near it another door standing ajar. The leaded window, which was very small, was firmly closed. The place had the same airless, dusty smell as the ones below, but with something else added, a faint warm pungency that struck the nostrils of both men as soon as they were inside.

"There's been a fire here," said Salt, going over to the grate. He and Pardoe looked down on a mound of feathery black ash, the surface lifting and trembling in the draught from the chimney. The sergeant, thrusting his toe into the middle, disturbed it thoroughly, then applied his fingers to the ash he had turned up.

"Warm underneath," he said. "It's burnt paper—they made a thorough job of it."

Pardoe felt it too, and put a hand to a poker that was propped against the fireplace. He drew back in time, remembering the possibility of prints, and stirred the charred mass with his fingers. It revealed nothing that had not been destroyed, but Pardoe took from his pocket a flat two-ounce tin that had once held tobacco and put a sample of the ash in it. While they were engaged at the hearth the room had been active with quick rustles and hops, a scratch, a patter, and the hard sound of bitten wood. Whoever had once lived in Titt's Cote the mice had it now.

"How long since they was gone, d'ye think?" Salt asked excitedly.

Pardoe shrugged. "Half an hour, at a guess."

He silently cursed the luck that had failed to set his own plans a half-hour earlier. They might then very easily have caught the intruder red-handed, for whoever it was had obviously believed the police visit fixed for Sunday at earliest. It was ironic that his scheme to enter the place by night had been made with the very premonition that so would the unknown party reason. What had found him unprepared was such prompt action on the part of their adversary.

"Look here," he said to Salt. "I'm going over some of the stuff for prints, but there's not enough to keep the two of us busy. I got an idea. While I'm clearing up, you get over to Miss Leith's house—you can go across the park, and once you're in the lane it's only about a quarter of a mile farther down. Suppose she's Gretton? It's been in my head since I knew she didn't turn up in Cloudy all spring."

"But what've I got to do?"

"Anything you like—pretend you're looking for the gardener and thought in the dark it was the lodge. Pretend what you like. The chances are a maid'll answer the door, but with luck her missus will. Notice how she's dressed, what her manner is. It isn't late, only about a quarter to ten. I'm going to see her tomorrow in any case. But you may get a line on something tonight. I'll come straight down from here and meet you at Spanwater gates at ten-thirty."

It was better it should be Salt. He had a deceptively ingenuous manner that might make such a blunder credible. Before his lumbering tread had died away, Pardoe was busy dusting for prints the poker and the tops of the small dressing table and washstand, the only articles of furniture the room contained. The bed was wooden, of the low, modern variety, and the door which was merely on a latch did not possess the inner knob which might have been useful.

Presently he went into the room beyond. The presence of a tall wardrobe made it appear even smaller than it was. A cane-bottomed chair stood forlornly in a corner. The mice had scampered freely here too, for their dirt was on the floor and the skirting had been gnawed in places. What was this? He bent to look at a cluster of small, pellet-like objects on the boards. They were only chewed bits of newspaper, discolored, hardly recognizable—the mice again. Looking round he noticed that there was a clear space between wardrobe and floor nearly six inches deep. Something light was sticking out from under one of the feet of the wardrobe. When Pardoe had eased the foot a little off the board and pulled the thing out he found it was a piece of newspaper roughly triangular in shape, its longest side measuring only about three inches and with every exposed edge mouse-nibbled. It was difficult to guess its age; except for the round spot covered by the wardrobe foot it had been yellowed by the daylight. He turned it over and caught sight of the name "Goulburn," followed by an incomplete reference to a street fire.

It puzzled him, because memory tantalized without providing an answer. Surely—yes, it was—Goulburn was a town somewhere in Australia. Australia—Pardoe's eyes brightened, though he was quick to reflect that that need mean nothing at all. An English paper might very well contain an allusion to an overseas town. But he remembered at the same time that Joyce Murray had been last heard of in Australia.

As he slipped the paper into his pocket something ran in and out of the ring of light thrown by the torch. Pardoe was in time to see a mouse skip nimbly round the far side of the wardrobe. He went idly to investigate, and found at the base of the skirting a large hole. He was turning away when the very shifting of focus entailed by the movement made him catch sight of a gleam of something white inside. Stooping, he pushed two fingers down and after a little probing extracted another piece of newspaper. It had evidently been dragged by the mice into a farther crack, for it tore in the process, but Pardoe had secured enough to make his find worthwhile. It was a portion of the running headline from the inner sheet of a newspaper. Complete title and date of publication were missing, but it was enough for Pardoe, who read "*Sydney Ch—*" on the scrap in his hand. It did not matter if it were *Sydney Chronicle* or *Sydney Christian*, or what it was. He would soon find out. His luck was in. Out of all the torn bits of paper that might have come his way, he had found the very piece that told him what he wanted. Miss Gretton had had in her possession an Australian newspaper;

better than that, a newspaper published in New South Wales. The bright-eyed creature that had fled to its hole from the disturbance above did not know with what benevolence it was at that moment regarded by the breaker of its peace.

Pardoe got down on his hands and knees and peered beneath the wardrobe. The boards there were badly gnawed, and in places seemed dropping away. He drew a finger across them. They were nothing like as dusty as the rest of the room. When he was on his feet once more, shaking the dust from his trousers, the inspector tried to reconstruct what had happened.

It looked as if Miss Gretton had spread newspapers beneath the wardrobe, with some idea, perhaps, of checking the activities of the mice. She might, too, have placed shoes there. Her visit tonight—or the visit of her confederate or enemy, Pardoe did not yet know which—had probably been to cast a last look round for incriminating evidence. She may have remembered there were still the Australian papers. So she had burnt them in the bedroom grate. Their presence upstairs explained satisfactorily what had puzzled Pardoe: why the fire should have been lit in the bedroom and not downstairs. She would not have bothered to carry them down. The missing letter which, by Dinah's account, ought to have been lying inside the front door, may, after being read, have shared the same fate. On the other hand, the intruder who clearly possessed a key to the house might have taken that away some time previously. But however neat and expeditious her raid tonight had been, she had overlooked three details: a nibbled scrap of paper caught under the wardrobe foot and so escaping notice, a mousehole, and the stains left by a pair of galoshes. Pardoe wondered for a minute how she had managed to ignore the last point, then remembered that the lie of the house was probably familiar to her and that the kitchen window was uncurtained. She had not cared to use a light downstairs where she was perhaps sure she had left no clues, so had put her galoshes down in the dark and taken them up when she left, again in the dark. That looked as if she knew before coming in that the evidence lay upstairs. And that meant that the presence of Australian newspapers was a source of danger to her.

Pardoe's spirits rose at having got even so much from his visit. He opened the wardrobe door, but as he expected, found nothing inside. He was about to close it when his eye was caught by a flaw in the jamb which had slightly splintered the wood at about the level of his own chin. A few short hairs were sticking out of it. In the torchlight they shone silver; it was impossible to tell their actual color at the moment. The inspector pulled them out and folded them away in a leaf of his notebook.

There was nothing else to be seen upstairs, and he prepared to leave the house. He confirmed his impression that the kitchen window had no curtain, tried the back door again, and left by the front. He walked round the cottage, flashing his torch from side to side. The scent of wet violets filled the windless air. At the foot of the dovecote, half-hidden by a bush of southernwood, he came across a sodden piece of cardboard with some of the letters of Miss Gretton's final instruction to the baker still legible on it. But it was pulpy with many rains, and he let it drop to the ground.

Pardoe followed the track that turned into Spanwater lane, and went on to the manor gates. As he turned the corner by the brick wall a sturdy figure loomed up in the darkness. He shone the torch on it, and saw that it was Salt. The sergeant had been thereabouts nearly ten minutes, he said. Pardoe instantly recognized a quality of excitement in his voice, and saw that he was carrying under his arm what looked like a parcel. He drew him back up the road towards Titt's Cote. There was likely to be a greater privacy in that direction.

"I didn't see her," the sergeant said hastily. "A maid come to the door—elderly body, deaf. What did I say? *Deaf?* I couldn't make her take in a word, an' I didn't know what she was driving at neither. I *think* 'er missus 'ud gone to bed. She said so, anyhow. But that's neither 'ere nor there. Look what I found," he finished triumphantly, and waved in Pardoe's face a pair of galoshes.

"Dammit," the inspector said softly. "That's too good." His next thought as he handled them was that they were incredibly small. Surely only a child could have put those on. "Where were they?"

"And where d'you think? In the bloomin' garden an' all—Leith's garden, I mean. Just inside the gate in the lane. I didn't see 'em when I went in, but when I come down I kicked the one a foot or two. I thought it was a cat. Gee, looks like she's a fool 'anding 'em to us on a platter like, if it *was* 'er in the cottage."

Pardoe agreed, some of the optimism with which he had left Titt's Cote wilting in face of this reversal of his theory. It was not impossible, of course, for Miss Leith to have worn the galoshes; he had not yet seen her, and was ignorant of what size shoe she might take. But it was certainly difficult to understand why any woman who had achieved a fair measure of success that night should have left such a patent clue knocking about at her very threshold.

They had turned back and had almost stepped into Spanwater lane when a car, headed for the main road, came nosing past with its headlights dimmed. Salt strode out in its wake and looked at the number plate.

"By all that's rummy," he breathed, "if it isn't Sandy. Now what's Dr. Smollett doing in tonight's little show?"

PART III

LIGHT

Let not the dark thee cumber.
ROBERT HERRICK: *The Night Piece.*

CHAPTER XV

CLOUDY SABBATH

No will-o'-the-wisp mislight thee.
ROBERT HERRICK: *The Night Piece.*

SUNDAY broke fair in Steeple Cloudy. Flying sun and shadow skimmed the pastures like wings, and the clouds that came piling up from the horizon like an arrogant armada were as white and dazzling as the sloe and cherry of the countryside.

Pardoe, watching the last of the congregation leave Steeple Church in quest of its comfortable Sunday dinner, felt a vigor of mind in tune with the general spring cleaning. Mr. Flood's salutary address may have had something to do with it, for the inspector had attended the eleven o'clock service and, sitting at the back where in a quiet observance of his fellows secular interests might be served with religious, had listened to a surprising condemnation of the gathering. Privately, Pardoe thought the rector a little severe. The villagers might, for all he knew, be the heartless sensation-mongers he made them out, but when you had a murder (and presumably a murderer) plopped down in your midst, you ought to be permitted a little mongering. Besides, Weir, with no attempt at disguising his identity, had settled down there less than two years ago, before the echoes of the Bunting case had died away. What did country rectors expect? Not what Scotland Yard did, it was clear.

Pardoe had watched the zealous little man with the lively interest he always brought to "the proper study," thinking, as he had thought more than once in the Old Bailey and in coroners' courts, how fatally easy it was to abuse the privileges of bench and pulpit. The mute acceptance by their audiences of whatever they cared to give them was too much taken for granted. What was it to be outspoken when nobody could call your bluff? Mr. Flood had reminded him of his portable wireless at home; how often had its bland assumption of authority provoked in him a desire to shout it down! Well, country congregations, no doubt, had as much of the masochist in them as any others; and it was plain that the Rev. Flood took pleasure in his own invective. You're getting cynical in your old age, Pardoe told himself. But with the manor so much in evidence this morning, was this diatribe even in the best of taste? Defense could be far more embarrassing than prosecution.

Pardoe had had an admirable view of them all from his pew by the font. Was it courage, piety, innocence, or just indifference that had made the family turn up in strength for the chief service of the day? Weir himself was not there, of course; he was an agnostic. But, to the inspector's astonishment, Augustus was, sitting between Dinah and Andrew Pitt for all the world like an archbishop without his lawns. Nick sat very quietly next to Andy. None of them wore mourning. Behind was Aurelia Brett, her face so white that Pardoe expected her to faint any minute. Why, he asked himself irritably, must people martyrize themselves if that's how they're going to feel about it? The only servant present was Lou Blessitt, her rosy cheeks getting rosier as Mr. Flood's eloquence waxed stronger. She clearly could not make up her mind whether his denunciations were directed against manor or village. Neither Mond nor the housemaid was to be seen. Mrs. Kingdom, with a vigor equal to the rector's, was probably punching in her tin shed close by.

In front of him and on the other side of the aisle, so that he had an unimpaired view of her profile, Miss Leith sat and knelt with perfect composure. Her golden skin seemed oddly allied, Pardoe could not have said why, to the precisely chiseled features. He caught himself wondering how much skilfully applied makeup would be needed to convert them into those of a woman who might be "sixty, but did seem lissome."

On the way out he met the eye of Dr. Fisher, who nodded curtly. By the south door, under the great yew that slanted so far forward on the tilted ground it seemed to be peering inquisitively into the church, the Coxes, father and son, were talking to a stocky man who looked like a horse-dealer.

"Right, Mr. Birchall," he heard Walter say as they parted, and recognized the name of the gypsies' patron.

He liked the church better when they were all gone and silence had dropped back into the nave. It was a tiny cruciform building with an apsidal arch and a finely carved minstrels' gallery. The pew finials, no two alike, were executed with an almost riotous imagination. Pardoe left the south door open so that the sunlight threw a shaft into the darkness, with a single dappled shadow from the yew. He went to look at the great alabaster tomb of the Ruffs in the chancel. The clothes of the recumbent effigies and the veins of their folded hands were exquisitely wrought. There they lay, Sir Thomas and Anne, his wife, indifferent in their proud security to the fear and distress that possessed their home. No wonder such serenity had captured the imagination of Matthew Weir.

The inspector turned to go out. Just before he reached the door his eye was caught by a slip of white on the matting at his feet. It was a little piece of paper torn from a shopping-pad, with a few words scribbled on it in pencil: "*E.M. Sunday*," with underneath, "*F. at night*," and below that, "*D.F. Thursday?*" It had been freshly folded, and fallen from a prayer-book perhaps. It was impossible to say who had dropped it; its proximity to the door failed to connect it with any particular pew. It was probably of no consequence, but Pardoe, who took no risks while at work on a job, placed it between the leaves of his notebook.

Once outside he set his course for Miss Leith's house, first calling at the Silver Fox for his car. It was still well in advance of the normal lunch hour. The sergeant was busy on his own lawful occasions. Church attendance, even in the interests of his work, went sadly against the grain with Salt. He was engaged this morning in keeping an eye on Spanwater and whoever it might contain, and in putting the notes of the case into some kind of order. Last thing Saturday night Pardoe had rung up the superintendent in Cottlebury and secured his cooperation for setting a watch on Mond. He had thought by the fellow's looks yesterday that he might be planning a getaway. Creed had promised to send a man to tail him on Sunday.

Miss Leith herself, in a deep blue frock that was becoming to both figure and complexion, opened the door to Pardoe and showed no surprise when he introduced himself.

"I've been expecting you," she said, taking him into a small drawing room on the right of the hall, and added at his questioning look, "Mr. Weir is, and Mrs. Weir was my friend. In a case like this, I understand it is the practice of the police to visit friends. Won't you sit down?"

Pardoe complied, feeling a little deflated. Was this a courteous way of taking the offensive? When they were seated she looked at him with a gleam of amusement in her slanting eyes and waited for him to return the attack.

"Your rector was in great form this morning," was all the inspector could think of. It sounded feeble in his own ears, but it brought the subject at heart close enough anyway.

"Oh, yes," she said coolly. "If you enjoy that sort of thing. For our own part, we'd prefer a less uncompromising vindication."

So she was identifying herself from the start with the manor party. That made things easier for Pardoe.

"Miss Leith," he said frankly, "I've come to you because I think you can help me. Will you first give me some particulars of yourself and your profession?"

"Of course. Name, Jane Leith. Age? Not necessary? Very well. I am a tutor in Classics at Osney Hall, a college for women in Oxford. When I'm not in residence I live here, with my maid." She smiled. "I'm afraid the other detective found it a little difficult to make her understand last night. But it was silly of him to go so far out of his way—the lodge is quite a quarter of a mile farther on."

She was laughing at him, Pardoe was sure.

"The country at night is strange to a town-bred man," he found himself saying curtly in Salt's defense.

"I know. I could see you were busy up at Titt's Cote, though exploring it in the dark must have been uncomfortable."

"How did you know it was the police at Titt's Cote?" he asked promptly.

"Who else would it be? Unless the tenant returned all at once in the night. I could see your lights."

"What time was that?"

She frowned. "To be precise, I saw your light twice. The first time was at eight o'clock. Then not again till about nine-thirty."

Pardoe felt excited. If she were last night's intruder she would know he had discovered the visit to the cottage. Was this a clever move to divert suspicion from herself?

"May I ask how you knew it was eight o'clock?"

She lifted the long brows that gave her a faintly Mephistophelian look. "Wasn't it you?" she said. "I knew it was eight when the light came on in the bedroom, because I have my supper at that time and I was just going down to it. I saw it from the landing window."

"Do you know when it went out?"

"Not exactly. I went upstairs again at twenty to nine. Titt's Cote was in darkness then. It was Meggy, my maid, who told me somebody was there at nine-thirty—she hadn't known about the earlier light."

"The light your maid saw," Pardoe said, "was ours. The eight o'clock one belonged to somebody else—I want to know who."

He glanced instinctively at her feet, and saw that they were small and slender. Suppose the galoshes had been worn directly over stockings? He looked up to find her watching him with a cryptic smile.

"Well, I hope the first visitor left you some clues"—she too looked down at her feet—"footprints, for example."

"Enough for our purpose," the inspector said evenly. He felt that a challenge had been flung and accepted. "Miss Leith, were you acquainted with Miss Alice Gretton?"

"The tenant at the Cote? No. I've been away from Steeple Cloudy since before Christmas when the cottage was vacant. When I came home nearly three weeks ago she had already left it."

This was what Pardoe wanted. "You didn't leave Oxford all last term?" he asked mildly.

She gave him a quick look. "I wasn't in Oxford. I had been ill in the Michaelmas term. The doctor advised a few months' absence from work. I spent Hilary recuperating."

"Would you mind telling me where?"

"Mainly in Dorset. I was combining recreation with a little research work in the village churches. I am preparing a book on Wessex brasses."

"You were alone?"

"Quite." Though her tone was still faintly amused there was a hint of impatience in it. "Is it important?"

"It may be."

She broke the tension suddenly by laughing. "Inspector, this walking round and round the thing is absurd. I'm not Miss Gretton. If I were I'd produce a better alibi. Though in real life a shaky one is supposed to be more convincing, isn't it?"

When Pardoe did not reply she looked grave, and went on more quickly, "I don't want to obstruct you by treating any of this lightly. Cruel and silly things are talked about in villages, as everywhere else—far more silly than wicked, in spite of the rector. I got to know Mr. and Mrs. Weir directly they came here. I admired them for their handling of the life misfortune and publicity had left to them. And I was deeply sorry to see what shock had done to Mrs. Weir. As she gradually drew away into her own world, where I think she was usually happy, my friendship for Mr. Weir continued. He and I alone in Cloudy have the same interests. He could talk to me about his work in Penmarket, knowing that my job was his job—that we spoke the same language. What interpretation a few people, they were really only a few, chose to put upon our friendship mattered only to themselves—and to the rector, of course, whose kind, indignant heart persuades his tongue to indiscretion."

She looked so little perturbed that Pardoe could almost believe the scandal had touched her scarcely at all. He was impressed against his will by what she had said, and had to remind himself that if she were indeed playing a part she might have prepared just such a speech. He murmured something formal about the necessity of extending the inquiry to everyone whose movements coincided with the times under review.

"You're not obliged to tell me anything, you know," he added as a somewhat belated consolation. "I mean, I can ask, but it isn't compulsory for you to answer."

"Of course I know," she said, an irritable note evident for the first time. "What conceivable purpose should I have for not answering questions to which in each case there's only one answer? I should be very glad to know I was able to throw any light on this unhappy business. But I'm afraid I can't." She hesitated. "I can only suggest one thing."

"Yes? What's that?"

"That the person responsible for Mrs. Weir's death may be the same person who poisoned Miss Bunting two years ago."

Pardoe admired the bold risk she took for Weir. "That's a possibility which has occurred to us, Miss Leith. But there's another too—that the person responsible for Mrs. Weir's death wants us to think precisely that."

She looked at him with a new interest. Then, the further implication striking her, her color rose. "Does that mean the police are satisfied they know who caused Miss Bunting's death?"

"Not at all," Pardoe replied, noticing that her voice was not quite so controlled. "Whether they are or not, that was not what I meant. But if the police can be led to think there is—to speak plainly—a single murderer, while it can be proved that the person actually guilty in Mrs. Weir's case was nowhere on the scene of the Bunting crime—you see?"

She nodded, the color bright in her cheeks, her queerly shaped eyes dark and luminous. "A reliance," she said softly, "on the power of suggestion. The person you are looking for in Steeple Cloudy hopes you'll not be able to rid your mind of the Bunting case, and that the resemblance this one bears to that will make you see only one hand at work. Isn't that it?"

"Something like it," Pardoe said noncommittally. He had placed on the table all the cards he intended placing—except one. Without relinquishing his hold of it, he showed her the slip of paper he had picked up in church. She frowned, and denied knowledge of it. Nor could she think of anyone locally whom the initials fitted.

Pardoe put it away, and questioned her on what she knew of the late Mrs. Weir's character and general disposition. It tallied neatly with what he had gathered from various sources, with an additional sidelight on Mrs. Kingdom.

"You are at liberty, Inspector, to discount my disapproval of Mrs. Kingdom on grounds of prejudice. But her fervent dislike of me doesn't determine what I think of her effect on Mrs. Weir, whose affliction made it easy for others to gain ascendancy over her. I think the housekeeper had a serious influence on her."

"In what way?" Pardoe asked.

"For one thing, her blighting religious views are the sort to produce melancholia in anyone who listened to them. For another, she is disloyal to Mr. Weir, whose unorthodoxy makes her bitterly resentful."

"I wonder why he goes on employing her," Pardoe said half to himself.

"She's a very old family servant of the Buntings. She was kept on to please Mrs. Weir."

He was interested in the eagerness, almost irreticence, with which she spoke. Defense of Matthew seemed the one thing calculated to loosen tongues.

He rose to go. "What date did you arrive in Steeple Cloudy this vacation, Miss Leith?"

"On March 28th," she said immediately. "I travelled down from Cottlebury in the same train as Mr. Augustus Weir, and in the same carriage as the companion—I forget her name—who came to look after Mrs. Weir. So there's not much chance of any of us practicing deception on you there."

At the door, with the light falling full on her features, he asked her if she had any galoshes.

"Yes. Would you like to see them?"

"Please."

She went indoors, and came out again the next minute carrying a brown pair, which were perfectly clean and at least two sizes larger than the ones Salt had found. Those had been black.

"Do you remember when you last wore them?" the inspector said.

"A few days ago. Yes, in the middle of the week when we had a thoroughly wet day—before you came."

He thanked her and, before returning to Steeple, drove slowly along the lane to see if Salt were still at Spanwater. It was difficult to assess at its proper worth the interview he had just had. His impression was that she had been speaking the truth, but she was clearly a woman whose self-possession and steady nerve might enable her to lie convincingly. Frankness did not necessarily connote innocence; hadn't there been something a little slick in her anticipation of the drift of his suspicions? He had not altogether liked the way she had introduced the subject of footprints.

Before he reached the lodge, he caught sight of Salt coming through the door in the shrubbery wall. The sergeant waited on the grass verge, and Pardoe, as he pushed open the car door to admit him, saw at once that he had something to report.

"Mebbe you'll want to look in at the manor," Salt said laconically as the inspector accelerated. "Stop by the gates a minute an' I'll spill the beans."

Pardoe pulled up round the corner by the wall, the bonnet facing Spanwater gates. It was warm there in the shelter of the bay, and the old brick glowed in the sun. While he listened to Salt his eyes watched with a kind of idle pleasure the ceaseless journeys of a wren to a cranny below the clustering ivy.

"Look here," the sergeant was saying, "it's going to be stable door and stolen hoss over again with tailing this bloke Mond. Creed sent a chap down just now, with the story he's having a look-see at the garage Pitt's car was in. But he'll get nix. Mond was out last night."

"When?"

Salt shrugged his shoulders. "They don't know. An' he's too blind drunk to answer. But the housekeeper an' Miles, the girl, swear that he was coming up the service stairs between three and ha'-past ack emma. Kingdom says she'd been wide awake some time when she heard him come slip-slopping up the stairs, an' Gracie, who was frightened and lit her light, says it was three-thirty by the clock in 'er room."

"Didn't he even have an excuse for walking about?"

"Nope. Came down late in one of 'is dumb fits, according to the Kingdom. She said he'd been drinking even then."

"What? At night, or this morning?"

"Ask me another. Both, if you 'eard 'er. And her jes' back from meeting too." He grinned, swerving himself round towards Pardoe so that he set the car creaking. "That's not all. Guess who gets the galoshes."

"Mrs. Kingdom."

The sergeant's face fell. "Right in one. Says she hunted 'igh an' low for 'em before she went to meeting this morning. Always keeps 'em in the boot cupboard under the service stairs. Ain't going to stay in the same house, she's not, where the butler rides a broomstick at night an' somebody is too light-fingered to know their own!"

"And what was she doing the while?" Pardoe cut in. "Smoking another witch out of Titt's Cote? Did you let on we'd picked up the galoshes?"

"No. I let her run on in the hopes she'd trip herself. Suppose it was her up at the cottage last night, an' she wants us to think it was Leith—suppose she's Gretton?"

Pardoe smiled. "The one thing she can't be, old man. Unless she knows the trick of adding cubits to her stature. No, but she could be a confederate—in which case her abuse of Alice Gretton's been a blind—or else she knows what's become of the woman and was destroying evidence last night."

"What say Mond was up there last night?"

"He could have been," Pardoe conceded. "But if he was the third party to go over it, I'll wager he found little for his pains." He looked sharply at Salt. "You think he's in with the housekeeper?"

"I dunno," the sergeant said reflectively. "They're not speaking to each other this morning if that's a pointer."

"Creed's put a fellow on?" Pardoe said, glancing at his watch. "Well, it's lunch time now—that'll make 'em stay put. We'll have ours too, and come back this afternoon to put Mond through it."

On the way back he ran over to Salt his interview with Miss Leith. Later, over the excellent mutton and apple-pie provided at the Silver Fox, and for nearly an hour after lunch was eaten, inspector and sergeant discussed the case from every angle. These talks with Salt always served Pardoe as an admirable clearing-house for ideas that too often seemed at their most confusing before light broke. All the better if Salt, as was frequently the case, propounded a conflicting theory. The clash of inference acted as a stimulus on the inspector, who had more than once pounced upon a truth hidden from both until they had found themselves in opposing camps.

It was plain that Salt had fixed the guilt on Matthew Weir, whom he suspected of collaborating with his brother and with Miss Leith in a plot to poison his wife for the sake of the £6,000 he was certain to gain. Opportunity, possible experience with arsenic in the past, and the subsidiary motive of getting rid of a sick wife in order to marry again, were proffered in sound support of his theory.

Pardoe nodded. "But what's Augustus doing in your show?"

"Well, he wants the dough too. He got a pretty hard knock when he knew Gow had passed in his checks before clinching the deal—if there ever was a deal."

"I know. But six thousand wouldn't do everything. If Weir's reckoning to pay for the education of Nick and Dinah Terris, put his brother's affairs straight, and marry on it as well, he's not overambitious financially. It's even arguable that Mrs. Weir alive might have been more profitable to them."

"There's that about it," Salt conceded. "But say he *knew* the Murray girl was dead?"

"That's better. That puts a different complexion on the money motive. But if he knows, why's he keeping quiet? He'll never be able to touch a penny till her death's clearly proved."

Salt drummed his fingers on the table. "Well, say she ain't dead then," he said eagerly. "Suppose she's in this with Weir an' they're going to split the hundred thou. It'll bring 'em. See? Then she'll turn up quietly after a bit, the lost heiress. An' when everything's lovely in the garden again she'll give Matthew an' Gus an' the boy an' girl an' Leith their wages."

Pardoe laughed. "Write a film script," he said. Then his face grew grave. "I don't say there's nothing in it, old man. But how does Gretton fit in? You mean she's Joyce Murray?"

"Or mebbe Leith. Either'll do."

"That's just it," Pardoe said quietly. "Nothing will do where Alice Gretton's concerned. The woman won't fit in anywhere. Think—if she was poisoning Mrs. Weir with minute doses of arsenic on different dates throughout February and March, why did she clear off with the job half done, or how'd she manage to finish it when she wasn't there?"

"If it was Leith she was there," the sergeant pointed out stubbornly.

"If it was Leith why did she ever have to pretend she was Gretton? There's a lot of pointless trouble in that impersonation if you ask me. Wait a minute—" Pardoe thumped the table softly with his fist. "Suppose Weir and Miss Leith wanted a red herring for the police, so between 'em they invented Gretton and Leith played the part?"

"I'd say she wasn't red enough," Salt rejoined, unconsciously paraphrasing Queen Victoria. "Not enough clues pointing 'er way." He added after a pause, "It's only a hunch you an' me got that Titt's Cote is mixed up in this."

"No." Pardoe shook his head. "Not only you and me. There's Mrs. Kingdom—she rubbed it in about the sickness coinciding with the visits to the cottage. And what about last night's eight o'clock visitor? No, if Gretton was only a red herring, the funniest part of it to me is the date she cleared out."

"You mean," Salt broke in, "it 'ud have been more phoney if she'd gone after Mrs. Weir was dead?"

Pardoe nodded. "That's about it. The way I look at it she ought to have gone later if they wanted police attention specially drawn to her. And why was there a piece from an Australian paper in the cottage?"

As he spoke he drew out again the few clues he had picked up at the Cote, and which he had shown Salt last night—the piece of paper and the fragmentary hairs from the crack in the wardrobe. To them he added, with a brief explanation to Salt, the leaf from the shopping-pad he had found in church a few hours ago.

The sergeant's stare was forbidding, as if he would hypnotize it into yielding up its secret.

"Looks to me like visitors to tea and supper," he said at last, flicking it contemptuously from him.

" 'Mm. Engagement memoranda," Pardoe said absently. "Perhaps you're right. Have a look at these in daylight, and tell me what color they are." He passed over the folded paper containing the hairs.

"Yellow," was the verdict after it had been carried to the window and its contents frowned upon. "Palish one end, brighter at the root."

"Yes. And Joyce Murray was fair."

Salt whistled softly. "I was right—she's Gretton. See what I said, it fits—"

"Not necessarily." Pardoe interrupted. "Only up to a point. Why the needless invention of Gretton, who you pointed out yourself was a washy red herring? If Joyce Murray was in this thing with Matthew Weir, why did she invent a woman that had to be left to the housekeeper to implicate? Another thing, why should Murray want to hasten Mrs. Weir's death so much that she was willing to split the fortune she'd have had entire by waiting?"

Salt was forced to admit the cogency of this. "P'r'aps she was in a jam too—like Augustus," he suggested. But it did not sound convincing even to himself.

There was a tap on the door and Walter Cox put his head in.

"A lad from the manor to see you, sir."

At the inspector's invitation the boy was sent in, a thin youth with startled eyes in a very white face. He wrung his cap between his hands and got his message out only with an effort.

"I'm Dick, sir. I help Comfort in the garden. It's Mr. Mond, sir—the butler, sir. He's dead."

CHAPTER XVI

AGAIN POISON

This is the haven
False servants still arrive at.
PHILIP MASSINGER: *A New Way to Pay Old Debts.*

MOND was indubitably dead. Both his person and his room had forcibly registered the fact from the moment, two hours ago, when the Yard men had set eyes upon them. Now it was close on five o'clock, and the procession that had individually tramped the service stairs since three had gone away: Superintendent Creed, the divisional surgeon, the camera man who had gone to work with cheerful disregard of the nauseous details, the ambulance men, and the corpse itself. Only a police sergeant from Cottlebury hung about unobtrusively in the domestic quarters and outside the butler's locked room, while the fingerprints man who had explored the furniture and taken the prints of the dead man himself remained at Pardoe's request to perform the same office on the household. There was Dr. Smollett too, who had arrived ten minutes after the police surgeon and had been drawn into conference with him.

When they had reached the manor, after telephoning Cottlebury, it had been Nicholas Terris who had taken them up to the room that was witness enough in itself of the butler's end. There was everywhere evidence of the vomiting which had preceded death. Pardoe had been even thankful for the reek of whisky which filled the place. The body was lying on its back on the bed, the clothes of which were horribly rumpled beneath it. One hand clutched the quilt in an agonized bunch, one dangling foot touched the floor. The head was thrown back, giving an unnatural strength to the weak jaw, and streaks of damp hair were sticking to the brow. Under the partially lowered lids the eyeballs were turned up. His face was a bad color, and some angry marks on the chin had attracted Pardoe's attention. The hands too—he had picked up the unclenched one and examined it.

The condition of both body and room had had a nightmarish quality, and it was hardly surprising to learn that Mrs. Kingdom, the first on the spot, had only managed to summon the cook and Aurelia Brett before fainting dead away. But in spite of the ghastly evidence of the wretched man's sickness, it was a disorder of another kind that interested Pardoe. There were signs of a frenzied treatment of furniture and clothes that had nothing to do with the agonies of physical suffering. Drawers had been pulled out and their contents tumbled onto the floor, boots flung across the room, an overcoat tossed inside out upon a trunk, the doors of a cupboard in the wall left a-swing, and even the outer pockets of the coat the corpse wore showing the lining desperate fingers had failed to replace.

"That pretty well disposes of the suicide theory," Pardoe had remarked to Salt. "Allow for a certain amount of disturbance when he was retching about the room—it won't account for this. Suicides don't have to conduct a feverish search of their own things before passing out."

"Unless," said the sergeant, "the guy who did it happened along when he'd just snuffed out and knew he had summat they wanted."

"Mrs. Kingdom? Work first, faint afterwards? You may be right, but I think the party who combed this over knew Mond was going to die."

The divisional surgeon, whose languorous air was a defense against the perpetual tyranny of life and belied the speed and economy he put into his work, was of the opinion that death had occurred not earlier than two o'clock that afternoon. The hour fitted adequately with the discovery of the body by the housekeeper at two-twenty. An autopsy would be carried out, of course. Meantime, it was safe to state that Mond had died from acute poisoning, probably by arsenic, the onset of which had been accelerated by excessive whisky drinking and the combined effect on a groggy heart. Questioned as to the scratches on the dead man's face and hands, the police doctor, after a second scrutiny, declared them to be recent and inflicted before death. They were not in his opinion self-inflicted. He asked if there were a cat in the house. Dr. Smollett, the only person present likely to know, replied in the negative.

They had not far to seek for the medium by which the poison had been taken. A bottle of whisky two-thirds empty stood on a small bureau close to the head of the bed, beside it a recently used glass. These had been removed for analysis.

The depositions of the family and of Dr. Smollett contained some interesting points. From the moment the doctor had come into the room Pardoe had thought him ill at ease, perfunctory in his remarks, absently endorsing medical opinion. As soon as the preliminary routine was over the inspector took him aside.

"What's biting you, Doctor?"

"You spotted it?" Smollett gave a diffident smile. "Only this—I fancy something I blabbed last night may have precipitated this mess. I ran into Sir Jacob Borth in Cottlebury in the evening. He's a patient of mine—so's Freddy, bad cess to him. It seems the old man came home to tea yesterday to find his secretary had supplied you with the address of the boy's coach. What does the old quiz do but go round to see if he could dig the story out of Freddy. I gather he wasn't too welcome at the hospital, but as usual he got his own way. He told me this tale of Mond being Fennick, and I'm afraid I passed it on to Mat—to Mr. Weir. I looked in on him professionally last night, you know. By the way, wasn't that you and the sergeant lurking in the lane when I went away? Now if this fellow's a suicide, I'm wondering if he got to know the police were on to his alias and took this way out."

"You can bet he knew we were on to it," Pardoe said bitterly, in his heart cursing the nosiness of old Borth, the doctor's easy tongue, and his own oversight in giving Mond a slack rein. "But I think we shall find that somebody else took the way out for him."

Matthew Weir had confirmed and supplemented the doctor's statement.

Pardoe took him into the library, noticing that though his voice was under control the hand he put out to the chair was unsteady.

"I gave Mond notice this morning, Inspector," he said. "I don't know whether it had anything to do with this."

"Why was that, sir?"

"He'd been unsatisfactory for some time. Then last night Sandy told me this tale about his actual name being Fennick. I said nothing to him then, but this morning when Bessie told me he had been out in the night I questioned him on both matters. He refused to answer. And he was so drunk in the morning that I dispensed with his services at lunch. I gave him his dismissal then, intending to repeat it when he was sober."

"When did you see him last?"

"About twelve. Just before the others came in from church. I told him to go up to his room and stay there until he'd got himself in hand. He looked ghastly. I said if he was not better by the afternoon a doctor should be sent for."

"When you say 'ghastly,' " Pardoe asked, "are you suggesting he was in pain?"

"Oh, no. I don't think so. I mean he was drunk, and he looked ill—stupefied would be the better word."

"Didn't he say anything, let fall anything, that would explain his condition?"

"No. He was silent most of the time. When he did speak he was quite incoherent."

"I see. Now was last night the first time you knew Mond's name was Fennick?"

"Yes—or at least," he amended gently, "the first time that I knew Mr. Borth had *said* he was Fennick. My nephew has now told me what happened last Christmas, but it didn't reach my ears at the time—probably because Freddy wasn't regarded as a reliable authority."

"Evidently not," Pardoe replied grimly. "All right, Mr. Weir. The Fennick part of the business will soon be settled. Another thing—would it have been easy for the butler to leave the house at night and return to it with none the wiser?"

"Perfectly. The key was left in the inside of the door at the north end."

Pardoe did not comment on this. "Had he been the worse for drink on previous occasions?"

"Not to my knowledge," Weir said. "But there had been a change in him lately—a change for the worse, I mean."

"In what way, precisely?"

Weir hesitated. "He was impudent in a covert fashion. He got slack too. Mrs. Kingdom had cause to complain of duties left to her which fell properly within his province. Miss Brett reported him once for rudeness. He seemed to have an unaccountable dislike for her."

The inspector nodded. "And when did you notice this change come over him?"

"About a fortnight before Easter. My brother was the first to draw attention to it the day he arrived. He asked me if Mond were ill."

Something here intrigued Pardoe. Somewhere a warning bell was struck. Things were beginning to click into place. He left Matthew and went to question Mrs. Kingdom, whom shock had up till now rendered inarticulate.

He found her seated by a fire in the otherwise bleak sewing room, with Blessitt, the cook, in a chair opposite. Both women were sipping strong tea and trying to extract from the situation the pleasure they thought their due. Mrs. Kingdom looked white and shrunken, only the eyes alive in her haunted face, but Blessitt's rosy cheeks were hardly less rosy than usual, and even brighter with anticipation than with color. Beholding this unnatural alliance, Pardoe wondered if there was to be found anything more callous than a kindhearted, insensitive woman; it had taken the ugliness of Mond's death to arouse in the cook any sympathy for Mrs. Kingdom.

He had resolved to speak to the housekeeper privately, but even when he had dismissed her, Blessitt was disposed to linger. Pardoe went irritably to the door, where she stood with an eye fixed imploringly upon him.

"Yes, what is it? Anything you want to tell me?"

She nodded and signed to him to follow her into the passage out of range of Mrs. Kingdom's eyes.

"It's this, sir." She turned away a moment in deference to modesty, diving a hand into the front of her frock. "I found it underneath the poor fellow. I was thinking maybe it was something would show why he done himself in. So I kept it for you."

As calmly as she might have lifted a kettle on the boil, she handed Pardoe a stamped letter.

The inspector glanced at it, then gave her a look of astonishment.

"Then you moved the body?"

"No, not really," she said. "Only his one arm. I wasn't sure he was dead. Didn't I ought to 'ave? This was on the counterpane under his elbow."

"All right," Pardoe said. "I'm glad you found it. Have you said anything about it?"

The cook winked unashamedly. "Not me. And I was the only one except Mr. Nick who would go inside the room. That Miss Brett," she added with a touch of tolerant scorn, "she took one look from the door and walked away and said she'd be sick. Too ladyfied like."

Pardoe scarcely blamed her. "Do you think anybody saw you take this?"

"Nobody didn't, sir. Mrs. Kingdom, she fainted right off, an' Miss Brett an' me took her into my room being it was the nearest, and Miss Brett stayed there with her. Glad too, I'll be bound, to be out of the sights. Mr. Nick came up jes' as I was coming out. I'd 'id it by then."

"You've done well, Cook," he said. "We may find this useful." He noted the naive pleasure on her face and softened his dismissal of her with a smile.

When he was alone he looked at the letter, stuck down and stamped ready for post. Across the thin envelope an uncontrolled hand had scrawled: "*Miss D. Flynn, 3a Wynburn Mansions, Little Whale Square, E.C. 4*." He had little doubt that it was the object of the search in Mond's room, still less that it was the butler's script. The contents would keep until he could examine them with Salt. He put it away in his pocket and returned to the sewing room.

Mrs. Kingdom was standing up when he went in. Something in her attitude made Pardoe suspect that she had not long left the door. Well, she had heard nothing likely to be of much profit to her, and the evidence, such as it was, lay snugly in his own pocket. She eyed his approach without speaking, but it was a silence which suggested that she had lost command of the situation. Pardoe would have been sorry for a less implacable woman, but it was neither expedient nor merciful to temper the investigation at this stage. She would have to submit to the same questioning as the rest. He invited her to sit down and tell him how it was that she had discovered Mond was dead.

With the curious inconsistency he had remarked before in witnesses who had seemed stunned to silence, she plunged into speech with a vehemence for which he was unprepared. It was clear, too, that she had not wanted to be left alone. Besides the relief found in words, she welcomed company.

Pardoe gathered that just before lunch she had been told Mond was unfit to appear and that he had received his dismissal. She had seen him herself earlier in the morning before going to meeting, at the time she had missed her galoshes, and had found him drunk and unwilling to explain his nocturnal adventure. What she described as anxiety for his condition, but what Pardoe read as natural curiosity allied to secret gloating over his disgrace, had prompted her at a quarter past two to go upstairs and see if he had made any sort of a recovery. When there was no response to her knocking, she had supposed he had fallen into a drunken sleep, had opened the door a little way to satisfy herself on this score and had witnessed the sight which had made her shout for Louisa Blessitt and the companion.

"Now, Mrs. Kingdom," the inspector said, "why are you certain that Mond went out of doors in the night? Why couldn't he have merely been downstairs—getting drink again perhaps?"

"He didn't need to. That's why. He kept it in his room. And I *know* he went out, because in my room you can hear the key turn in the back door that opens by the garridge. I was awake before he come in. So I know."

Pardoe made a note to remind him to test this statement by experiment, then quickly changed the subject.

"I want you to tell me all you can remember of the clothes Miss Alice Gretton usually wore when she went out."

She looked at him as if she had not quite understood.

"You saw her sometimes, I think, even though you didn't speak to her?" he said impatiently.

At that she gave him a graphic enough description. Trust a jealous woman, Pardoe thought, to be accurate on the subject of another woman's style of dress. He jotted down the items: dark blue cloth coat, black and white woolen scarf, small black felt hat with a dark blue feather, black shoes and stockings.

He shut his notebook, and in the act of putting it away looked at her with a deceptively mild expression.

"I ought to tell you, Mrs. Kingdom, that we've found your galoshes.

They were in the kitchen of Titt's Cote."

This was perhaps a jesuitical treatment of the truth; but Pardoe felt the setting might be more productive than that of Miss Leith's garden. He saw her stiffen and look at him with incredulity, followed by a flash of fear.

As she did not answer he continued, "Did you perhaps break in there last night?"

She protested then so fiercely that it was as if a cat had spat at him. "Me? *Me* go to Titt's Cote? And for why? Tell me that. I wouldn't ha' gone to the place not if I was carried there!" She drew a sharp breath and looked sly all at once. "That would be Mond."

"What would he want there?" Pardoe asked, thinking it unnecessary to enlighten her as to the disparity in the times.

But she could not say. Pardoe, recognizing the remark for nothing more important than a futile bit of malice against one who could no longer refute the charge, did not press it. He could see that she was inwardly shaken with fear. He leaned forward a little and said with quiet emphasis: "Have you ever wondered if perhaps Mrs. Weir and Miss Bunting were poisoned by the same person?"

There was a short silence in which she sat rigid in the chair, her small sinewy hands tight in her lap. Something in her look chilled Pardoe's blood. But the impact of the question at that moment achieved its purpose: and for the simple reason that it carried her two years away from the present, she fell neatly into the trap.

"That couldn't be."

"Why?" The inspector sounded casual.

"Because Miss Leah is dead."

Pardoe and Salt returned to Cottlebury in the evening, leaving Creed's man, who had never had a chance to shadow Mond, to nose awhile round Spanwater. The village post had been collected long ago. In any case, Sunday or not, Pardoe preferred manual delivery to the editor of the *Cottlebury Chronicle* of the appeal he had drafted relating to the disappearance of Miss Alice Gretton. A description of the clothes she had probably been wearing was based on the account given by Mrs. Kingdom and confirmed afterwards by Dinah Terris. Fortunately Miss Gretton's unsociability had not extended to an invisible cloak; several who had never exchanged a word with her were still able to say what she had looked like. The *Chronicle* was published daily, and was on sale in Cottlebury by 3.30 P.M.. and in the surrounding district by evening. There was the hope and the chance that in addition to the cranks who would prove to have seen her in a dozen places simultaneously some genuine memory might be stirred.

Recourse to the railway and bus timetables showed how she might have left Steeple Cloudy for Cottlebury and Cottlebury for London or Birmingham at various times between 5.30 P.M.. and midnight, which constituted the period on March 21st when she was most likely to have gone away. Besides these, Pardoe checked the train and road services for the following morning up to the hour at which the snow had stopped. It was less likely, however, that she had left Titt's Cote either in the small hours when the snow was at its heaviest or later when she ran more risk of being seen.

There remained the problem of what she had carried; probably a single suitcase. She had moved into Titt's Cote with noticeably little, nothing apparently beyond what a weekender would hold, and had made shift with the inadequate furniture the cottage contained and a few accessories acquired later. Since nobody, however, admitted to entering the cottage during her tenancy, exactitude in this respect was impossible. If other means failed, the cooperation of the BBC would be sought for the tracing of both Alice Gretton and Joyce Murray. Pardoe could not expect a reply cable from Sydney before Wednesday morning at the earliest, probably later if the inquiry at that end should be at all protracted.

Meantime, on Monday morning the inspector proposed returning alone to London. In addition to making his report in person at the Yard, he wanted to examine Augustus Weir's affairs and to visit Miss D. Flynn.

Back in Steeple with Salt, Pardoe slit carefully the envelope addressed to her and removed a piece of cheap notepaper on which an almost illegible message had been scribbled. It lacked both date and address and was bitterly concise.

"*I am getting out. It is too hot here. A. wants too much. Better drop F.P. Meet me you know where Monday. Bill.*"

"Dashed off in panic," Pardoe commented. "Would you say that was an 'A.'? It isn't the Roman variety and that unjoined curl in the middle might make it a 'G.' "

The sergeant did not answer. He was thinking hard. It was quite usual for anybody christened Augustus to be called Gus, especially by a fellow of Mond's class.

Pardoe felt a keen satisfaction as he deciphered the uncontrolled scrawl. While it might be suggested that Mond's opening sentence hinted at suicide, it went unquestioned that a man about to take his own life did not arrange a rendezvous for the following day.

Other news was not so accommodating. Pardoe had left Salt to check the eight o'clock alibis of the household for the previous evening. With dinner at seven-thirty it seemed to him to be running it rather fine for any one of them to be up at Titt's Cote half an hour later. They had come to a dead end, however, for the dinner hour had been changed that evening to seven-fifteen to oblige Augustus, who had a portable wireless in his room and wanted to listen to a reading of his own poetry on the National program at seven-fifty.

"And it was there too," said Salt savagely. "But here's a funny thing. Why didn't he let anybody else listen with him? He could have been faking his alibi. You notice 'ow quiet he is on his feet? Like a bloomin' cat. Suppose he let 'em read his pawtry to the empty room while he crept out, pinched the galoshes on the way—"

"Well, don't tell me he put them on," the inspector interrupted with a grin.

"Rubbed 'em in a puddle," the sergeant continued imperturbably, "an' made the prints in the cottage. Then he could have tossed 'em into Leith's garden on the way back, to make it look as if Kingdom had got rid of 'em that way, or to implicate Leith an' pretend *she* was putting it on Kingdom."

"You're too clever," Pardoe groaned, holding his head. "But it could be. Anything could be."

A few hours later a tall gypsy with a touch of the wolf in his loping tread walked into Steeple to report to the village sergeant the disappearance of his mother. Unfortunately that worthy arm of the law, scorning to connect the troubles of the O'Malleys with those of Spanwater, was inclined to make short shrift of the matter. Morning was time enough anyway. He knew these plausible, every-man's-hand-against-me fellows. What was more important from a wider point of view, he was unaware of Inspector Dan Pardoe's interest in Esther O'Malley.

CHAPTER XVII

PIE WOOD

Light thickens; and the crow
Makes wing to the rooky wood.
William Shakespeare: *Macbeth.*

Sergeant salt had spent the morning carrying out the instructions of his chief, who had taken the car and gone off to London immediately after breakfast. If the sergeant should need a car in his absence he would have to requisition Weir's Hillman. Salt felt a pang of envy that was almost homesickness at watching the inspector leave behind the secrecy of the country for the city's noise and bustle. He went back to his job with a grunt, and by midday had got into communication with the Mendips in the person of Mr. Paul Benedict, helped the man deputed to shadow the manor folk at what might be called the home end of the business, and spent the bulk of the time subjecting Mond's room to a minute examination.

That it had undergone the minimum of cleaning added materially to his depression. He found nothing more exciting than an array of empty bottles in the cupboard attesting to the magnitude of the butler's thirst, a coat minus the second button, and thrust out of sight beneath the bed a pair of dirty boots, the soles and heels caked in fresh mold to which a number of blackened leaves still clung. Minute gritty specks that glittered in the dirt proved to be coal dust. Salt looked at them closely and went away thoughtful.

After lunch Andrew Pitt decided to go for a walk. Not far away a cuckoo shouted encouragement of such intention, or mocked him for a stay-at-home perhaps, and the sky from horizon to horizon was as blue as the forget-me-nots he had seen growing in the water under the shrubbery bridge. The truth was he was sick of being forced to kick his heels in a place from which decency, had he been a free agent, would have expelled him long ago; sick of feeling miserably shy of everyone because bogies kept jabbing his mental ribs and sticking doubts between them; sick, above all, of every conversation with Nick coming to an uneasy full stop because he carried with him a knowledge he was unable to share. Anyway, he would take himself off this afternoon if only out of courtesy to his hosts.

He strolled into the garden first, then innocently round to the shrubbery to see if he could catch the police shadow disguised as a tin of weedkiller. A nice jolly walk he'd have if the fellow spotted him. "Like one that on a lonesome road," thought Andy, trying to feel jocular about it all; but he remembered that his own particular fiend always trod close behind now, and the fun faded.

There was nobody about, but as he came back again and in by the front door he met Aurelia Brett turning to go upstairs. Though he had not had the chance to say much to her since that silly squabble on Friday and didn't really want to, it was impossible to avoid her now. She was looking white and edgy like the rest of them, but her blue eyes shone brilliantly in her pale face, and her hair looked as misty and innocent as the hair of angels in German Christmas cards. She was perfect with her hand laid like that on that lovely balustrade.

Andy blushed and, lifting his eyes to hers as she paused on the last tread but one, gave her a look of mingled admiration and recklessness.

"I'm going for a walk. Won't you come too?"

She did not answer for a moment, but smiled in a way he could not understand. "No, thank you. Your car wasn't safe. Would a walk with you be, I wonder?"

His flush deepened. Good Lor', she couldn't possibly think— He must have reached the limit of his nerves if he couldn't meet a joke in the right spirit, but there had been something double-edged in the words.

"We should only be followed," she went on less provocatively. "I went into Steeple this morning to buy stamps and there was a police hound waiting outside. They must be fools if they think we don't know."

A savage note in her voice stirred him unpleasantly. He was moved to involuntary defense of the police.

"They've got their job," he muttered. "It doesn't matter after all if you're not up to anything."

She laughed at that, looking at him with narrowed eyes, disdaining words. Then she turned round and went slowly upstairs.

The laugh followed Andy like an echo as he left the house and swung himself over the wall to drop into the field by the bowling green. He would take this direction for a change, climb the meadows across the road, and explore Pie Wood that streaked the horizon like a black smudge. She had not forgiven him then. In a way that made things at once easier and harder. He had almost made up his mind what to do. His sister, Zoe, who had that morning written a characteristically clear letter, was quite positive what he ought to do. Not, of course, as he assured himself hastily, that he would let her advice influence him. She was younger than he. It was funny, though, how perceptive she had sometimes shown herself.

When he gained the empty, sunlit road he exulted in his solitude. He had thrown off the sleuth, he was sure. With that knowledge the host of dark fancies that had fluttered in his brain for a week took wing and left him. They would roost at home, he knew, but that didn't matter for the moment. He pushed open a five-barred gate—twin to Freddy's higher up the road, which had been temporarily replaced by a hurdle—and for twenty minutes climbed the pastures, stubbing his toes lightheartedly into the tussocky molehills. At the top he came to a ditch of nettles with a stile into the wood. For a minute or two he sat on the step to recover his breath, looking back at the sunlit country below the vast dome of the sky. Unpeopled like that, it was wise, tender, drowsy, giving life, not death. Then he turned, swung his leg over the bar, and the wood closed in on him.

It was abnormally dark, he thought, for an April afternoon. There seemed to be no proper path. As soon as the stile was crossed a succession of jutting boulders formed a natural zigzag stairway in the damp earth. Faced with this unpromising ascent, Andy debated if it was worthwhile going on. On consideration he thought it a little towny and flaccid perhaps to be daunted by the initial difficulties of a walk, and decided to scramble up and see if the top was any more attractive. The steps were slippery from recent rains, moss-grown, obviously little used. At the top he straightened his back and, holding on to the naked arm of a beech sapling thrust out at him, blew a slow breath over his warm face.

Pie Wood—why Pie? Evidence of pastry there was none. The magpies, of course—didn't they call them pies in the country? Silly creatures to want to live where eagles should have been more at home if only there had been room in these smothering trees for them to spread their wings. At the thought of having mounted to an unknown eyrie Andy grinned.

Though the trees pressed closely, there was a little more light here. New spring foliage broke green against the occasional patches of sky. A path of sorts, rich with the ooze of rotting leaves, dived straight into the heart of the wood. As he followed it through that breathless place where even the faraway cuckoo was muted, it occurred to him that woods more than anywhere else have a secret life of their own. Perhaps it was that trees drawn together in company generated a peculiar spiritual force. They were exclusive, like the gypsies that were said to live somewhere in their depths; not inimical exactly, but so indifferent as to be unsocial. At the thought of a tree becoming unsocial Andy laughed aloud. But he checked himself because it was rather like laughing in church—not the tamed church of civilization where the vision of the worshipper was too often bounded by the ritual, but a primitive temple where religion was spontaneous and not always, perhaps, holy.

He had been walking a quarter of an hour when he noticed that twilight had retreated before the broader day. Shadows began to run beneath the trees where the clear, thin sunlight fell. Woodruff grew here in lacy abundance and the delicate, veiny windflowers with their sharp green, appetizing leaves. In the middle distance were masses of bluebells still in close bud, and beyond young, curly bracken in a wash of sunshine.

He came out into a clearing that was really like a small plateau with slopes running to left and right. Some distance below on the left a byway ran, bounded by hedge and gate. Far in front to the right and only just visible a cottage roof appeared. The gypsies, thought Andy, but there was no sign of life. Only from this angle the cottage seemed crouched and ready to spring.

He looked across at the narrow road and the corner of his eye was caught by something unnatural in the lie of the ground at the edge of the wood. Turning his head he saw that a little behind him where trees, road and clearing met was a deep depression partly overhung with brambles and nettle clumps. On approach it proved to be a pit of some sort, and in one place where the bushes grew more thinly at the lip a mass of earth had slipped inwards, leaving the staring gap that had caught his attention.

The soil must have given way very recently, for it was raw and moist and at the slightest touch still dribbled in. He bent closer to peer into the basin below him, fifteen feet or so deep, frowned, drew back suddenly with a gasp, then cautiously bent farther over again, edging his way from the gap to the firmer bush-grown rim. He knelt down, one hand pressing hard on a bramble shoot. But he was unconscious of the pain. Somebody had slipped down, down with the slipping earth—those were stockinged feet he could see. But would all that mold have fallen *above* its victim? And would anybody caught up in the bushes like that die of such a slip?

Andy looked wildly round at the empty, watching country, as if he expected a posse of police and doctors to invade the spot. But he was alone with the dead. He scrambled to his feet, slipped, grabbed the stocky roots of a bush, and accompanied by a rattle of loose earth slithered down the inner side of the pit. It was comparatively easy then, in spite of the brambles that snatched peevishly at him, to work his way to the spot where the earth hung in a dark cataract. He was sure he could see an arm, in death perhaps still groping for the edge and safety. With a breath that was half sob, he pressed his feet into a sturdy bush that grew from an outcrop of stone and started to dig frantically with his hands, throwing, pushing, scattering the concealing earth. His efforts were rewarded with grim suddenness. The freshly disturbed soil started again to slide, first with a slow movement, then increasingly fast, until the bulk of it dropped with a thud into the tangle below. But it had not taken the body with it.

Slung face downwards across the bushes about six feet below the edge of the pit and spattered with mold, was a dead woman. Her feet were nearest Andy, but by leaning out and sideways he could touch the waist of her long coat. An inch or two farther—at the sight his heart was thumping in the roof of his mouth—and the back of her head appeared. Or what had once been the back of her head. One glance, and a wave of nausea for a second clouded the whole hideous scene from his gaze. When he had steadied himself his feet were slipping. He clutched the treacherous earth above him, but it broke in his hand, and only by pressing his back against the pit could he keep his balance. He wondered if alone he could ever drag the body to the surface. He would have to get help. The cottage—

There was a sound behind him. By alternately wriggling and wedging his shoulders into the slope he managed to roll over on to the grass and draw his legs up after him. A yard or two away a man was coming across the clearing from the direction of the road. Andrew Pitt had never in his life imagined that the sight of a police officer would have been to him more delectable than that of the choicest houri in paradise. Sergeant Salt would never have thought so either.

"What you up to?" he called sourly, for he had dogged this youngster for the best part of two miles with scant hope of gaining anything but sore feet, and had left the wood for the road ten minutes ago so as to cut off his retreat that way. "Come on outa that."

"I'm out," said Andy feebly, and pointed with a finger far more vocal than his tongue.

The next half-hour was not among the times Andy cared to recall in after years. He could remember standing by, dumb and helpless, while Sergeant Salt, his homely, flatfooted personality swamped all at once by one whose efficiency dominated the scene, looked at the body from every angle, took notes, examined the slippery, trampled ground. Then he had a picture of himself kneeling at the edge to receive the body which the sergeant, taking on the heavier job inside the pit, hoisted up at the expense of much effort and the risk of letting it and himself fall into the mess of thorn, bottles, pots, pans and miscellaneous rubbish below.

When at last they got her to the surface and she was lying on the ground, they saw that she had been a tall woman with darkish gray hair, horribly matted now with blood and rippling in a curious fashion at the sides. She wore a long dark blue coat and a black and white woolen scarf knotted loosely round her throat. In the briars at the bottom of the pit Salt had seen a black felt hat with a blue feather in it. A queer feature of the clothing was the stockings she wore: thick woolen ones, the darning badly cobbled. And there were no shoes on her feet. Salt felt them. They were dry.

But it was the face at which Andy looked, and decided not to look again. Even the back of the skull was better than that. A corrosive acid had done its work properly. Salt knelt to look at her ears. The lobes were torn and blood had dried in the lacerations.

"Gretton," said Salt softly. But he was frowning. His eyes, that kept returning there, wandered again to the feet. He looked at the trodden earth beyond. Half embedded in it something shiny glistened. The sergeant stooped and, poking it out, saw that it was a button of the type found on men's coats. A few threads still clung to it.

Andy felt cold as ice. He moved off to the hedge by the road and was quickly and thoroughly sick.

Chief Inspector Pardoe was not much pleased with his day's work when at teatime on Monday he turned the nose of the car home.

The seedy character of Little Whale Square had been discouraging to start with. Wynburn Mansions was a group of gaunt houses of blackened brick, inhabited by the less hopeful members of the class that keeps just above the poverty line. Pardoe talked to the dispirited landlady, but received only bad news. Miss Dora Flynn, it was true, had occupied a room there since February, but less than two hours ago she had received a telegram and had left hurriedly soon afterwards on a bus from the bottom of the square. She had paid up her rent all right, but had not said where she was going, an omission which plainly aggrieved her landlady. On learning that it was a police matter the woman's demeanor brightened perceptibly, and she consented to show him the room. But in spite of a careful search it told him precisely nothing. If Dora Flynn had ever possessed anything of interest she had been careful to dispose of it or take it with her, including that morning's wire. Well, that at least was traceable.

"Did you ever know Miss Flynn by the name of Fennick, perhaps Mrs. Fennick?" he ventured.

She had had reluctantly to deny it. But the question evoked something. It clicked in her mind with what Miss Flynn had said more than once lately, namely, that soon she was likely to come into a lot of money when the lawyers had settled up her affairs. That was interesting. So was the description of her as a thin, fair girl with pink cheeks and bright blue eyes. But the landlady had thought her "a bit on the soft side," and that did not fit so well.

Pardoe did not immediately take steps to trace Miss Flynn's movements. He drove instead to the offices of *The Archon* in Bloomsbury, and there met with better luck.

Considering Augustus Weir's esthetic bias, his place was unexpectedly businesslike. Sir Ronald Edwy was a little surprising too. Pardoe saw an earnest, spectacled youth with a deep, clever brow and an absent manner. At first inclined to reticence, his reserve broke down when the inspector, sizing up his man, shamelessly let him believe that Augustus had given *carte blanche* for the inquiry.

"Well, I don't know what about *proof* of Mr. Gow's interest in our paper," Edwy said, with a gentleman's distaste for probing beneath a man's mere word, "but will this help you?"

From a file he handed Pardoe Augustus Weir's letter of April 5th. The inspector scanned it quickly. Was the boy a fool after all? Either that, or else he was damned sure of Augustus.

"Who's Rice?" he asked abruptly.

"Franklin Rice, the essayist." He was gently tolerant of official ignorance. He suddenly became more human and added, "He's very expensive."

"I'd better keep this for the time being," Pardoe said.

He had gone from there to the post office which had received the telegram for Dora Flynn, and in a very short time had secured a copy of it. It ran: "*Go at once to R. Writing. A.*" It had been handed in at Cottlebury General Post Office at 9.40 A.M. His last call was at Scotland Yard where authority was not too happy about recent developments. For an hour the A.C. listened in helpful silence to what he had to say, and agreed to send a couple of men straightway to Rochester to locate the roadhouse Mond had said his brother-in-law kept. Even if he had spoken the truth in that respect it might be a tedious job, and it was preferable from every point of view that Pardoe should be back in Steeple Cloudy as soon as possible. His superior was sympathetic, if not exactly encouraging.

"If it's what you think you'll have a devil of a job still to bring it home. When they like to sit tight and keep their heads—and in spite of the butler's death this one seems the sort to—what are you to do?" He sighed. "Pray for the novelist's evergreen, old man—the Murderer's One Mistake."

At eight-fifteen, Pardoe passed through Cottlebury, busily engaged in building a castle in the air round his prisoner.

At eight thirty-five he reached Steeple, where Salt greeted him with the news that Alice Gretton's body was in the mortuary. Whereupon his castle crumbled into fragments—until the sergeant told him something else.

An hour or two later, Miss Flora Hickey of New Albany, Indiana, U.S.A., in her hand a copy of that day's *Cottlebury Chronicle*, was telling her story to Superintendent Creed at the police station.

CHAPTER XVIII

THE TRUTH

> Agam. *We go wrong, we go wrong.*
> Ajax. *No, yonder 'tis;*
> *There, where we see the lights.*
> WILLIAM SHAKESPEARE: *Troilus and Cressida.*

"IT WAS the ears as much as the arms that clinched the identity for me," Pardoe was saying to Creed and Salt in Cottlebury on Tuesday morning. "If Alice Gretton had ever worn earrings, the murderer wouldn't have had to rip them off, and more than one of the people who described her to us would have observed them too. There's plenty, besides her son, to testify that Esther O'Malley wore copper rings in her ears. Then the extensive burns on the arms and chest—when we know that the gypsy received just such injuries when she saved the Birchall children years ago. And the hair being unfastened—you noticed the wavy lines of it. She wore it in plaits at the sides—he had to loosen it. Other points, equally telling——"

"Found what he killed her with?" Salt interrupted.

"Not yet," Creed answered him. "But we're combing the wood. What'd the medical report say? Heavy, blunt, narrow. Probably a spanner, or something like it."

The inspector nodded. "The stockinged feet were queer. So were the good black shoes with their laces hanging loose, found in the pit. Her feet were too big for them. So he chucked them down instead, and in his hurry forgot or didn't stop to change the stockings she must have pulled on to go to the door when he roused her. She was in bed when he got there, you see. There was hardly anything on under that coat and frock and scarf."

"But he didn't kill her there?" Creed said quickly.

"No. If he had O'Malley would have found signs of it in the cottage. She was a plucky old thing. She must have opened the door. She may even have thought it was her son come back at an odd time."

"Lucky for O'Malley he's got an alibi," Salt remarked.

"Yes. They got to know, of course, that he went up weekends to work on Birchall's other farm and took the kids with him for a treat. The old woman was alone there from Friday afternoon to Sunday evening, sometimes to Monday."

"Funny thing O'Malley didn't take a look in the pit."

"Why? Funny to us, not to him. It wasn't close to the house, and to them it was merely a hole where they emptied their rubbish. He was looking for her, remember—not for her corpse. It was dark, too, and he had the kids to take back to the laborer's wife who used to house 'em at the other farm. He says he thought his mother might be back by the time he returned. When she wasn't he walked over to Steeple, and didn't get back to the cottage till the small hours. In the morning he went over to Birchall's."

"And her clothes?"

"Bundled away in a little coal-house at the back, and the coal actually shoveled on top of them. Her boots too. If O'Malley had found 'em in the cottage he'd have jumped to foul play. As it was he wondered why she'd gone out without locking up. And he couldn't make out why the bed had been slept in. That gave him the notion it must have been Saturday she'd gone out, and met with some accident."

"Good thing Pitt an' me didn't hoof that button out of sight," the sergeant observed.

"Yes. It's from Mond's coat all right. A reconstruction suggests that she tore at his clothes and his face—by the cottage before he finally struck her—hence the scratches. He hit her more than once. Then the button dropped off when he was dragging her to the pit. After that he must have put Gretton's clothes on her, and then gone back to the cottage to hide old Esther's own things."

Pardoe was silent for a moment. Remembering the vitriol he found himself viciously regretting that the butler had died before suffering the more protracted punishment of his trial. But, he reflected grimly, the brain whose instrument and, finally, victim Mond had been still lived.

"And the vitriol," Creed interposed, as if reading his thoughts, "told us at the start there was a reason for destroying the features—if it wasn't just spite."

"Hasty murder by night doesn't leave much time for that form of bestial spite. They wanted to give us Alice Gretton without Esther O'Malley's face."

"A clumsy bit of work," Salt said contemptuously. "Gretton vanished four weeks ago, and the doc says Esther O'Malley's not been dead more than two days."

"That wouldn't have stopped them. It might be claimed that she'd been kept alive by somebody to whose interest it was her mouth should be shut, and killed at the last because she was too dangerous. There's one thing about it—Esther O'Malley's murder is indication enough that they're seriously rattled."

The report on Mond had come in. The butler had died of acute arsenical poisoning, and the whisky in the bottle was impregnated with weedkiller. Prints on bottle and glass were his own; on the bottle they were significantly superimposed on smudgy marks that might have been made by gloves.

After Salt had brought in news of the discovery of the body in the pit, Creed had taken the precautionary measure of increasing the number of men deputed to shadow Spanwater. By one of these a report was made that would bear investigation.

Directly after breakfast Aurelia Brett had been followed to the subbranch post office in Steeple where, as was subsequently ascertained, she had merely bought a book of stamps. The shadow had stopped a few yards farther along the path by the post office. As she came out a bus from Cottlebury going to Steeple Cloudy stopped close to her. At the same time a bus in the opposite direction headed for Cottlebury met the first bus and pulled up a yard or two down the road on the other side. The man swore that he saw Aurelia Brett mount the step of the bus bound for Steeple Cloudy and go inside. Thinking his quarry was safe and not wishing to make himself conspicuous, he had turned his back for a few seconds to light his pipe. When he looked round again both buses were moving off. He returned to Spanwater, but Aurelia Brett was not there. She did not reappear till close on lunchtime. It was clear to Pardoe that by a neat bit of head and footwork she had outmaneuvered the police shadow by descending from the Cloudy bus and mounting the one bound for Cottlebury. It could be an innocent enough ruse, of course; the normal reaction to the knowledge that one is being followed is a determination to outwit the pursuer.

Pardoe, who approved American women, liked Miss Hickey as soon as he set eyes on her. She was staying at the Crown Hotel in Cottlebury, and when the inspector was shown into her sitting room his immediate impression was of a genial vitality too expansive for the size of the room. She was forthright too, and in five minutes had given him the story she had told Creed last night. At the end she handed him a little book in chintz covers, first finding two places.

"It was certainly Alice Gretton," she said firmly. "Trust Flora Hickey. She was in the ladies' waiting-room on the platform at this station at eleven o'clock on the night of March 21st. And so was I. I'm traveling to and fro and staying right here in Cottlebury—I mean it's my headquarters. My mother's folk three generations back came out of the Cotswolds. They were Sheptons, and they were born and married and died all round here. I've enjoyed myself so much collecting my ghosts to take home with me."

Though her meaning was unmistakable the picture conjured up was, Pardoe felt, a little uncomfortable.

"And Miss Gretton?" he reminded her.

"Oh, yes. Well, there she was, coat, scarf and hat all as you've described. I was sitting in a corner of the waiting-room reading. The attendant was there too. Then the woman you are looking for came in carrying a suitcase."

The inspector frowned. "This happened a month ago, madam. Do you usually remember chance meetings for that length of time?"

Miss Hickey laughed. "Now you're making fun of me, Officer. Of course I don't though I'm very, very interested in people and a great many of them go into my diary. But I wouldn't have forgotten this lady, you see, because of the brooch."

"What brooch?"

"The brooch that I saw when she opened her case on the table to look for something. It was pinned to a crêpe-de-chine blouse packed on top, a pretty thing you wouldn't have expected a plain old lady like your Miss Gretton to wear. And the brooch was very attractive."

She described it to Pardoe: carved in ebony, she thought, of heavy design, it had represented the head of a Bacchante, the short wild hair rippling up and back.

"It was lovely," she repeated. "She'd bundled it back into the case in a minute, but not before I'd seen. And then a week later—you'll see in my diary it was March 28th—I saw the same brooch again. Well, I thought it was the same, but a different person was wearing it then."

"Yes? Who?" Pardoe's words dropped like stones.

"A tall, slim girl waiting for a train to take her to Spanwater Manor. She was wearing the brooch on the front of her jumper. It's all in my book."

The silence that followed stirred Miss Hickey's drop of Scottish blood to a queer chilly ferment. After all, this man was a policeman.

"You don't think—the poor old lady that's missing—well, I surely would like to know she's not dead," she faltered.

"She isn't dead," Pardoe said harshly. "Please tell me, were you dressed the same on both occasions, March 21st and 28th?"

She shook her head. "Well, no. The first time I had my hat on, and being night a big coat over my suit. The next time I wasn't wearing a hat—I was painting one!"

She sat through the few questions that remained, a look of kindly concern on her face, more than half her mind given to the delightful composition of today's entry in the diary the police officer was clasping so affectionately.

"You've wilfully kept back important evidence," Pardoe said sternly. "A bit more and you might have jeopardized Miss Brett's life if, as you think, she is using an alias while at Spanwater for her own safety's sake."

Andy dropped his eyes unhappily. He did not think so, and what was worse he did not think the inspector thought so, but he had inserted that bit of romanticizing to sweeten the gall of his betrayal and to numb his own conscience.

The inspector and Sergeant Salt had returned to Steeple Cloudy after tea. In Cottlebury Pardoe had gone straight from his interview with Miss Hickey to the post office where he had made certain inquiries, and had then put through a long call to Scotland Yard. From there he had gone to the police station for a hurried consultation with Superintendent Creed. Now he sat in the library at Spanwater and heard Andrew Pitt tell the story he should have told four days ago.

"Let's get this clear," Pardoe said. "You say that in August 1936, when you were still a sixth-form schoolboy, you spent a holiday with your parents in Malvern. There you met Miss Brett whom you knew as Mary Paskin. She was then a governess and was staying with her employers at the same hotel as yourselves?"

"Yes. I remember so clearly because of the afternoon I went up to the summit of the Worcestershire Beacon. It had been a fine day, but just after leaving the top to come down thunder clouds rolled up and there were some wopping splashes of rain. There was hardly anyone up there except Miss—Miss Paskin and me, and I suppose they sheltered at the summit anyway. I hadn't spoken to her before, but I'd seen her for three or four days by then. The rain came down in torrents. She had on a thin frock, no coat." He hesitated at the memory, looked profoundly uncomfortable as the past glided swiftly into the present, and blurted out, "I put my raincoat round her. We talked. She told me her name. We were a long time getting down, you see—you can't run on the Beacon slopes. It was thundering wildly all the time, but she didn't turn a hair. She was the coolest girl I've ever known," he finished admiringly.

Pardoe gave him a thoughtful look. As he saw it, it had been a clear case of calf-love, cutting deeper than most.

"Did she tell you anything else? Her future plans, for instance?"

"As a matter of fact, she did." Andy would not meet his eye. "She said they were going to Australia in the spring—the Australian spring, I mean. They sailed in September."

Salt made as if to whistle.

"And who were 'they'?" Pardoe asked more gently.

"Her employers. The name was an odd one, so it stuck—Gay-Pevening. There were two children she was looking after. I wrote once to her, care of the family, but she didn't answer." He blushed furiously.

"I see," Pardoe said. "And when you arrived in Cloudy you recognized Miss Paskin immediately, and were astounded when she denied it?"

"Yes. I had to believe her, of course—though I couldn't," Andy said, logic retreating before the Public School code.

"Now listen to me," the inspector said. "It's a grave matter that you should have been so tardy with your information. It will be a still graver matter, and may cost another life, if you mention to Miss Brett or to *anyone else* what you have told me now, or the fact that you have told me anything. *In her own interests* you will keep quiet. Do you understand?"

"Yes," said Andy with a simple dignity. A look of comprehension that made Salt uneasy had passed between the two.

Half an hour later when Pardoe and Salt had returned to Steeple, two of the men deputed to shadow the manor withdrew more ostentatiously than they had arrived. Indeed, one of them had a rather indiscreet talk with Lou Blessitt before he went, expressing his pleasure at being relieved of a cold job.

Events after that moved swiftly and with a certain predictable neatness for which Pardoe, coveting a clean break, was grateful.

At eight twenty-five the door at the north end of the manor opened. A woman came out wearing a raincoat and a felt hat pulled down all round. Her gloved hands were empty. She paid very little attention to her surroundings, but walked fast and lightly down the path to the door in the shrubbery wall. In less than ten minutes she had reached the road, where, hands in pockets, she stood waiting. Some yards farther down a young fellow, carrying a newspaper, leaned on a bicycle and chatted with another man. She looked hard at them. They were laughing, and snatches of their conversation about the day's racing reached her. She tapped her foot impatiently on the road and dismissed them from her thoughts.

The headlights of the Cottlebury bus threw their beams round the curve of the road. In another minute it had passed the men and pulled up alongside the woman. She stepped up and took her seat just inside the door. The young man with the bicycle gave the machine over to his companion and sprinted for the bus, swinging himself in as it moved off. As soon as he was seated about halfway down he became engrossed in his paper.

At Steeple the bus stopped near the Silver Fox. Nobody got out or in. The young fellow with the paper got up hurriedly and went out to the step, but did not alight. He looked a little bewildered, removed his cap, scratched his head and, muttering something, returned to his seat. The bus lurched on again, and about five minutes later was followed at a respectable distance by a car which did not attempt to overtake it. Once when the bus stopped at a hamlet to put down a passenger the car drew in to the grass verge twenty yards behind.

Still in this order bus and car ran into Cottlebury at nine-five. The bus pulled up several times to allow passengers to alight before the depot was reached. At the third of these stops by St. George's Cinema in the High Street, the woman got down. She was followed a second or two afterwards by the young man, who dropped his newspaper and had to stoop momentarily to retrieve it before walking in her wake along the crowded pavement. People were going into the last house of the big picture, others were surging out. But the brilliant facade of the cinema was no temptation to either the man or the woman. She pressed on briskly, looking straight ahead, her hands in her pockets. He followed about five yards behind. A little behind him the car that had tailed the bus gutter-crawled quietly along.

All at once the woman turned the corner by a fishmonger's shop and went down a dark entry that was hardly a street. But at the end of it there was a bright light. The young man quickened his pace. Directly she passed into the pool of light she turned left and vanished from sight.

The car had drawn up a few yards from the High Street entrance, and the two men who got out were walking quickly on the trail of the first man. All three turned left at the bottom as the woman had done, and found themselves in a slightly wider street of squalid houses. The corner house on their left, with lighted windows on the entry and a door in the larger street, swung a dingy sign that proclaimed it the "Peregrine Family and Commercial Hotel."

The woman was nowhere to be seen, but on the opposite corner a man stood offering lavender for sale. The young man with the newspaper crossed to give him a penny, and received a nod. He in turn nodded to the men behind and then strolled some little way past the hotel front. The vendor of lavender came over and took his stand by the entrance.

Pardoe and Salt went inside. The clerk was expecting them.

"No. 4, first corridor, on the right," he said.

They passed quickly through a swing door and found themselves at the foot of the stairs. As the inspector, with Salt close on his heels, started to go up, a girl came running down, hesitated at sight of them, then as they stood aside, came on. She was not dressed to go out. She was of medium height, fair, thin, with a pink-cheeked, rather foolish face. She looked at them again, then tentatively pushed open the door and went through. At a sign from Pardoe Salt followed her. The inspector ran upstairs on the balls of his toes.

The door of No. 4 was a little ajar. Pardoe opened it farther and went in quietly. The gas was burning low in a cheaply furnished bedroom. A figure stood by the washstand with the water-bottle in one gloved hand and in the other a piece of paper, the contents of which she was recklessly tipping into the bottle.

She saw Pardoe an instant before he reached her. She dropped the paper and ground her heel into it. She made to dash the bottle down too, but Pardoe had her wrist. Her free hand went in a flash to the pocket of her raincoat and pulled out a cork, which rolled away. She raised her hand, Pardoe ducked sideways still holding her, and a little bottle smacked the opposite wall. There were more footsteps on the stairs. Salt and the lavender vendor came in, and between them got the bedroom bottle from her without spilling the water. The sergeant produced a pair of handcuffs.

"You can put those away," she said viciously. "It's all right. What fools you've made of yourselves."

"Mary Paskin," the inspector said, "alias Aurelia Brett, alias Alice Gretton, I arrest you on the charge of attempting to murder Dora Fennick, alias Flynn."

"How?" she said quickly.

The other men held her arms as she stood breathing hoarsely. Pardoe stooped and gathered from the floor what she had trodden upon.

"Medinal, I fancy," he said.

"Fennick," she said with a sneer, but remembering too late. "You mean Joyce Murray."

As they took her out into the passage, Salt glanced at the ugly stain on the wallpaper made by the flung bottle.

"Vitriol," he said, and shuddered.

That night an order was obtained from the Home Office to exhume the body of a Mrs. Kempson who had died at Fycliff in October of the previous year.

CHAPTER XIX

THE WHOLE TRUTH

Lo! the spell now works around thee,
And the clankless chain hath bound thee.
LORD BYRON: *Manfred.*

BY WEDNESDAY AFTERNOON a cable had arrived for Inspector Pardoe from police headquarters, Sydney, N.S.W. It informed him that in July 1937, Fenella Pagan had sailed for England, a fortnight after a girl with whom she had been lodging had died of tuberculosis. The dead girl had been buried in Sydney Cemetery under the name of Dora Fennick.

It did not matter so urgently now, except that it rounded off the story Pardoe had listened to in the morning. The long notice he had had Mr. Kirk insert in the various agony columns of the London papers, asking for news of Fenella Pagan, had borne fruit. He had spent an hour at Scotland Yard, taking down the voluble evidence of a Miss Berenice de la Faye, who had been christened plain Molly Potts and was nicer when you thought of her that way.

In the same company as Fenella Pagan she had toured the coast of N.S.W. in 1936–37. In the late summer and early autumn of 1937, according to the Australian seasons, a theater had been leased in Sydney, but they had not done very well there and by June were packing up to return home. But Fenella, whom none of them had known as Joyce Murray and who had never referred to her family, had not been able to accompany them. She had been in poor health for months, "always coughing, poor kid, and she lost weight terribly, till at the last you'd have thought the hacking would have broke her in two." She had finally been obliged to give up her job in the company, a month or two before it left for England. They had done all they could for her, but she had been too ill to venture on the return voyage. She had got about, though, almost up to the last, and had been seen a number of times with two girls who were strangers to the theatrical folk and whom she never introduced. The one was tall and handsome with golden-brown hair, the other bore a certain likeness to Fenella, especially since the rapid progress of the disease had deepened the pink of her cheeks. Some of them used to wonder if it was a relative. Fenella moved to their lodgings late in June and they had seen little more of her.

But a strange thing had happened a few months later. On her return to

England Miss de la Faye had written to Fenella, begging her to let her know where her people could be found.

"I had her on my mind. I said if she wasn't well enough to write to get somebody else to. But a couple of months later a letter came from the landlady of her digs, enclosing the one I'd sent, to say that Miss Pagan had sailed for England in July after her friend's death. I couldn't understand it at all. I puzzled like billy-o over it. Then I supposed the woman had got the names mixed, and Fenella was dead."

That was all. It was enough. Dora Fennick, charged with being an accessory to the murder of Mrs. Weir, was slowly breaking down under cross-examination and supplying the missing facts.

On an evening three days later when Scotland Yard, sending out its feelers north, south, east and west, had amassed enough material to build a background to the conspirators, Pardoe and Sergeant Salt were in the assistant commissioner's room. They had been discussing the case.

"If I'd not given Fennick his head with the express purpose of making him lose it," Pardoe said moodily, "neither he nor Esther O'Malley would have been murdered."

The A.C. shrugged. "That's assumption. The girl might have killed her."

Pardoe was doubtful. "With the butler under lock and key, so to speak, she'd have been playing a lone hand, sir. I think she'd have held off."

The A.C. reverted to facts. "And they've found arsenic in Mrs. Kempson?"

"Two grains, and a bit over. Brett brought weedkiller with her from Fycliff after Fennick had told her the kind in use at Spanwater. There's no doubt she kept it at Titt's Cote, and brought enough away with her to poison Mrs. Weir. That's why Creed found none when he searched the house. What she poisoned Fennick's whisky with she got from the cottage when she visited it last Saturday night and burnt any remaining evidence."

"Now you've got your facts what exactly was the starting point of her game?"

Pardoe sighed. "If you put it like that, sir, ten years ago, when her family was on the rocks. She was the eldest child of a Nonconformist minister named Paskin, who was ruined by a share-pushing swindle in 1929. His children had to dree their own weirds, as the Scots say. And a struggle they had. Mary was first a probationer at the local hospital, and a bit later on nurse in a North London ward—so she had, after all, the knowledge it suited her to disavow."

"There's a gap there, isn't there?"

"Yes. Some arrogance on her part brought matters to a head with the matron. She had to go—that was in 1934, and the next news of her is as governess to the Gay-Pevenings.

"That was how she got to Australia. And it was on the boat she fell in with Dora Fennick, William Fennick's sister, who was a lady's maid crossing with her mistress. It was all innocent at first, if anything could have been termed innocent even in the days when Mary Paskin was only a potential criminal."

Salt grunted skeptically. His private view was of a long list of murders antedating Mrs. Kempson's.

"So you think she conceived the plot of setting up a bogus heiress before she knew of Leah Bunting's death?" the A.C. asked, a little puzzled.

"She certainly did," Pardoe said. "We've got that on Dora Fennick's evidence where lying would be pointless. They picked up with Joyce Murray and remarked her close resemblance to the Fennick girl. When she'd told them who she was and what she was heir to and how, probably, she preferred her own mode of life to all the money in the world, they left their own jobs because they—or I should say Paskin, for the other girl's a moron—saw a gold-mine opening at their feet. All that money go elsewhere, indeed? Not if they knew it. Joyce Murray was dying. Well, let her be. But Joyce Murray dead should still be alive. They moved with her into fresh digs, probably concealing from the landlady just how ill she was, and by doing everything for her themselves managed to transpose the two names so that the woman believed it was Dora Fennick who died and Fenella Pagan who went home. They stole Joyce's passport and left her Fennick's. And when they came home they were all set to push Fennick's claim when opportunity arose."

Pardoe paused. "Then they heard, probably through Fennick's brother, details of the Bunting case and Weir's acquittal a month or two earlier. That made them stay their hand, because Mary Paskin's brain had conceived a deadlier plan. It's probable that like thousands of others she honestly believed Weir had murdered Leah Bunting—"

"Wait a minute," the A.C. interrupted. "Now that the housekeeper has confessed the Bunting woman committed suicide to get her brother-in-law hanged, there'll be a perjury case pending."

"Nothing doing, I'm afraid, sir. The woman's too near the borderline—religious mania, and the kind of one-track mind that can't distinguish between right and wrong nor realize the magnitude of what she did. She didn't know till after Bunting was dead, when she found weedkiller among her things and a sort of crazy journal the woman had kept, and never said a word about either discovery."

"Borderline?" Salt grumbled unexpectedly. "She's right in the loony bin."

They laughed, and Pardoe continued. "Mary Paskin knew that it's the accepted belief a successful poisoner will strike again. And if Weir actually didn't strike soon enough to satisfy her she'd make it appear that he had.

She bought all the papers she could lay hands on giving full accounts of the trial, and laid her plans accordingly."

"What about the Australian paper found at Titt's Cote?" the A.C. remarked suddenly.

"Probably the lining of her suitcase, I'd say," the inspector returned. "The other papers she burnt may have been accounts of the Bunting case." He thought for a minute. "In the meantime, while her scheme was ripening she had to live. So in September, 1937, she changed her name, bleached her hair, and got the post of companion to Mrs. Kempson—got it easily, I imagine, because nobody would stay with the old slave-driver."

He broke off to remark, "By the way, sir, our man's picked up a good bit from Mrs. Friend, the niece who was with Mrs. Kempson when she died. She verified the rumor that had gone round about a legacy for Brett."

"What? The £500?"

" 'Mmm. Only it turned out to be fifty. Brett—we'd better call her that now—poisoned her when she was genuinely ill for a hypothetical bequest she never got."

"The prompt, devilish, cold-blooded greed—"

"I know. We've seen how murder got to be a game with her. Well, having polished off Mrs. Kempson to her satisfaction, she was free to cast round for higher game. And she felt it was time to tackle the Weirs. Mr. Weir unfortunately showed no inclination to oblige in the matter, so she meant to do it for him. I'm pretty sure the £50 she got at Mrs. Kempson's death, when she'd thought to have ten times the amount, finally determined her to murder Mrs. Weir.

"For a few weeks she was in digs consolidating her plans. She unfolded the scheme in full to Bill Fennick. She'd got both the Fennicks completely under her thumb by dangling the Bunting thousands before their eyes. Fennick himself may have thought in his mean little heart that once they'd got it they'd be able to dish Brett of her share. Anyway, he left the Mendips suddenly in November—Benedict's identified him without hesitation—and in the name of William Mond got the post of butler at Spanwater, with faked references because Weir was known to be glad to get what servants he could."

"A good thing he gave the Rochester roadhouse away," the A.C. put in.

"Yes, because he knew they'd give him a false alibi if necessary. A married sister and her husband crooked enough to do a dirty spot of work if they thought there was money in it."

"And put Dora Fennick up when necessary," Salt added.

"Yes. So the plan developed. Brett was to take Titt's Cote after Mond had been a month or so at Spanwater and had supplied her with all necessary information. As a safeguard for the future and to get friendly with

Mrs. Weir she had to assume a new personality, so she became Alice Gretton. She wore heavy clothes to disguise her figure, a far more sensible precaution than most, and she had the uncommon wits to know how easily age is betrayed by the neck, so she covered hers up well.

"Mark you," Pardoe leaned forward earnestly, "her original scheme never included her entry into the Weir household. We know that from her own hasty improvisation whereby Gretton disappeared suddenly and Aurelia Brett took her place, and also from Dora Fennick who says her brother was dead against Brett taking the post of companion. From the moment she came into the house he was the complete jitterbug. And he never regained his nerve. She made the most dangerous of all mistakes, that of being careless with the material she worked with. She took it for granted Fennick was the same fiber as herself."

" 'He travels fastest who travels alone,' " the A.C. murmured. "Play a lone hand when next you do a murder, Sergeant."

"There she was," Pardoe resumed, "Alice Gretton, living at Titt's Cote, ingratiating herself with Catherine Weir and feeding her minute doses of arsenic. It's an important period in more than one sense. Remember, Dinah Terris told us the gypsy had been calling at the Cote and had been repulsed by Gretton? Now putting all superstition aside, we can't shut our eyes to the fact that people of old Esther's race are frequently endowed with a sense we tamer ones haven't got. She probably knew there was something evil in the wind, and that day she met Mrs. Weir out with Brett she must have recognized Alice Gretton in the new companion and made the sign of warding off the evil. And I think on Easter Monday when she was so importunate at the back door there was some idea in her prophetic brain of getting at Mrs. Weir and warning her."

"Interesting, only 'tisn't evidence, Mr. Policeman," said the A.C., but he did not smile.

"Agreed. The Devil himself isn't evidence in this prosaic world, yet it's questionable if he's ever been so busy as nowadays. Well, by the middle of March there was thought of getting a companion for Mrs. Weir, and the poor woman herself spoke of it to Gretton. This revolutionized Brett's plans. If she could get the post she would. If she failed she could still carry out the Gretton plot, though less easily if a vigilant companion were engaged. So she encouraged Mrs. Weir for all she was worth to fall in with the idea. She was, of course, familiar with Weir's objection to trained nurses. What she couldn't get to know was the date the advert was likely to appear. When it did, she had to go off in a hurry.

"She went to Gloucester to post her letter of application, wise to the fact that she stood a better chance of an interview from a nearer place. When she got the post and mentioned living in London to the doctor it was a kind of involuntary caution prompting her to suggest remoteness from Steeple Cloudy. On that fateful March 28th, she returned there as Aurelia Brett. There were other arrivals for Spanwater, and Miss Hickey's observant eye took pleasure in a brooch she recognized. She wrote to Dora Fennick, of course, to hammer into her weak head the change of plans, and even then the girl was fool enough to write to Titt's Cote a day or so later—the letter Aurelia Brett pushed in and afterwards retrieved, the letter, by the way, that she was careful not to mention. But Mrs. Weir had told her niece. We've been through Dora Fennick's stuff too—unlike Brett who destroyed as she went along, the girl kept too much, and there's a letter Fennick wrote warning her not to write again. There's a queer phrase in it: 'M. can corroborate some.' In its context we can take it to mean that Matthew knew some of the facts about Joyce Murray, and that they, the conspirators, had them all."

"Is it clear why she picked on Easter Monday for the murder?"

"Quite. There were two main factors to account for that. Andrew Pitt, who was nearly my Waterloo, arrived on the Saturday, and Monday was the day on which she'd been promised a longer time off. The first event shook her badly. Instead of inducing her to hold her hand, his coming urged her to get the murder done with—and fastened on Weir. The second thing presented opportunity. From her point of view Monday was an excellent day. You remember she went straight from her walk with Mrs. Weir to catch a bus into Cottlebury a couple of hours before lunchtime, and she didn't return till after nine? That is, she went *before* the herb tea was made, much less strained, and came back *after* Mrs. Weir had gone to bed. But what was an odd feature of her outing?" Pardoe finished, looking from the assistant commissioner to Salt.

"The lunch case she was carrying," the sergeant replied.

The inspector nodded. "By her account we know that she must have taken that case out on her walk with Mrs. Weir, because she never returned to the house till night. But why? She had a handbag as well, and she lunched in Cottlebury. The answer is that it contained something she would need on her way in at night. Namely, arsenic with which to dope the herb tea in the kitchen and a thermos flask to carry some of the drink upstairs."

"Suppose she'd found somebody in the kitchen?"

"She had her excuse ready for the cook. She wouldn't have done the poisoning—that's all. Or came down in the night afterwards and put in the arsenic. And if she'd been caught pouring some into the flask she'd have been doing it at Mrs. Weir's request, and it would still have been free of poison in the jug.

"Now the arsenic was shown to have been in the herb tea *after* straining. The plants were free of it. Aurelia Brett, apart from having no obvious motive, seemed automatically eliminated from suspicion by having been out of the house the whole period from before the stuff was strained till after it was drunk. But—"

"I know this answer," the A.C. cut in. "She thought only Mrs. Weir ever drank it."

"Yes. She'd heard the others say they wouldn't touch it. She'd also absorbed the reports of Weir's trial which mention in some detail the uncertainty in a case of arsenical poisoning of fixing the exact time when the arsenic was taken. When Miss Terris drank some at seven o'clock without ill effects a different complexion was put upon the case. When we knew of it explained why Mrs. Weir's symptoms appeared so late, a point which had puzzled Dr. Fisher. It meant further that the stuff had been poisoned at night, which, while it did not eliminate the rest of the household, made it possible to include Aurelia Brett in our list of suspects. On her own evidence she had gone to the kitchen that night.

"Of course from the very start, though there was nothing to connect her with a motive or an opportunity, there were some peculiar features about her testimony."

"All that stuff she wasn't asked for," Salt interposed. "To blacken Weir and Smollett. You let her run on."

"Yes. That's how people give themselves away. She didn't emulate Iago in that respect. She'd prepared a great deal to say, and she meant to say it. And it was very lucid. I was interested. Remember how she collared us in Mrs. Weir's bedroom? But it wasn't just the general tone was odd. There were particular things too. Why did she give us a gratuitous alibi for herself for the Monday? Why, since she was so suspicious of her engagement as a companion, didn't she once mention to us or to Smollett that she knew about Weir's trial for murder? How was it that having such suspicions she yet admitted never locking her door until *after* the medinal was put in her drink? And though she said she'd gone to the kitchen to get a cup of tea, she hadn't been thirsty enough to drink any of the water in her room until an hour or so after going to bed, else she would have been drugged earlier of course. She'd doped herself, and she did it clumsily.

"Then there was the matter of the wild flowers. She disclaimed all knowledge of them, yet she knew directly what I meant by wild arum, by no means a common name for cuckoo-pint. Then she told us that Mrs. Weir sometimes called her 'Alice' by mistake, thinking we should get to hear of it, and excused it on the ground that she got people mixed. And at the end she threw in an apparently irrelevant remark about carrying her lunch case."

"Because Dr. Smollett had seen it?" the A.C. said.

"Yes. There's every chance he would never have thought of it again, but that doesn't, *dares* not, occur to a guilty mind. So she tried to forestall him by admitting her visit to the kitchen and by introducing the case."

"And when she put it in the thermos," Salt added, "she poured out too much, poisoned the drop left in the jug, an' went upstairs to tell Mrs. Weir she had brought her a nice drink of herb tea."

"Why too much?" said the A.C. quickly.

It was Pardoe who answered. "Because Dinah Terris noticed the big difference in quantity later when Dr. Fisher investigated. Brett could have poured the remainder down the lavatory, and thoroughly washed the glass she gave Mrs. Weir which would have contained the poison."

"And Mrs. Weir, of course, had meant Brett when she repeated the name 'Alice'?"

"That was interesting," Pardoe said. "Mrs. Weir was deaf and her mentality was failing. But an inflection of the voice will sometimes catch deaf ears very surely. That pointing could have been, as Smollett suggested, towards a photograph. Or it could have been meaningless rambling on the part of a dying woman. But when one remembers the juxtaposition of furniture and doors in her bedroom it could have been to *the communicating door of Miss Brett's room* she pointed, which was in the same line as the dressing table."

"Brett planted the cuckoo-pint in the bin, of course?"

"What's that, sir?" The inspector was thinking of something else. "Oh, yes. She never supposed it would deceive us. It was to point to somebody who *wanted* to mislead us but who had bungled his job—Matthew, in short."

"What were you going to say, Pardoe?"

"Only about Freddy Borth, sir. Actually he elucidated a good deal. Indirectly he precipitated the murder of Fennick, for when I got Benedict's address old Borth told Smollett what he'd found out, Smollett told Weir, Weir told Fennick, and Fennick as the weaker vessel relying on her to bolster him up told Brett—and sealed his own doom. Not but what I think she intended getting rid of him in any case after the gypsy's murder. He was cracking up, and an unnerved accomplice is the worst chink in the armor. Besides, that bit of paper I picked up in church—except possibly for the third item about Dora Fennick, is a revolting piece of murder memoranda relating to Esther and Mond, with the killing of the butler expedited by some hours when she knew his identity was out."

"Didn't she know of young Borth's recognition of him at Christmas?"

"I'd say not. It scared Fennick, but those were early days, and the last thing he'd want then would be to put any obstacle in the way of Brett moving into Titt's Cote."

The A.C. frowned. "Look here, when Joyce Murray's people were killed the December before last and she was advertised for, why didn't they push their claims then?"

"For several reasons, sir. Primarily greed—they stood to gain an immensely larger fortune by Mrs. Weir's death. Also, while Mrs. Weir lived she was a stumbling-block to such a plan. She had known Joyce much better than her husband had known her, and as her mental powers were stronger at that time she was in a position to expose Dora Fennick as an impostor."

"And you think Brett decided at the last to kill the girl?"

"Yes. She sent her that wire on Monday from Cottlebury after giving the slip to the man tailing her. 'R' was Rochester, we know. Then she booked a room at the 'Peregrine' by phone and wrote her to come. By then, you see, it was a case of saving her skin, not securing a fortune. When she got to the hotel she sent the girl down on some pretext about seeing that there was nobody about to spy on them, and so made the opportunity to poison the water."

The A.C. sighed. "You thought it was Fennick striking at Andrew Pitt?"

Pardoe grimaced. "I came a cropper there. In a sense, of course, it was—it would be Fennick damaged the car. What I didn't guess was that he and Brett were in it together. It was handed me, too, on the night she put up the magnificent bluff of defying Pitt to tell me something, and then later made the irrelevant remark about the likelihood of breaking one's neck in his car. I was on the wrong track. I'd intercepted a devilish look Fennick gave Pitt, and I thought he and Freddy had hold of the same damaging knowledge about the butler."

"You're human, not a superman," the assistant commissioner said with a smile. "And you had a massacre on your hands. Look how she was helped—the Murrays dying opportunely to leave Joyce heir, young Terris advocating euthanasia, Augustus Weir's debts, the general need of money, Miss Leith's absence from Cloudy—unconsciously they played into her hands. What a foul woman."

" 'I have seen the wicked in great power,' " Pardoe said softly. He added, "Murderers are oddly conservative. In the best traditions she stuck to arsenic—Mrs. Kempson, Mrs. Weir, Fennick. Only her attempt on the girl showed variation."

"Poisoners," said Salt with unnecessary emphasis, "aren't like you an' me. They run in blinkers."

EPILOGUE

Naught's had, all's spent.
WILLIAM SHAKESPEARE: *Macbeth.*

NOTHING BUT THE TRUTH

Being the closing passages of a letter written by Miss Muriel Hart to her nephew, Andrew Pitt, July 8th, 1939.

. . . and you will have seen by now that the wardress found her dead yesterday morning—not suicide which would hardly be possible in the circumstances, but cerebral hemorrhage, the brief report says.

Better as it is, Andy. Fiendish as it all was, indirectly this spares everyone as well as herself. It will make a bit of blather in the popular press and then silence.

It was a mistake for the defense to produce her letter to Mrs. Lessing. Not that anything would have made any difference with the other girl turning King's Evidence. But there was such a prepared note about it. In any case, written when nothing had happened, its unnecessary frankness came very near libel. If there was no ulterior motive why tell one's landlady such dangerous things? And neither Mr. nor Mrs. Weir's name appeared in the transaction when Spanwater was purchased.

I gather they're not proceeding with the charge of perjury against Mrs. Kingdom. A footnote on the Bunting case catches my eye—*the authorities* (all-embracing term!) *are satisfied that*, etc., etc. It's enough. Anything more would rake it all up again and we "have supp'd full with horrors." Anyway, Mr. Weir's execrators are now miraculously his champions—with as little reason. With the British public's superb lack of logic everyone is indignantly convinced of his innocence two years ago because of his innocence now!

Of course all the happy things will have reality now. Even caviare, like *The Archon*, is selling like fish and chips! Only don't tell Augustus Weir I said so. Well, it's some consolation for his unfortunate name beginning with an "A." And you will certainly come to me before you go and see Mussolini—Zoe, Nick, and Dinah too, please, and that poor little Freddy if the ogre will let him (I don't mean Mussolini, of course, but the other one).

Your loving
MEW

THE END

If you enjoyed *Shadows Before*, ask your bookseller about its predecessor, *Postscript to Poison* (0-915230-77-1, $14.95). The Rue Morgue Press intends to publish all five of Bowers' books.

About the Rue Morgue Press

"Rue Morgue Press is the old-mystery lover's best friend, reprinting high quality books from the 1930s and '40s."
—*Ellery Queen's Mystery Magazine*

Since 1997, the Rue Morgue Press has reprinted scores of traditional mysteries, the kind of books that were the hallmark of the Golden Age of detective fiction. Authors reprinted or to be reprinted by the Rue Morgue include Dorothy Bowers, Joanna Cannan, Glyn Carr, Torrey Chanslor, Clyde B. Clason, Joan Coggin, Manning Coles, Lucy Cores, Frances Crane, Norbert Davis, Elizabeth Dean, Constance & Gwenyth Little, Marlys Millhiser, James Norman, Stuart Palmer, Craig Rice, Kelley Roos, Charlotte Murray Russell, Maureen Sarsfield, and Juanita Sheridan.

To suggest titles or to receive a catalog of Rue Morgue Press books write P.O. Box 4119, Boulder, CO 80306, telephone 800-699-6214, or check out our website, www.ruemorguepress.com, which lists complete descriptions of all of our titles, along with lengthy biographies of our writers.